LINDA LAEL MILLER

THE *Marriage* SEASON

HQN™

HQN™

ISBN-13: 978-0-373-77933-8

The Marriage Season

Copyright © 2015 by Hometown Girl Makes Good, Inc.

Recycling programs for this product may not exist in your area.

This edition published by arrangement with Harlequin Books S.A.

For questions and comments about the quality of this book, please contact us at CustomerService@Harlequin.com.

® and TM are trademarks of Harlequin Enterprises Limited or its corporate affiliates. Trademarks indicated with ® are registered in the United States Patent and Trademark Office, the Canadian Intellectual Property Office and in other countries.

www.HQNBooks.com

Printed in U.S.A.

Dear Reader,

Thank you for joining me in Bliss County once again! It's a great place to visit during the summer (well, at *all* times of year, but I think it's fair to say that Wyoming is uniquely beautiful right now). And of course June is the traditional wedding month, hence my title—*The Marriage Season*.

In this story Becca (Bex) Stuart, the third member of the girlfriend trio that also includes Melody Hogan and Hadleigh Galloway, gets her turn to find the man who's right for her—and that man is Tate Calder, widower and single dad. I love to write about kids—and animals—so this gives me a chance to do both!

You won't be surprised that the story focuses on some of my favorite themes: the importance of family, friends and community, as well as the possibility of second chances, especially when it comes to love. And, as always, the setting is crucial to my storytelling, that setting being the American West. Places like this (Wyoming, with its stunning landscape, its mountains and rivers and ranches, its lovely small towns) really shape people and their lives. That's certainly true for Bex and her friends; in Tate's case, it *re*shapes his life, since he's a newcomer to Mustang Creek. And of course meeting Bex changes his life, too! And that of his sons…

I hope you enjoy *The Marriage Season* and that you'll visit Mustang Creek again this Christmas. Please visit my website, lindalaelmiller.com, and share your thoughts about the story, the setting, my blogs or anything else you want to talk about. Check it out for news of my upcoming books and contests, too.

Wishing you, your family (and pets!) a lovely and restful summer—or an exciting one, if that's what you prefer…

With love,

Linda Lael Miller

For Kate, the lifesaver. Thank you!

CHAPTER ONE

Leaves floated down like rain and littered the path with bright color, red and aspen gold. The air had a crisp bite to it, clean and fresh, the scent of autumn. Above, the sky was cloudless, a pure Wyoming blue.

Perfect training weather.

Becca "Bex" Stuart flashed by another runner with a nod. The trail was busy on this Saturday morning. Mustang Creek had put in a series of municipal paths specifically for walking, biking and running, and the money had, in her opinion, been well spent. She sure took advantage of her tax dollars every chance she got.

Just a light run. That was her goal this fine morning. Luckily, Bex had access, thanks to her business, to the finest athletic equipment available, so she could get an accurate time. The upcoming marathon was the usual 26.2 miles, and her strategy was to gradually work up to that. And then she'd begin tapering down. By next Saturday she should be ready.

Her friends thought she was insane.

From experience, because this wasn't her first endurance race, Bex knew they could be right. Mile nineteen was where you just wanted to chuck it all and quit, but if you got past it...you were home free.

Her phone, clipped to her shorts, beeped.

A text.

She could read it as she ran; however, she couldn't answer, not without stopping, and she wasn't going to stop now.

It was from one of her best friends, Melody, recently married, so now Mrs. Spencer Hogan.

Meet us at the ranch for lunch? Hadleigh and I want to talk to you.

It was, according to her high-tech pedometer, a manageable time frame as long as they meant around noon. She was able to type K without breaking stride.

There was definitely a shower in her future before she sat down with other human beings to eat—as a favor to them. Despite the cool temperature, Bex was perspiring, as she should be, or she wasn't trying hard enough.

"Bex? Bex Stuart?"

Male voice. Familiar.

The sound jarred Bex out of her endorphin haze, brought the world around her back into focus.

She'd just reached the second loop around Pioneer Park, and the place was filled with small, noisy kids celebrating life in general. The male voice belonged to Tate Calder, she saw with dismay, his two young sons among the crowd of children crawling all over the playground equipment.

Tate looked, as usual, put together and handsome with his clean-cut features, wavy chestnut hair and dark eyes. He wore a leather jacket and nice jeans, while she was arrayed in the scruffiest outfit she owned—and, naturally, sweaty, as well.

Great.

"Hi," she said. Not exactly brilliant, but polite at

least. A little breathless, Bex ran in place, her body on autopilot. *Keep that heart rate up.*

Not that it was a problem. Just *looking* at this man seemed to have an aerobic effect on her.

She'd encountered Tate two or three times before, since he was a friend of Hadleigh's husband, Tripp, both men having flown for the same company as charter pilots back in the day, before Tripp decided it was time to sell the firm and come home to Mustang Creek.

Tate's dark eyes were amused, missing nothing. "How've you been?"

"Good." Now *there* was a snappy answer. Yes, she was on a conversational roll, all right, a regular genius with words.

Tate grinned. "You seem to be in a hurry, so I won't hold you up. Tripp tells me you're training for a marathon." A brief, measured pause. Meaning what? "Really?"

"Really," Bex replied. She managed a small smile, friendly enough, but wobbly. "Nice to see you," she said, trying to distance herself from him, still running. Still going nowhere fast. "What can I say? Guess I'm a glutton for punishment." *Terrific. More snappy repartee.* Annoyed with herself, she sprinted off, probably improving her time slightly, since she didn't particularly want him to remember her with a shiny face and a messy ponytail.

Of all the luck.

Make that *bad* luck.

Tate was tempting as hell, no denying that, but Bex got the nearly subliminal impression that he was as wary of involvement as she was. His wife had died, and she'd lost Will in Afghanistan—it wasn't hard to do the psychological math.

Thoughts in a muddle, Bex finished her run and headed for home. There, she took a hot shower, put on her favorite red sweater and black jeans and, perhaps as a nod to the cosmic forces that governed vanity, she spent a few extra minutes doing her hair and adding lip gloss.

Satisfied that she looked okay, Bex left the house, got into her sporty SUV and, after making a brief stop downtown, zipped off to meet Mel and Hadleigh.

Reaching the Galloway ranch minutes later, Bex felt a twinge, a bittersweet sensation somewhere in the back of her heart. Tucked among the looming mountains, crystalline streams and venerable trees, the house and barn and other outbuildings—even the fences and corrals—seemed to *belong* there, organic to the landscape itself.

Tripp had taken over the place after his stepfather, Jim, long a widower, had finally remarried and moved into town. The house itself wasn't fancy, but it was spacious and solid and homey, with a welcoming air.

Secretly, Bex had always wanted to live in the country. She loved her work, felt she was making a genuine contribution to people's health and all-around well-being by furthering the cause of fitness through her ever-expanding business. And, if not actually country, Mustang Creek was certainly no clamoring metropolis. There was something…*nurturing* about being out here, with all this unspoiled nature.

Before she could even get out of the car, Mel and Hadleigh stepped onto the side porch, smiling and waving.

Both her friends were pregnant, and both of them were more beautiful than ever.

Bex felt a pang of affection, tinged, alas, with mild envy.

Hadleigh was farther along than Melody, her baby bump more pronounced. She'd married first, and she and Tripp had been eager to start their family.

All systems go.

Melody, running a close second, was just starting to show, a bit rounder than usual, her loose shirt disguising her pregnancy. If you didn't know her, you'd never guess, but they'd all been friends since they were six years old, so Bex was attuned to every change. She was living this with them, sharing the experience in a way, and she couldn't have been more pleased by their obvious happiness.

They really did glow.

They knew Bex felt slightly left out—there wasn't much Melody and Hadleigh *didn't* know about her—and they not only understood, they were also convinced her turn at marital bliss and motherhood would come. Soon.

When Bex's own hopes flagged, these two never failed to notice and offer encouragement. She was so lucky to have them in her life.

That choked her up for a moment, brought the sting of tears to her eyes. Romantic flings, career highs, fun times—all those things came and went, but friendships like theirs were as permanent as bedrock.

She paused, took a breath and squared her shoulders.

"I brought dessert," she announced cheerfully. "Don't kill me, but it's those puff pastries from Madeline's. You guys can't drink wine or coffee, so you need *some* sort of vice." She paused, chuckling. Some fitness guru *she* was, she thought wryly. "One pastry won't hurt." This was true enough, in her opinion. One pastry *wouldn't* do any harm. The problem arose when the rate of consumption ratcheted up to three or four tasty treats—or ten. Feeling cocky, she added, "Considering that I just ran eighteen miles, I can afford a reasonable level of indulgence."

Motormouth, her inner moderator gibed.

"Give me that bag." Hadleigh grabbed for it as Bex came up the steps. "I'm having mine *before* lunch, so no lectures on nutrition, please. And if Tripp has the gall to say a word—he has the metabolism of a shark, the rat fink—I consider it your solemn duty as my friends to drop him in his tracks." Paper rustled as she peered inside the bag. Sniffed appreciatively. "Oh, dear heaven," she lamented happily, in a near moan, nudging Melody lightly with one elbow as she spoke, "it's the ones with lemon whipped cream."

"Yep," Bex confirmed with a twinkle. Judging by the current reactions, if she hadn't surrendered the bag willingly, one or both of these watermelon smugglers would have tackled her for it.

Melody, feigning greed, made a comical effort to snatch the fragrant sack from Hadleigh's hands, and Hadleigh, in turn, pretended to dodge the move.

"Hey, share and share alike," Melody said with a grin. "If you think you're going to snarf up my share right along with your own, sister, think again."

Hadleigh laughed, still employing diversion tactics, an awkward endeavor under the circumstances, and Bex wondered if the third pastry, intended to be hers, would survive this good-natured tussle.

Hadleigh correctly read Bex's expression. Yes, she was fit and yes, she ran a fitness empire, but she loved Madeline's lemon-cream dreams as much as anybody did. "*You* can drink wine," Hadleigh continued, cheerfully accusatory. "*We* can't. Coffee?" She waved one hand in a dismissive gesture while holding the pastry bag just out of Melody's reach with the other. "Gone. A distant memory."

Bex had to giggle at her friend's histrionics.

Hadleigh took in her friend's trim figure with a mock glower. "Laugh if you want, Becca Jean Stuart, but one of these days, you'll be pregnant and craving all kinds of things you can't have, and we'll be the ones rubbing it in."

"Yeah," Melody agreed staunchly, making another grab for the bag.

For all the joking around, a whisper of sadness brushed Bex's soul.

If Will, Hadleigh's older brother and the love of Bex's life, had made it home from Afghanistan, everything would be so different.

She'd loved Will Stevens so much.

Maybe the phrase, "better to have loved and lost than never to have loved at all," was poignant, but it really didn't offer much comfort in reflective moments like this one.

Tough up, woman, Bex told herself. Then, after a beat or two, when she could trust her voice again, she went on. "Once you two get a handle on dessert, what's on the menu for lunch?" she teased. "I heard a rumor that we were going to eat an actual meal, and I could use some sustenance here."

Hadleigh closed the bakery bag and rolled it shut with a little sigh of resignation. "I made spinach lasagna," she answered. "Garlic bread, too. The guys will be here soon, so maybe we ought to fill our plates before they get back with the boys."

"Boys?" Bex asked cautiously. *Guys* usually meant Tripp and Spence. *Boys* implied someone else.

"Tate and his sons," Hadleigh explained airily.

It figured, Bex thought, unsurprised. She was going to have to deal with Tate Calder *twice* in one day? Just one more indication that God had a sense of humor.

Cosmic complaints department? This is Bex Stuart and I—

Please hold for the next available operator. Your call is very important to us...

THERE SHE WAS.

Again.

Tate had spotted Becca right away, back at the park. With looks like hers, she would've been hard to miss. She was trim, compact, with the kind of curves that drew a man's eye, even beneath baggy sweatpants and a faded T-shirt. And then there was all that silky hair, trying to fight its way out of a crooked ponytail.

At the time, he'd hesitated to say anything because he was rusty, to say the least, when it came to the whole man-woman interaction thing. Out of practice.

This *particular* woman stirred him, deep down, in ways he couldn't quite explain, rational thinker that he was. She made him want to take chances again, live for himself as well as his children.

But what if he fell for Becca—Bex, as the others called her—and his young sons got their hopes up, let down their guard, started to believe they might have a mother again, only to see the whole thing crash and burn? Would there be survivors?

He had no choice but to be philosophical.

Like it or not—Tate both did and *didn't* like it—he and Bex were face-to-face again.

The boys had both scrambled out of the truck the minute he pulled to a stop. He was grateful that they enjoyed visiting the ranch so much, and were distracted, as always, by the dogs and horses and all that space to run wild in. It meant the kids probably hadn't noticed that their dad had been flash frozen before their very eyes.

Tate worked up a smile, acknowledging Tripp and Hadleigh and Melody and Spence's existence with a slight wave of one hand as he approached them. Odd, how, just a moment before, he'd been so focused on Bex that she might've been standing all alone on the ranch house porch.

In fact, she might have been the only other human being on the planet.

Still, he was nothing if not a left-brained realist, and his attention had slowly widened, after that first weird instant, to include the others.

The cognitive dials in his head began to click, registering further details. Construction had started on the new house, for one thing.

Tripp and Spence looked like what they were— happily married men. *Satisfied* men, maybe even a little smug.

Their wives, he noted, were downright radiant, the way women tended to be when they were not only cherished by their husbands, but gloriously pregnant, too.

And all the time he was formulating these observations, his sons were tearing around the yard with the dogs, overjoyed, high on blue skies and green grass and every blessing in between.

Of course, part of this boyish exuberance was for his

benefit; Ben and Adam had been actively engaged in a campaign for a furry friend of their own for quite a while now. Although Tate wasn't averse to the idea—he'd always loved animals himself—they lived in a rented house, and the landlord didn't allow pets. So for the time being, anyway, adopting a critter was out of the question.

In the meanwhile, Muggles and Ridley filled the canine-companion bill.

Tate shifted mental gears, centering himself in the now. It was a beautiful afternoon, Ben and Adam were healthy, balanced kids and they were having fun.

Plus, they had a decent meal to look forward to. Tate's version of Saturday lunch was usually something along the lines of canned tomato soup and grilled cheese sandwiches. He had the feeling that they'd get something a little more appealing from Hadleigh Galloway.

Inevitably, since Tate was flesh and blood, reasonably young and completely normal, his gaze strayed back to Bex. Ms. Stuart had looked two notches above terrific in her jogging clothes. Now, in a pair of well-cut jeans and a red sweater that showed off her feminine figure, she was downright distracting.

Just a few yards from the casual gathering on the porch, Tate almost froze again—so much for getting centered—but an amused, all-too-knowing glance from Tripp kept him moving forward.

"Hello again," he heard himself say, his voice suddenly husky.

Damned if the Galloways and Hogans hadn't evaporated once more, leaving him and Bex alone on the planet. He gravitated toward her, like a passing asteroid yanked into the orbit of some strange new sun, and then—*then* he literally collided with the woman, for God's sake, right there at the top of the porch steps.

What the hell? he thought, but what he *said* was, "Sorry. I was thinking about the boys."

Fool.

Flustered, Tate looked back over one shoulder, trying to lend some credence to his fib, and saw no sign of the kids *or* the dogs.

Bex pointed in the direction of the barn and said, "They went thataway."

He gave a muffled laugh, realized he'd gripped Bex's shoulders at some point, and that he was still holding her, as though he'd expected her to fall. He let go. "Thanks."

After that brief expansion, the universe zoomed in again, with a swiftness that left Tate's head spinning.

She smiled, which only increased the sensation, and her voice seemed far away. "Good luck catching up with them, though. All parties were moving fast. They could be in Canada by now."

Tate struggled to regain his equilibrium. "That's a definite possibility," he agreed. "They're both a little hyper."

This was a routine, even mundane, conversation. So why did everything seem so awkward?

Bex appeared to be at ease, but that could've been an act, he supposed. The air around them practically pulsed with electricity, and if Tate knew one thing, it was that the invisible charge was flowing both ways. "Don't worry about the kids," she said lightly. "Mel and Hadleigh are both in mama-tiger mode, which means nothing bad would *dare* happen—not on their watch."

Mel and Hadleigh? Oh. Yeah. He remembered who

they were now. Two of the other people populating the earth, in addition to him and Bex and, somewhere in the immediate vicinity, his children.

Get a grip, Calder.

But a light breeze lifted Bex's hair just then, and she had beautiful hair. It seemed to curl naturally as it fell past her shoulders, emphasizing her graceful neck.

She was right, of course. The boys were okay. The ranch was as safe as anyplace else, safer than many, and besides, the dogs would raise hell if they sensed danger.

"So, how was the run?" he asked.

He'd meant to sound simply polite, asking a casual question that didn't reveal *too* much interest. The truth was, he wanted to know everything there was to know about Bex Stuart—which movies she liked, what kinds of books she read, the shape of her dreams, both waking and sleeping.

As she answered, something along the lines of, "Oh, it was fine," he found himself wondering about her favorite colors, songs, scents, memories.

Was she a morning person or a night owl?

Did she talk in her sleep?

Despite all that, another part of Tate warned him to keep his distance, circumvent whatever emotional minefield might be lying in wait.

He was not, never had been, the impulsive type.

And yet…

And yet.

He sighed. Shook his head, hoping to break whatever spell he was under.

Trying to act like a grown man instead of a teenager on hormone overload.

How's that workin' for ya? he chided himself.

Not worth a damn, that was how.

Okay, yes, he reasoned doggedly, Bex was beyond hot, and it had been a while since—well, it had been a while. Still, the world was full of attractive, available females, and Mustang Creek, small as it was, had more than its share of them. He got lonely sometimes, and he'd planned on remarrying at some point, but he'd been in no particular rush.

After all, he was busy, raising two kids on his own, starting a business, not to mention building a house. In other words, life was already complicated enough without throwing a relationship into the mix. And he knew instinctively that, with Bex, there would be no half measures, no holding back, no taking things slowly.

And then there was the color of her eyes. Hard to describe, even if he'd had his wits about him, which he clearly didn't.

Before now he would've said they were green, but in the slanting sunlight of early afternoon, they looked more gold. He noticed threads of gold in her hair, too, maybe artificial highlights, although he didn't think so. There was a natural quality about her, a lack of artifice in both her manner and her appearance.

She was one of the only women he'd ever met that he would describe as *striking*. Hadleigh was very pretty, it went without saying, and Melody Hogan was truly beautiful. But Becca Stuart was *more* than pretty, more than beautiful.

He'd heard her story, or some of it, anyway. Tripp had told him about his best friend, Hadleigh's older brother, Will. Bex had loved Will from the time she was young, and when he was killed in Afghanistan, she'd been understandably devastated. As far as Tripp knew, she'd been guarding her heart ever since.

Tate knew the feeling.

The best thing he could do now, he figured, was keep his mouth shut. Trouble was, he couldn't seem to do that. "Rumor has it we're going to have real food today," he said, just to end the silence. "The boys won't know how to act."

"Yep. Hadleigh makes the world's best spinach lasagna." Bex's lips turned up at the corners, as if she'd seen through his effort to lighten things up. He resisted the urge to kiss those lips—but just barely. She drew in a breath, blew it out audibly. *"However,"* she added, "you might be better off if you don't mention the word *spinach.* I'm no parent, but kids are kids. If I were in your place, I'd just hand them a plate and stand back. Once they taste the stuff, they'll dive in."

Tate relaxed a little. "Good advice."

His head was beginning to clear, but it wasn't happening fast enough to suit him.

He was still bewitched, still awkward. If the two of them had been in kindergarten, he'd probably be shoving her off the playground swing or pulling her ponytail.

Moreover, he could see that she hadn't been fooled by his effort at casual conversation; she knew he was off his game. But maybe she was off her own, just a little. Faint color had come into her face, and it wasn't just because of the cool fall breeze.

Finally, Tate stepped aside. "I'd better round up the kids," he said.

"I'm going back to town for more pastries," she told him, dangling her keys.

That announcement startled him for some reason, and it must have shown in his face.

Bex laughed again, but at least the awkward moment dissolved as she explained. "I brought pastry and I'm sure the pregnant ladies are going to need more. Plus, your boys probably wouldn't mind a few chocolate chip cookies for dessert."

The decision seemed sudden. Was she trying to escape?

He couldn't bring himself to ask. "You'll be idolized. Elevated to instant goddess status."

"I've always wanted to be a goddess." She breezed past him.

He shouldn't have looked back but he couldn't resist watching Bex as she headed for her car. She had a very nice posterior and a graceful way of moving…

"Tate." The use of his name was like a verbal poke in the ribs.

"Huh?" He turned to face Tripp, who descended the porch steps and slapped him on the shoulder. Hadleigh looked on, smiling, from the kitchen doorway.

"How about pulling your eyeballs back into their sockets and rolling up your tongue?" Tripp joked. "If you don't, some of us might get the impression that you're finally ready to stop acting like a monk and get on with your life."

"About time," Spence put in gruffly. Tate hadn't noticed him, or Melody, who stood beside her husband, one arm around his waist.

"Leave the man alone," she said. "It isn't as if *you* were in any big hurry to get with the program."

Spence's mouth opened, closed again.

Both Tate and Tripp laughed at his bewilderment.

Then, as if by tacit agreement, Hadleigh and Melody disappeared into the house.

"Hey, Tripp, let's have a look at that stallion you just bought," Tate suggested, anxious to shift his attention to something—anything—other than the mysteries of women.

Half an hour later, when Bex had returned with a stack of bakery boxes in her arms, and the men and boys had washed up, lunch was served.

Bex's earlier advice concerning any mention of spinach was proven right. Although his youngest, Adam, was infamous for his disdain of vegetables in general and eyed the green in the tomato sauce with suspicion, with a glance from Tate he took a bite—and quickly became enthusiastic about the lasagna, even taking seconds. Tate had to agree that the food was delicious, never mind that it was vegetarian and he was more of a meat-and-potatoes man.

After the meal, Bex got up from her chair, crossed to the counter and returned with the boxes from Madeline's.

The boys, both of whom had hollow legs, cheered.

"It's nice to be loved for something," Bex said, opening the boxes with a flourish. "Peanut-butter cookies and other variations with chocolate thrown in have arrived, plus more puff pastries. Those of you not running a marathon next Saturday may help yourselves."

Tate, who'd been trying to ground himself again ever since Bex had left for town, drew a breath, sat back in his chair and looked around at the spacious kitchen.

It was a well-appointed room, designed to be both functional and welcoming. The space was rustic, and he appreciated the simplicity of it. An island with a flat stove and a ceramic top had been added, an ideal fit with the hand-hewn cabinets Jim had built himself, years before. Even when Tripp had remodeled the place after he'd sold the charter jet service and moved back to Mustang Creek, he'd left the best parts unchanged, so the other appliances, however sleek and modern, actually enhanced the relax-and-stay-awhile effect. A natural rock fireplace filled one wall, and a quilted runner—Hadleigh's own handiwork—brightened the long plank table, with its sturdy pine chairs. The overall effect was warm and inviting.

Tate wanted that sense of hominess for his own place, for his boys. Tricky, in an all-male household.

Just the same, he maintained certain standards. Although he let a lot of house rules slide, one thing he insisted on was the supper ritual. Both Ben and Adam would happily eat in front of a TV or a laptop, but he insisted they all sit down together—every single night.

That particular dictate meant he wasn't always popular.

Just then, someone's phone rang, interrupting Tate's thoughts.

Bex was the lucky winner.

Or maybe not so lucky, judging by the worried frown that appeared on her face.

She answered her cell with a murmured, "Tara?" and got up, moving away from the table, phone pressed to her ear. Hadleigh and Melody, meanwhile, exchanged glances, looking concerned.

"This isn't good," Hadleigh said in an undertone.

Melody nodded in irritated agreement.

CHAPTER TWO

"Slow down. I can't understand you." Bex was several years younger, but decades calmer, than her volatile sibling, Tara. "What's going on?"

"I left him."

"Greg?"

"Who else would I leave?"

Bex could have done without the petulance in her tone.

Her sister had a point—it was a dumb question—but Bex was trying to process the situation, and the hysteria on the other end wasn't exactly conducive to rational thought. "Okay, where are you?"

"Your house."

Good choice. So much for an enjoyable, relaxing lunch. She wasn't going to rush home, because Tara and Greg had split before, but it sure ruined her day to have to worry about it. There was the usual blowup, and then they both changed their minds…

"I'll be home soon so we can talk," Bex told her after a few minutes.

There was an empty chair at the kitchen table and she took it. Melody looked at her inquiringly and Bex said, "The usual nothing."

Hadleigh rolled her eyes. "Let me guess, she left Greg again."

It was more than a little embarrassing to admit it in

front of Tate. "They had a dustup, it seems. I got no details. So I have no idea what's really going on. She and Joshua are at my house." Bex sighed; she couldn't help it. "I'll deal with this later. Every single time I rush to the rescue, Tara and Greg immediately make up. What I want to do now is eat something decadent."

Hadleigh pushed the box toward her. "The carbs will help."

It wasn't until the men took the boys back outside that Bex revealed the latest. "He's been cheating on her."

No one said anything.

She reiterated. "Greg's been *cheating* on Tara."

Still no comment.

She glanced from one expression to the other. "You both *knew*?"

Melody took another cookie and nodded. "Bex, here's a heads-up. This is Mustang Creek, remember? Where you live? Come on. Besides, he's cheated on her before and she always goes back. Like you said, you rush to the rescue, and it does no good. I'd love to help but Tara constantly makes bad choices."

It was so true.

If she could step up and defend her sister she would. Greg was bad choice number…what? She wasn't sure where he fell in the lineup. Tara's friends in high school hadn't exactly been on the high-achieving end; she'd dated some real losers before she'd settled on Greg, who definitely was not a prince. She'd also eschewed college in favor of the basic secretarial job she was offered at the local hardware store, keeping their books and answering the phone. But she'd done one thing very, very right, and Bex pointed it out. "Josh is great."

"Josh," Hadleigh said stoutly, "is adorable."

No question there. Despite his parents' acrimony, Josh was such a nice kid. Bex folded her hands on the table, her attitude one of surrender. "I am uninterested in this mess. I didn't want my sister to marry Greg, but she did it, anyway. I didn't want her to have a baby with him because they had problems before they ever walked into that church, but she did *that*, too. I'd love to know what I'm supposed to do now."

"It isn't your rodeo." Melody said it with quiet resolve, and Hadleigh nodded. "I wish this was your choice, but it's not. Tara needs to figure it out on her own."

"Josh has to be so afraid and freaked out."

"Well, let's go get him." Both Hadleigh and Melody were on their feet. "We have dogs, horses, food, acres of land and other boys his age. You brought these fabulous cookies. If that doesn't make him feel better, I'm not sure what would."

"My sister—"

"Tara isn't six years old, Bex. Josh is. He's six. We'll rescue him, not her." Hadleigh said it pleasantly enough, but her tone was unrelenting. "Let's go. Tara can do what she wants—stay at your place or come with us. Up to her. The important thing is Josh. We need to bring him here, give him a chance to relax, play with Tate's boys, hang out with the dogs. You're just going to sit and worry about him, anyway."

They had a point, and it was true. Her house didn't offer much entertainment for a young boy, while the ranch was a virtual playground of endless child fun. As they walked to the car, both of Tate's sons ran past, the dogs in hot pursuit, and there was definitely a cowboy theme going on with whatever game they were playing. Tripp and Tate followed at a more sedate pace, talking companionably, and when Tripp saw them getting in the car, he said, "I can guess where you're headed."

"I don't think Josh's shoulder should be the one Tara cries on," Bex said, remembering her sister's hysteria. "It can't be good for him to see her so upset. We're taking two cars. She can do her ranting and raving to me, while Mel and Hadleigh bring him back here."

And there went a lovely afternoon. Greg was a piece of dirt, but Tara was a bona fide drama queen with a capital *D*. Her sister wasn't blameless in all this.

She added quietly, because she was unaccountably embarrassed over something that wasn't her fault, "I especially don't want him there if Greg shows up with his usual apologies, which always involve a great deal of arguing. Besides, I can't prove he's ever gotten physical with Tara, but I've wondered. This time she seems serious about divorcing him. He might not take it well."

Tripp took out his phone. "I'll see if Spence can meet you at the house or at least send a deputy. That'll keep things calm. Otherwise, the three of you aren't going anywhere without me." Spencer Hogan, Melody's husband, happened to be the chief of police...

"I agree with that," Tate said, his chestnut hair ruffled by the breeze, his expression serious. "I haven't met the guy, but from what I've heard he's not exactly sainthood material. You shouldn't be there alone with your sister. Bring her back and then if he wants to talk to her, he'll have to go through Tripp and me."

If nothing else, she certainly had a wonderful support group.

If Tara stuck with her divorce plans, and Bex had her doubts, it was going to get interesting. For one thing, her sister didn't have a job any longer—when she got pregnant she'd quit the hardware store—or the skills to obtain a new one. Greg worked as a mechanic, but they constantly borrowed money from her parents as it was. Lawyers would have to be paid, there'd be child support and Bex was pretty sure their finances were already in bad shape.

With an inner sigh, she knew she could give Tara a job at the fitness center she owned in town, but she didn't trust her to make an effort if she did. The story of their lives. Tara was stunning, and Bex had always thought she was smart, until the day she married Greg. *Well, let's not forget those high school loser boyfriends...*

Downhill slide. A mess. A low-down, convoluted mess.

Spence said he could take care of it, no problem, and their little caravan took off. Mustang Creek was hardly a rockin' and rollin' kind of place, but on a bright fall Saturday it was busy, and Bad Billie's, a favorite local hangout, was packed. To her dismay, she recognized Greg's restored orange Corvette in the lot.

So he was drinking. Not surprising, considering his rift with his wife, but not good, either.

When they pulled into her driveway, she got out and went over to Melody's car to say, "Hey, can you ask Spence to call Junie? Have her get Billie to water down my soon-to-be-ex-brother-in-law's drinks?"

Junie McFarlane was a dispatcher for the police department, and Spence had been as good as his word; there was a deputy's SUV parked across the street.

Mel was right on it. "Junie and I are tight. I'll call her myself. Good idea. I know Billie would do it for me, but for Junie, Billie would flap his arms and fly to the moon."

Billie was a little older than Junie, who was in her late thirties, but everyone knew he had a serious crush on her. It was cute, coming from a rough-and-tumble guy like him, but she didn't seem to mind. Junie was a regular at Bad Billie's, and she flirted with him shamelessly.

So that was taken care of, anyway. Greg would soon be drinking a lot of water. Yep. It was healthy to be well hydrated. Bex had just done him an enormous favor, not that he deserved it.

Tara was sitting in the living room on the couch, her face splotchy, tissue in hand, and Joshua was intently watching a cartoon until he saw Bex walk in. His face lit up, and he scrambled to his feet.

"Hiya, cowboy." Bex went over and bent to kiss his cheek. "Isn't it a beautiful day outside? Muggles, Ridley and Harley told me to point that out. Is there any chance you want to go to the ranch for a while and see them? They sure are missing you. Tripp has some new horses, and Ben and Adam are there. Interested?"

"Yeah!"

The child was always too solemn in her opinion, so the enthusiasm was welcome.

"Ask your mom if it's okay for you to go with Aunt Mel and Aunt Hadleigh."

Tara waved an apathetic hand.

Bex walked him out to the car, saw him settled and buckled in, then mouthed to her two best friends, *Thank you*.

He was in good hands.

When they pulled away, she braced herself and went back inside. Her sister had definitely looked better. Runny mascara, foundation just a memory, and her entire face was puffy. Never mind her hair, which was a tangled mess. Bex said, "I'll go make us some tea. Then you can tell me exactly what's going on."

"That double-crossing son of a bitch is on his own now," Tara said a few minutes later, holding her steaming cup in shaky hands. "I've put up with him for ten years and he can't seem to get the concept that marriage includes fidelity. I'm done."

Bex had chosen an antique rocking chair that was her favorite whenever she wanted to reflect. "Do you mean it?"

Tara gave a jerky nod in response. "I know he's sweet-talked me back before, but it isn't going to happen again. I know you've heard this a dozen times, but I mean it. I really mean it."

At least Bex could say that, as of this moment, she was officially *not* an I-told-you-so kind of person. "You and Josh are welcome to stay here as long as you need."

"I already knew that." Tara sniffled and attempted a wan smile. "It's the first place I came. Thanks."

"The only trouble is that this is also the first place Greg will look if he wants to *sweet-talk* you, as you put it." Bex pointed at the front window. "See that deputy sitting out in his car? He's there courtesy of Spence Hogan and the Mustang Creek Police Department. Let's go out to Tripp and Hadleigh's ranch now, and you can take a nap. You look worn out. Then if Josh needs you, you'll be right there."

"That sounds good."

IT WAS IMPOSSIBLE not to recognize—and understand— the shell-shocked look on the face of Bex's nephew. Tate had seen it with his own sons the day he'd explained that their mother wasn't coming back. That she'd gone someplace peaceful and that from then on, she'd live in their hearts forever—as she would in his... Luckily, three dogs, acres and acres to run and two enthusiastic playmates made up for a lot.

Little Joshua was fortunate enough to have his aunt, who seemed to be handling the situation in a very efficient manner.

He was impressed, but the last thing he needed was another reason to like Becca Stuart.

The boys were whooping it up. They knew each other from school, Adam and Josh being in the same class, and he was glad to see them running around like a pack of small wild animals. The dogs loved it. Tripp said, "There's something about hearing kids laugh... I can't wait."

"Let's talk diapers." Tate said it drily.

Tripp burst out laughing. "Okay, got me there. I can wait for that part, but I'll man up."

"What if you have a girl?"

"Could happen." Tripp pointed at the boys running around. "But I understand those guys. I *was* one of those guys. Girls are a different story."

It might be irrational on Tate's part, but he'd always wanted a daughter. He leaned on the railing of the corral. "I'd like a girl. Someday. A different experience, I'm sure. Walking her down that aisle and giving her away, as they call it, to some other guy would sure be a leap of faith. Even the idea of that first date is daunting. So, if you don't mind, what's up with Bex's sister?"

"My personal opinion is that her husband isn't a bad guy—or a good guy. He's not perfect, but I know him. We went to school together. Greg was the direction

Tara chose, for whatever reason. Bex is just too good at picking up the pieces, so this isn't the first time she's been stuck with the Tara-and-Greg mess, not to mention poor little Josh. Like I said, you're getting my personal opinion here. Without Bex to turn to, Tara would simply put up with Greg. But Bex has loyalty nailed down and Tara knows it. He fools around, Tara leaves him, he apologizes and she goes back, and Bex is the only one, as far as I can tell, who even worries about what it's doing to their kid."

There was a plume of dust in the driveway. Tate asked, "You expecting company or could that be him now?"

Tripp exhaled loudly. "Orange Corvette… That's him. Might be best if the kids aren't around for a bit. I know he has rights as a dad, but if they've really split, I'm going to let Josh stay here until I see a court order— unless his mother decides differently." As he moved off, he added, "You might have to lasso Bex if her sister changes her mind. At any rate, the kids don't have to hear this conversation."

Tate had taken his wedding vows seriously, so he was hardly going to balk at stepping in, either, and he could easily see Bex getting in her brother-in-law's face. He said laconically, "I'll bring the kids inside and be right back in case there's trouble."

He whistled for the dogs and called out to his sons and Josh. "Time out. Come on in the house. Everybody."

Ben looked really put out. "Dad!"

"For a few minutes."

"But Dad, I—"

"Now. Don't argue."

At least his son understood when an order was an

order. Nothing ambiguous about it. Ben sighed as he motioned to the dogs. "Come on, boys."

They followed, lumbering along at his heels, with the two younger boys close behind. It was telling that even when Josh glanced over his shoulder and saw his dad's car, he still went in.

To Tate, that said a lot. It touched his heart, but not in a good way. Once the kids and dogs had filed inside, he hurried over to Hadleigh. "Greg is here, so keep them inside, okay?"

She nodded. "No problem."

He went back out, joining Tripp in the drive. "Just how 'not bad' is this guy?"

They'd both dealt with difficult situations, back when they were pilots. As the authority figure on the plane, they usually had to deal with passengers who got out of hand. "On a scale of one to ten?" Tate added. He wasn't worried, just curious.

"He's maybe a six," Tripp informed him, hands in pockets as they walked up to the car. "Plenty of bluster, but there's no real juice behind it. We know each other—so that should help."

"Galloway." The man in question slammed his door and walked toward them. A big guy, Tate noted, but soft, with a shock of dark hair and a five o'clock shadow. He must've been at work because he still wore his shirt with his name embroidered on the pocket. "My wife here?"

"Yep."

"I figured my sister-in-law would drag her out here or to Hogan's place. Can I talk to her?"

"Nope."

Anger flared on his face. "You heard the *wife* part, right?"

"Doesn't matter. This is my land. So these are my rules." Tripp didn't budge. "Tara's not receiving company at the moment. Seems to me she needs a little peace and quiet."

"Then I want my son."

Tate was truly not one to butt into anyone's business, but he'd seen the look on the poor kid's face. "He's inside playing with two other children. Why would you make this harder on him? Get in your car and go, and when you and your wife choose to have a sensible conversation—with lawyers involved or not—he doesn't need to be part of that, either. Like I say, it's time for you to leave. That isn't negotiable."

"Who the hell are *you*?"

"A father. The boy's not a pawn, so don't even try getting to him. 'Cause that's not going to happen."

At least Greg had enough sense to realize that neither he nor Tripp was planning to back down, so, muttering under his breath, he stomped to his car and drove off in a sputter of gravel.

When Tate turned around, he saw Bex standing there.

She gave Tripp a quick hug. "Thanks. Both of you were great."

When she came over to him, the kiss was more on the corner of his mouth than his cheek, Tate noticed—and appreciated. Not quite the real deal but...

A very nice start.

CHAPTER THREE

BEX TOOK THE CALL absently, at the desk in her office, assuming it was her accountant calling to schedule their monthly meeting. "This is Bex Stuart."

"Bex, this is Alma. Joshua gave me your cell number. I don't like to bother you, but I don't know what else to do."

Alma was the school secretary. A shudder of dismay went through her. "Is he sick? I'll be right there."

"No, he isn't. Don't worry about that. But I would appreciate it if you'd come in. We have a problem. Tara's not answering my calls—they're going directly to voice mail—and Josh's father, quite frankly, told me in no uncertain language that he wants nothing to do with it. He was downright rude."

Why did *that* not surprise her? After nearly a week of constant harassment in his quest to talk to Tara, who was still at Bex's place, Greg had finally barged in to the club. He'd brushed past the receptionist and marched into Bex's office, where he'd planted both hands on her desk, looking her in the eye. "If this is how you want it, they're your problem now."

She wasn't about to yield to his bullying. "Considering the way you've treated my sister, that's *exactly* how I want it." Tara wasn't without some responsibility in this whole mess, but Bex had no intention of discussing that with Greg.

"You got it, Bex." He'd swung around and left, leaving a hint of motor-oil aroma in the air.

She grabbed her purse and told Alma, "I'm on my way."

"I'll tell Josh and send him back to class. He's very anxious over this matter. That's my main concern." She paused. "I'll explain later, when you get here."

What matter? she wondered as she unlocked her car and slid in. There was no disputing Tara was a wreck, watching television half the night and sleeping most of the day. She really needed to get herself sorted out, but Bex didn't know how to advise her. She'd never been married, much less through a divorce, so how could she relate?

The school was a low-slung, modern brick building, only a few years old. Their beloved former school had finally reached the stage that the town had determined that a new building would make more sense than doing endless repairs, and while she'd mourned the loss, there was no doubt this facility was to-heck-and-gone better. The playground equipment alone made her inner child envious.

She parked the SUV in the parent lot and walked through the double glass doors. The office was right inside, and every visitor had to check in and sign a log, so she dutifully did that, and was directed to Alma's desk right down the hall.

Alma Wainwright was an institution in Mustang Creek. She'd been there when Bex was in elementary school, and she didn't look a whole lot different now. She still wore her hair in exactly the same bob, with a pair of spectacles constantly perched on the end of her nose. She glanced up and pointed to a chair. Bex sat. Old habits were hard to forget.

Alma picked up a piece of paper and handed it to her, across the desk. "Here's the problem. No one's paid for Josh's school lunches this year. With the new program it can be done online. Or his parents could apply for the free lunch program sponsored by Bliss County and the state of Wyoming if they qualify, but they won't respond. He's very self-conscious about not having a lunch card, and even though he's only six, he understands that no arrangements have been made. We would never allow a child to go hungry, so of course he gets a tray like everyone else, but we do have to account for every meal, so could you *please* ask your sister to address this?"

Bex couldn't restrain a deep inner sigh. Poor Josh. Such a simple thing. Why would Tara let this slide? "I'll pay it right now. I'd appreciate if you'd give Josh a lunch card immediately. He's not having an easy time at the moment, and I don't want this to be harder on him than it already is. Why didn't he just tell me?"

"He's a child. He's embarrassed." Alma adjusted her glasses and peered closely at her. "That, my dear, is why I called *you*. This is Mustang Creek. I know his parents have separated—again. Joshua's a very nice little boy and frankly, deserves better. The school system can take the loss on his meals, but I'm afraid he can't take the blow to his self-esteem."

Maybe Alma should've been a child psychologist instead of a school secretary; maybe in some ways it was the same job. Bex wrote the check on the spot, making it for the entire semester. After that she decided that with the marathon tomorrow, she could use a run. A light one, because it wasn't a good idea to push herself too hard the day before a race. The other benefit was that when she ran, there was nothing to do but think, and she needed to get a grip on the current situation.

Of course, as she exited the building, she bumped into Tate. Or rather *slammed* into him, her head down since she was searching for her keys and not paying attention. He caught her by the arms. "In a hurry?" he asked with a low laugh.

"Kind of." She flushed. "This is getting to be a habit."

"Seems to be." He let her go. "Ben forgot his math homework. I thought I'd do him a favor and drop it off, although he'd better remember the next time or take a zero. I'm trying to teach him about responsibility but he *is* only eight, and he did do the assignment without having to be reminded. So he gets one free pass. What are you doing here?"

Bex steadied herself and fabricated a smile, which she usually never did. However, Tate Calder shook her normal composure. "Josh forgot his lunch card."

He frowned. "They keep it here at the school."

She gave it up. "Fine. That's true. His parents *forgot* to pay for his lunch card. I ran over to take care of it, but I'm new to this experience. I'm going to go home, ask my sister why *she* isn't on top of it and then go for a run. I have a marathon tomorrow morning."

"Want someone to run with?"

He meant himself? "You're a runner?"

His smile was addictive. She could become a fan. Wait, she already was.

"I sure am."

"Ten miles," she warned. "I usually go longer, but tomorrow's the race."

"Ten miles is no problem. I've run marathons, so I know you're right about not pushing too hard the day before."

"Really? I mean, you've run marathons?" She felt a little foolish repeating his own words back to him, but verbal dexterity seemed to have deserted her.

"I have," he replied. He had the most delicious smile, spontaneous and easy. "Where should we meet and what time?"

She sensed that he was issuing a challenge, and she was always up for that. "Pioneer Park, top of the trail, and give me about twenty minutes."

He opened the door wider. "Will do. See you there."

That was one dangerous man, Bex concluded as she walked to her vehicle.

Those flashy good looks concealed a sensitive interior if he was dropping off his son's homework. Besides, he'd definitely stood up to Greg and he'd had no obligation to do so, other than his friendship with Tripp. Even more than his support of Tripp, his obvious concern for Tara and Josh—especially Josh—had particularly appealed to her.

So he was a runner. Huh.

She'd show him the true definition of *a run for his money*. She had some frustration to work out.

Predictably, Tara was in bed when Bex got to the house to change her clothes. Her sister was bleary-eyed and seriously in need of coffee when she emerged from the guest bedroom.

It was almost noon.

Bex went into the kitchen, pressed a button on the

coffeemaker and prepared the coffee. The lunch money mattered not at all. Josh did. As she delivered the coffee, she said, "Tara, I get that your life is upside down, I really do. But you need to talk to Josh. Make sure he doesn't have issues you haven't addressed."

"Like what?"

How could the woman be so self-involved? So obtuse? And about her own child! Oh, boy, Bex *really* needed this run. "Can you just talk to him? That's all I'm asking."

She'd have to leave it at that for now and hope Tara discovered her better self—not to mention her maternal instincts—in the next few hours.

TATE MET HER at the top of the path in a dark T-shirt and gray sweatpants, and she had to admit to a small—well, not *that* small—heartthrob moment.

It wasn't just that he was handsome, or tall, or all-around gorgeous. Oh, he was all those things, but none of that meant as much to her as dropping off his son's homework at school in the middle of the day. She wasn't sure why that was such a turn-on; it simply was. The single dad at the elementary school who was also a sexy former pilot. She went for interesting when it came to guys, and he qualified.

She pointed. "This way."

They took off, and she immediately had to tone it down, because she was such a competitor and this wasn't the time for it. He was definitely very fit from what she could see, and she was *really* looking. She knew he'd be able to outpace her. "Ten *easy* miles, okay?"

He ran with the grace of a natural athlete, and she

liked the symmetry of his stride. "Easy is better for me. With the boys, I don't have much opportunity. I'd love to run more often. I can't manage it."

She wanted to ask about his wife, but shied away. Will was still an unhealed wound for her, so she should give Tate the same consideration by avoiding the places that remained raw and sore. Instead she concentrated on the path. "The temperature is perfect. Not cold, but cool enough."

"The scenery is perfect, too."

It was true that the mountains were magnificent with their forested sides and snow-covered peaks, but he was studying her. She said wryly, "I have a feeling I was paid a compliment and I have no idea how to respond— except to point out that I probably look as tired as I feel—and there are a lot of miles between me and that finish line tomorrow."

"What if I take Josh and the boys out to eat and we watch the finish? I'm sure they'd want to be there when you cross the line. The boys would think it was fun, waiting for you to show up. Would that work?"

For her, yes. And it was generous of him to include Josh. Tara was like a bulb that went on and off. Sometimes she was a great mother and sometimes—now, for instance—she just wasn't there. "I'm not his guardian in any way, so I'll ask my sister, but I suspect you're on. Thanks for the offer."

"Seems to me you're very much his guardian right now." He said it seriously. "Of course, I do need his mother's permission. Tripp mentioned your brother-in-law's visit to the club. I've met him, and he doesn't seem dangerous, but he is angry."

Naturally she'd shared the whole story with Hadleigh

and Mel, which was why Tripp, and no doubt Spence, had heard it, too. Bex shook her head. "Greg doesn't like me and the feeling is mutual. I wish Tara hadn't told him I tried to talk her out of marrying him in the first place, but she did, and after that there was no going back. He was running around on her when they were engaged and, needless to say, after they tied the knot. The entire town knew it, and she married him, anyway."

They rounded a curve. "Fidelity in marriage is not negotiable."

Curious at the vehemence in his tone, she looked at his profile as they ran. His expression was suddenly remote, as though he was thinking of something else. No woman in her right mind would cheat on *him*, so that couldn't be it.

Could it?

"I agree." She was hitting a comfortable pace now, and hoped the same thing happened tomorrow. She decided to change the subject. "So you're building a house from the foundation up and going into horse-breeding as a new business, plus you're a single parent. Sounds like you have a stress-free life."

"You bet. I am completely without cares in this world. Hey, didn't you recently franchise a chain of fitness centers? Does that mean you're as happy-go-lucky as I am?"

"Sure thing." She grinned and then responded in a more serious voice. "The reality is somewhat different from the dream, but I worked hard to get this far, so I refuse to complain."

"Do you always wear that bracelet?" That question came out of nowhere.

He was referring to her bracelet with the three charms from the marriage pact.

He'd noticed.

She said, "Always."

Tate sent her a sidelong glance. Damn him, he wasn't even breathing hard. He obviously did run on a regular basis; he hadn't made that up to impress her. "Yeah, Hadleigh and your other friend, Melody, wear them, too."

She just nodded, didn't explain.

A moment later, he spoke again. "Not that you don't have enough on your plate—what with Tara and Josh and all—but I'm supposed to make some decisions about the finishes in the house so they can be ordered. Would you mind, if you have a free evening, going shopping with me? I'd like a second opinion. Otherwise I'm fairly sure everything would end up brown. Not because it's my favorite color, but because the boys can do the least harm to brown. They're dying for a puppy. I get asked on a daily basis and you've seen them with Muggles, Ridley and Harley, so we all know I'm going to give in once we have space for a pet. Which means more brown will be needed for the obvious reasons, like muddy paws. If there's another option, please save me."

Bex laughed. "Looking at paint and wallpaper, hmm. Are you asking me out? I hope I'm not being presumptuous here—but it sounds like an interesting first date."

"Personally I consider running ten miles together a first date. So that would technically be our second date. Dinner's on me."

Date. She'd rarely said that word out loud since she'd heard about Will's death. Sure, she'd danced at weddings and even flirted once in a while, but for the most part, she'd gone out with her friends and immersed herself in her business. She hadn't given any serious thought to a relationship in many years.

Tate Calder wouldn't be the place to start, though. She didn't have time for a built-in family, especially since she had Tara and Josh living with her these days. And if Greg was unwilling to even pay for his son's lunch at school, it was going to be a very messy divorce. At least Tara recognized that she no longer had any option, other than divorce…

What she hoped would happen was that Tara would finally get control of her life now that she'd actually made the decision. Some depression was natural, of course, but she needed to think about her son.

"I'll make you a deal," Bex said as they jogged along, sticking to the runners' side of the path as two cyclists whizzed past. "I'll be more than happy to offer my unbrown opinions in exchange for advice on six-year-old boys. Lunch cards? I remember them from when I was in school, but you couldn't load them online then. It never occurred to me to ask Josh if his was paid for. What else am I missing? He's a sensitive kid, and he doesn't discuss whether he misses his dad. I don't have video games or anything like that yet, and if I asked Greg for anything, he'd tell me straight where he wants me to go."

"He'd better not." Tate's voice had a hard edge.

Nice to know that between him and Tripp, not to mention Spence, she had some male backup.

He added, "You have a deal. His class has a field trip coming up, and they have to bring a sack lunch. It's next Tuesday. If you like, I'll pack a couple and send them both with Adam. I have two cupboards, one labeled What You Want Them to Eat, and the other What

They'll Eat When You Aren't Watching. I've learned to combine them and hope for the best. I've tried to stare down young Ben Calder over his aversion to cooked carrots before with no success, and then discovered he *would* eat them raw. The bonus is that they're actually healthier that way. I pick my battles, and with that one, I figure I came out the winner."

This new responsibility scared her a little. Well, more than a little. Tara would emerge from her emotional stupor—she had to—but when? Until then, Bex knew she was in charge by default.

"I'm not up for this, am I?" she said ruefully.

"It is definitely a learn-as-you-go process, and it seems to me that you're doing just fine."

She wasn't too sure about that, but at least she had another ally now, one with on-the-ground experience, so to speak. "I'm trying."

"If you really don't mind helping me out, would you like to see the house sometime soon? Maybe it'll help you visualize the project."

"Sometime soon," Bex agreed, with no hesitation at all. "How about after the marathon?"

CHAPTER FOUR

THE NEXT MORNING, Tate found himself riding herd over three boys as opposed to the usual two.

He could handle it, but they were kind of a wild bunch. They'd eaten a civilized breakfast—he'd insisted some fruit be included, not just pancakes and syrup—and then they'd gone to the park. Josh seemed happy enough, and he and Adam got along well, while Ben obviously enjoyed being the kingpin.

Bex could've requested a better day for the marathon, though. Later on, about two hours into the race, a storm front rolled through and the weather turned bad.

Into every life some rain must fall, but a lot was falling at the moment. He did carry an umbrella somewhere in the back of his rig and he dug it out when the clouds began to gather. True to form, the boys were immune to the inclement weather, especially when the first person crossed the finish line to a chorus of cheers and shouts. "I thought Aunt Bex would win." Josh looked deflated all of a sudden.

This was the delicate part of being a parent, Tate knew. The smallest nuances could make a major impact, so situations like this had to be addressed carefully. In as offhand a voice as possible, he said, "The men will come in first for the most part. We're built a little differently. We can run faster. It's just how it is. She might still win, but in the women's race."

"It's the same race," Josh pointed out.

Interesting territory.

"But the male and female runners are judged differently, with different times." He handed Josh a juice box.

"Why?"

A kid who took things literally. Tate considered his response. "It's like flying a Cessna," he eventually said. "Those are sleek planes that can do just about anything, but you don't want to be the pilot in a storm. On the other hand, a 757 can generally handle all sorts of weather."

The plane analogy was lame, but he meant well, and it was what he knew. In the end he put it in simpler terms. "Men and women aren't built the same. It's a biological thing. In plenty of ways, the female of the species has the advantage over us guys."

He might have elaborated but more runners were crossing the finish line. As predicted, all men so far, but the boys were enjoying the spectacle, soaking up the excitement, the thrill of achievement, and that was never a bad thing.

When the kids spotted Bex, they started hopping up and down, yelling and waving, and she managed a smile and a small wave as she crossed the line and began to walk it off, accepting the bottle of water one of the volunteers handed her.

Bex hadn't won, as it turned out, but she placed third. Tate was impressed. He kept the boys corralled until she finally walked over. He was merely going to give her the lightweight jacket she'd left with him; instead he draped it over her damp shoulders in what felt, for some reason, like a very intimate gesture.

She met his eyes and said, "Thanks."

"You're welcome. Well done, by the way."

Despite the umbrella, the boys were completely wet because they couldn't stay still, but luckily it wasn't all that cold out. She limped next to him as they walked to his vehicle. Her smile was rueful. "No matter what I do, my feet are always bleeding after I run one of these."

"And you feel like Rip van Winkle, I know. Asleep for twenty years and just woke up." He wasn't quite sure, since she was already drenched, why he felt the need to hold the umbrella over her, but he did it, anyway. "A hot bath will do wonders. How was your time?"

"Personal best." She smiled as she said that, looking pleased.

And beautiful, even soaking wet and exhausted, with no hint of makeup on her face. He had a hard time keeping his gaze from slipping downward to where her shirt clung to her breasts. For someone so athletic, she still had very feminine curves, not to mention those long, toned legs.

He realized she'd caught him staring when her brows went up a fraction. "Please tell me my shirt isn't transparent now. I'm too tired to look down."

"Unfortunately not." He pressed a button on his key fob to unlock the SUV. The boys had scampered ahead and had almost reached the back doors. "But it wouldn't hurt my feelings if it was. If you need any help getting out of those wet clothes, just call me."

"Generous of you, but I think I can manage." Her wry expression changed. "How was Josh?"

"Well behaved and polite," he assured her. It was the truth.

"Good." She smiled in relief, a smile that turned into a look of concern. "I mean, he usually is, but then again, he didn't tell me about the school lunch thing, either."

"I'm sure he's anxious about what comes next, once his parents are divorced, but I saw that in Ben and Adam when their life underwent a big change. All you can do is be there and answer the inevitable questions as honestly as possible. For the record, I'm not a child psychologist, but I believe that 'I don't know' is a perfectly acceptable response if that happens to be the case. Those words have certainly come out of my mouth more than once."

"The trouble is, he's not really asking." She stopped to face him, her lashes starred by raindrops.

Those incredible eyes. He was back to thinking they were green again.

This attraction was getting out of hand, and he needed to put an end to it, but he had a feeling *that* wasn't too likely.

"I learned the hard way that you don't have to be a superhero. I was determined to make everything okay for my sons, but the truth is, I couldn't fix…what had happened."

That sounded preachy, so Tate amended it with a grimace as he opened the passenger door. "It's like flying without controls, if you ask me. You take the plane up and hope for the best possible landing."

She laughed and shook her head as she put a foot on the running board. "You and Tripp. He says stuff like that all the time. You do realize I'm going to get your car seat all wet."

Tate looked at the boys in the backseat, equally soaked and laughing loudly about something or other, Ben leaning over to punch Adam in the arm. Tate said, "I suspect the vehicle in general might need to dry out, so don't worry about it. Do we still have a date tonight or will you be too worn out?"

She sat down and reached for the seat belt, clicking it in place. "I believe I owe you. I'll be fine tonight. Who's watching the boys or are they coming along?"

He loved his sons, but no way.

Tate went around and got into the car. "Can you picture them selecting bathroom tile or kitchen countertops? Hadleigh offered to watch them. I accepted. She said she'd be happy to have Josh, too."

"You do know she's matchmaking."

He almost didn't hear what she'd said because the boys were getting rowdy and he'd just flipped the ignition switch. Bex sat there, dripping, looking straight at him, as if life was like the marathon she'd just run, something to be met head-on and conquered.

Tate conceded. "Yeah, I've noticed." What else could he say?

THE RED SILK DRESS was too much for what was essentially a trip to the hardware store, so Bex changed again. Black pencil skirt and white camisole with a pale gold sweater. Okay, that was better. Besides, after 26.2 miles, heels weren't an option, so plain black flats were, at any rate, comfortable. Her toes needed some TLC.

Bex had no idea where they were going for dinner, so for Mustang Creek, this outfit was middle ground. A little upscale for Bad Billie's, but dressy enough for

O'Henry's on a Saturday night. There weren't a lot of other decent choices.

Tara was watching television again, but at least she was with Josh. She'd readily agreed to the idea of his spending the evening with Hadleigh and Tripp, which wasn't entirely reassuring. Bex felt almost guilty for going out.

Almost, she told herself firmly. Josh would have fun at the ranch, as he always did, and she deserved a night out.

"You look nice." Tara stirred, finally showing some animation. "Tate Calder must be worth the mascara and lip gloss."

She thought about Tate's wavy chestnut hair and those magnetic dark eyes. He *was* worth the effort, no question about it. "He saw me sopping wet earlier. It seems like the only time I see him is when I've been running. I thought I might try to make a better impression."

"You're always pretty, Bex." Her sister's eyes were glassy with tears. "Thanks for everything you've been doing for Josh. Thank Tate for me, too, will you? I can't deal with it right now."

Bex had to admit she wished Josh hadn't heard that. "I love Josh, so everything's okay. We're going to meet Tate at the ranch. You ready to go, buddy?"

He grabbed his backpack. "Yep."

"Maybe give your mom a hug before we head out?" She suggested it gently. It was their relationship, Josh and Tara's, and they didn't need her interference, but *she* couldn't figure out how to deal with her sister at the moment, so he was probably even more confused.

Tara held her little boy close and murmured against

his hair, "Have fun with Aunt Hadleigh and Uncle Tripp."

They made a quick exit and Bex debated again about asking him how he was feeling as she pulled out of the driveway, but decided to take Tate's advice and wait.

If Josh himself mentioned it, that would be different. At his age, she, Hadleigh and Mel hadn't had any secrets from each other, but she wouldn't have shared them with an aunt, either, so that was something to keep in mind. Maybe Ben and Adam were the key; Josh might talk to them.

Tate's truck was already parked by the house when they pulled in, and all three dogs swarmed out to meet them. It was heartwarming to see Josh jump out and laugh as they greeted him, tugging at his backpack and leaping up to lick his face. He loved it and he needed it. She'd get him a puppy—she'd thought about getting a dog more than once—but for all she knew, Tara would move out tomorrow, and dogs needed to be walked and trained, and her own schedule didn't permit it. So far, Tara had no place to go, since Greg was still living at their rental, so with everything up in the air, a puppy was the worst decision in the world. In theory it sounded great, but if Josh had to leave his new dog behind, and she had to find someone else to take care of it… Good intentions, sure. But a really, really impractical idea.

She could swear her life had been simple at one time.

Tate came out to greet her, that unforgettable smile firmly in place. She was relieved to see that whatever he had in mind, he'd dressed like her to the extent that he wore khaki slacks and a button-up blue shirt, but no tie.

The dogs and Josh raced into the house. He took her elbow and guided her toward his car. "Let's get the hell out of here while it's calm. I brought over every game system we have. Tripp will be as riveted as the boys. He's hooking it all up now. Hadleigh's already figured out she can watch a movie in another room with her feet up and toss a frozen pizza in their direction. You can say hello when we pick them up. Let's go select the paint, the appliances and whatever else goes into a kitchen and be done with it."

"I know Hadleigh, and she won't feed children a frozen pizza." Bex climbed in the truck and he closed her door then got in on the driver's side.

"I was joking. She did say something about roasted chicken and broccoli. I wish her luck with the latter, but anything's possible. They're now sold on her spinach lasagna, although I have to take some credit, since I told all three boys the spinach was a wild plant cowboys used to eat."

"Clever."

"It seemed to work." He backed out of the drive. "Ben was probably on to me, but Adam bought it and he's the picky eater. Speaking of which, if *you* are, tell me now, because I was thinking Thai food for dinner."

There was certainly no Thai restaurant in Mustang Creek, so Bex sent him a quizzical look. "I love Thai. Mel, Hadleigh and I used to eat it all the time in college, but the closest place I know of is pretty far away."

"Not if you fly."

"Oh." That hadn't occurred to her. "You have a plane?"

"Sort of."

"How do you *sort of* have a plane?"

He shrugged. "Technically it belongs to my father. He doesn't like flying commercial, which means we have an arrangement. He bought the plane, he pays for the hangar and if he wants to go somewhere—business or pleasure—I man the cockpit. My aunt gets to keep the boys while I'm gone, which she loves. So everybody wins."

Bex felt a certain amount of curiosity about the kind of business that allowed a person to buy a plane, but she didn't ask. It sounded as though Tate came from a well-to-do family, but she was lucky that money wasn't actually one of her problems. "Sounds like it," she said. "What are you going to do with the horses if you have to pick up and leave?"

He pulled out onto the road and headed in the direction of the municipal airport. "Tripp introduced me to the local vet. Nice guy and he wants to go in with me. We've met a couple of times and I trust Tripp's judgment. Another win-win, since I'd obviously have to hire him, anyway. I know horses, since I was raised with them, but I don't know a lot about breeding them yet. Nate Cameron has that part down, so I'm on board with taking care of the day-to-day and building the stables, and he's willing to come and stay at the house if I have to fly out. We're still hashing out the business details, but it looks good."

It did sound good and Bex also knew Dr. Cameron; he was pleasant, reliable and competent. He'd gone to high school with Tripp and Will. His practice was mostly large animal, but he did have a clinic for small animals open several days a week with an older veterinarian who was close to retirement.

That brought her thoughts back to Tara. She'd dated Nate Cameron for about six months during her senior year. Why couldn't she have married him instead of Greg?

Tate distracted her from that thought, which was just as well, since it was going nowhere. "My boys want to go fishing," he said, "and I have a friend with a cabin on a nearby lake. Do you suppose Josh would like to go? I don't know Greg, but if he's inclined to join us, that would be fine with me. The place is rustic, outdoor facilities, woodstove, and there's nothing to do but hike and fish. If Greg's the outdoor type and wants to come along, he's invited."

That was generous. Very.

Score another point for Mr. Calder.

"I'll ask my sister to have that conversation with Josh. I'm sure he'd love it. And I'll tell her to mention it to Greg." Who probably *wouldn't* love it. Not one bit...

CHAPTER FIVE

HE SUSPECTED IT was unfair not to prepare her for his family, but then again, it was impossible to be prepared, so Tate had made an executive decision just to hope for the best. As the plane touched down sweetly on the landing strip, he thought it might be prudent to say *something*.

"You're probably about to meet my aunt and my father. Unless they're out, in which case we're in luck, but my aunt's usually there. After my mother died, she moved in and took over, sort of like a certified dictator at large. She's terrifyingly efficient."

Bex looked startled, and he didn't blame her. Her gold-green eyes widened.

He pointed at the house. It was far away but there was a Jeep parked near the airstrip to get back and forth. "There'll be a lot more decorating choices around here than in Mustang Creek. The builder suggested I go to a more cosmopolitan area to pick out what I wanted and have it shipped. I'm hoping this will be a forever house for me, so why skimp at this point, right?"

"Right," she said, but the word wasn't loaded with enthusiasm. She was gorgeous in a slim skirt and a sweater that set off her eyes, and he knew his family would embrace the idea that he might be seeing someone. Meeting them so early on, though—that was asking a little much. He figured the run together didn't count, so this was their first date.

The house was like a minicastle minus the turrets. Most people found his father's place a bit...overwhelming. Should he have given her more warning, some kind of initiation, so to speak? Well, too late now. He'd better get this out of the way. He opened the Jeep passenger door in what could only be described as a gentlemanly fashion and, despite her tight skirt, she climbed in with matching grace. That shouldn't surprise him; she an athlete, after all.

The more he told himself he didn't have the time or inclination to date Becca Stuart, the more he was convinced he was going to override the system and do it, anyway. Ben and Adam liked her, and that *really* counted.

Then there was the undeniable sexual attraction. Tate was drawn to Bex on a very basic level—other interests aside. That had never been in dispute, not from the moment they met.

Not exactly what he needed at this point in his life, perhaps, but things didn't always go as predicted. Or as planned.

Aunt Gina *was* home. She'd heard the plane, so there was no going back. She was already on the front porch, waving hello, when he pulled up in the Jeep; she hesitated briefly when she saw that he wasn't alone.

"Hello." Tate didn't even turn off the ignition, but jumped out, returned the offered hug and stepped back. "We aren't staying. We're on a shopping trip, so I'm taking the Jeep into town, then we'll fly back to Mustang Creek from here. This is Bex Stuart, by the way."

"Pleased to meet you," Bex said, looking—and sounding—a little shy.

"And you, as well. Surely you can stay for dinner." His aunt, petite and dark-haired, was eyeing Bex with a speculative gaze, her size no indication of her force of will, which could blast the top off a mountain. He sensed approval on the appearance front, but there was plenty in Bex's appearance to approve of—all of it, in fact.

Maybe he was just being hopeful that they'd get along.

He sidestepped the dinner invitation. "Some other time when I can give you advance notice," he told his aunt gently. "We'll grab a bite in town. Bex has had a long day, so we need to make it an early night."

For once, Gina let it go. "Your father's on a conference call at the moment, but at least stop in and say hello on your way back."

A clear order.

"Will do," he agreed hastily, all but saluting.

As he and Bex drove away, turning onto a street that was lined with discreet driveways and manicured lawns, Bex asked him, "Is every date with you this interesting?"

"Wait until you get to the exciting part where we look at kitchen countertops and built-in ovens," he said drily.

"This is quite the neighborhood." She gestured at the massive rooflines they could glimpse in the distance, behind the professionally landscaped grounds.

"Not what you'd call homey, is it?"

"It's impressive, anyway. May I ask in general terms what your father does for a living? Oil wells? Gold mines? Diamonds?"

At her joking tone, he shot her a sidelong glance.

"Nothing so glamorous. He owns a manufacturing company that makes engine parts for almost every major car company in the world. I'm sure the conference call is with Japan or Germany or someplace like that. He does a lot of business in the US, but there's a high demand overseas, as well."

"Rich kid, huh?"

He had been. Part of that had been good, part of it not so good. "I've made my own way. Other than my college tuition—and I had an athletic scholarship, so I essentially paid for some of the tuition myself—Dad doesn't give me a dime, and I don't ask for anything. Never have. I earned the money to pay for the land and the new house by working some long hours and making a few decent investments. I thought about asking my father if he wanted to invest in the breeding venture, but he's still ticked off at me because I turned down a corporate pilot's job arranged by a friend of his. I would've been away from home a lot, sometimes for weeks at a time, so I said no. Dad's great, don't get me wrong, but growing up, I barely saw him, he worked so much. I want to *raise* my children."

"You do seem emphatic about it."

He was. Tate couldn't have explained why he was telling her so much, but he'd been dated for his trust fund before, although he already knew Bex wasn't the type to marry for money. His wife, Sandra, had felt differently, though, so he wanted to be clear on that before he entered into any potential relationship. Making that mistake once was definitely once too often.

He continued, his voice even. "The plane is a compromise. I don't mind being able to fly now and then, because if I didn't love it, I wouldn't have done it in the first place. And I don't mind letting the boys have time with their great-aunt when I take my father here or there on short business trips. But Mustang Creek is the kind of place I wish I'd grown up."

"It's great," Bex said. "Hadleigh and Mel and I had a ball as kids, riding our bikes everywhere, eating ice cream in the park, playing Optimist softball… Small-town stuff, but those are good memories."

He turned on to Cheyenne's main thoroughfare, busy with traffic, and headed toward the warehouse store his builder had recommended, saying he often did business with the company. They were reliable and carried quality materials. "Seems to me the three of you are still making them. Good memories, I mean."

"That's true—not that everything's quite as simple these days." Bex laughed, her profile serene. "Hadleigh's the impulsive one, and Melody can be outspoken, not to mention stubborn. I have my faults, too, of course. I can be really competitive, but I'm also the peacemaker in the bunch. If we were all the same, I doubt we'd get along so well."

"I'd really like it if Ben, Adam and Josh formed that kind of friendship. They're young boys, so they're over-the-top sometimes, but they seem to enjoy being with each other. It's good for all three of them. My kids are new to town, essentially, and Josh is going through a tough time."

"The fishing trip is a wonderful idea."

Tate spotted the building and pulled into the lot. "You aren't the one who's going to be taking all those minnows off the hook." He chuckled. "Hey, we'll have fun. They'll learn to pee in the woods, like real men."

"Don't you dare encourage them to do that," Bex warned, but she was laughing again.

"Males are born with that instinct," he informed her, "so I won't *have* to encourage them." A pause. "Okay, let's get the hard part over with, shall we? The shopping, I mean. Even though I can make decisions with the best of 'em, choosing kitchen cabinets isn't one of my strong points."

IT WOULD'VE HELPED if he'd taken her by the construction site so she could get a feel for the layout and materials of his new house before he'd flown her halfway across Wyoming to do something as important as advise him on his "forever house," as he'd called it. He'd mentioned something earlier about seeing the place, but that idea had fallen by the wayside.

Still, Bex had to admit, it was fun to look at the different kinds of granite and marble, backsplashes, faucets and other fixtures, spending someone else's money. Tate had asked for her opinions, after all. He approved the spruce cabinets she suggested, and the perfect bronze handles, too, and offered no resistance when she steered him away from granite to a poured concrete countertop a slightly darker color than the cabinets.

"A farmhouse sink," she said firmly as they surveyed that aisle. "It's beautiful and it'll suit the rustic nature of the house."

"I don't even know what you mean by a farmhouse sink. Feel free to enlighten me," he added mildly. "To me, a sink is a sink. That's why I asked for advice."

At first he balked at the six-burner gas stove, not because of the price, although that was substantial, but because he claimed he could cook about five dishes, and none of them required more than two burners. Bex reminded him that preferences tended to change over time, and so did circumstances. He might meet a woman who practiced the culinary arts in a serious way...or he might develop a passion for them himself. Plus, his sons would grow up and most likely have wives and children of their own, which meant there'd be family gatherings—Thanksgivings and Christmases and birthdays and who knew what other celebrations. *Then* he'd see the wisdom of a properly equipped kitchen.

Tate seemed enthralled, if a bit amused, by the broad picture she painted.

Finally, her case made, she brought the speech full-circle. "It's your forever house, right?" She ran her hand lightly, almost wistfully, along the gleaming top of the stove. "I think I can speak for most women and say that I'd love to have something like this. My rule is, if you're going to do it, do it right."

A stainless-steel side-by-side refrigerator with a bottom-drawer freezer came next, and by then they'd covered the basics. Tate put the total on his credit card—a massive amount—and didn't blink an eye when the woman obviously assumed Bex was his wife.

Beyond a doubt, this had to be the most unusual first date ever.

"Food," Tate said succinctly as they left the building. "Next order of business. Apparently, making domestic decisions, especially about kitchens and fridges and stoves, causes intense hunger."

Bex smiled and agreed that it was time to eat. Privately, she was glad he hadn't accepted his aunt's invitation to dinner. The people in Tate's family were probably quite friendly, but sitting down to a meal with them might be too much, too soon.

Besides, she had no idea where this was all going— or if it was going anywhere. Tate was a widower and he'd never mentioned his wife. He had two young sons to bring up, a major construction project to complete and a new business to organize.

Bex's own situation was hardly less complicated; she had her sister and nephew living with her all of a sudden, plus fitness club franchises opening across the country, which meant that, of necessity, she traveled a great deal. There were "significant learning curves" attached to "growing the business," as her financial adviser, who had a great fondness for corporate clichés, constantly told her. And, deep down, she wasn't completely sure she'd ever gotten over Will's death a decade ago.

Bex grasped the permanence of that loss, accepted that there were no guarantees in life. But emotionally... well, some part of her still expected her lost soldier to come marching home.

Granted, things were different now. Tate wasn't fighting in a war. Unfortunately, there were other dangers besides bullets and bombs and, like anybody else, he could die. He was a man who flew small planes and would be working with large animals, both situations that could put him at risk... Death could happen close to home, not just on a faraway battlefield, as it had with Will.

Bex pushed those thoughts to the back of her mind. She was with an attractive—make that sexy-as-hell— man. No need for any big decisions yet. If ever...

Why not simply enjoy the moment?

The restaurant was busy, since it was a Saturday evening, but they got a table for two fairly quickly, which might have been due to the flirtatious hostess and her interest in Tate as he explained that, no, sorry, he hadn't made a reservation. Bex was still trying to decide if she should be amused or annoyed when they were seated.

"Does that always work?" she asked, settling in.

"What?" Oh, so innocent.

"That suave, charming way you have. That smile."

He pretended to be puzzled, picked up his menu and finally grinned at her over the top of it. "Assuming that I *am* suave and charming, with a memorable smile, I have only one question. Do any of those things work on you?"

Now they were getting onto unstable ground. In fact, this was a quicksand sort of question. Bex felt a flutter in the pit of her stomach, unrelated to hunger, and took her time answering. "The way a man smiles certainly makes a difference to a woman," she said seriously, feeling like a humorless fool, but unable to respond in kind. "And yours just happens to be wicked."

He flashed it then, full force, with that hint of a dimple in his left cheek included, no doubt, to increase the wattage. "Fear not, fair damsel," he teased. "You're safe with me. Translation—lighten up a little." He watched her for a long, silent moment. "I think you just gave me a compliment. I'm still processing that." Another pause. "My aunt liked you."

Bex had managed to relax, ever so slightly. "She saw me for about thirty seconds."

"I know Gina Calder pretty well. She has the instincts of a barracuda when it comes to sizing people up." Another of those conversational hairpin turns followed. "Are we ordering separately or do we want to share?"

This entire evening she'd been outmaneuvered. Bex gave up. "I say we share. You choose for both of us because I'm too hungry to think. I am planning to have a glass of wine, though, and I'll feel guilty you can't, but my feet still hurt and you didn't tell me I'd be meeting your family. So we'll be even."

"I would never drink and fly a plane or drive, but I supervised three boys for at least half the day. Do I get sympathy points for that?"

"Absolutely. Once we touch down safely, I'll be the first to hand you a cold beer."

"Like a serving wench? You'd wear the outfit? I want a low-cut bodice."

"Don't push it."

In the end, ordering was a joint process, and they chose spring rolls and mango salad to start, followed by shrimp pad thai and lemongrass chicken; everything was delicious. Her glass of California chardonnay was exactly the kind she liked and accompanied the meal perfectly.

She did meet his father briefly later that evening, when they stopped by the house. Tate's dad was an older version of his son, with some silver at his temples and a genial smile.

Later still, as they taxied along the runway before takeoff, she was already yawning. "He seems nice."

"Most of the time he is. But appearances can be deceiving."

"Duly noted. I might point out, though, that none of us are nice *all* the time."

"That's the third yawn. Feel free to nap. It's a short flight, but you still have to take Josh home." He pretended to be concentrating hard. "Let's see, you ran a race, took a flight you didn't know you were going to take and helped a hopeless bachelor organize what I suspect will be a killer kitchen. Like I told my aunt, you've had a full day."

Bex sighed, admiring Tate from the corner of her eye.

He had a clean profile and handled the plane so effortlessly he didn't even seem to be thinking about it. She *was* tired, but pleasantly so. It had been a lovely evening, and a treat just to get away. Her feet did hurt; tomorrow, she knew from experience, they'd *really* hurt. Something to look forward to, although she'd signed up for it, so there was no one to blame but herself.

"You, on the other hand, supervised three boys all morning—as you modestly pointed out. You took them to the race, then you flew us to Cheyenne, drove us around and also did the shopping. And now you're flying us back," she said with a sleepy smile. "You've had a full day, too."

The night sky was brilliant with stars, the earlier inclement weather having headed south into the Midwest. A vast arch of velvet black was studded with diamonds, almost like something Melody would make. That gave Bex an idea.

Tate had already done a lot for Josh—and he'd met her nephew mere days ago. She wanted to thank him. Melody had made an impressive clock for her husband, Spence. Everything she did was one of a kind, and in this particular case, she'd used an outline of their ranch house as a background, Tripp had cut the metal pieces required by her design and a local artisan had made the frame from wood found on the property. Everyone who saw it urged Melody to expand her jewelry design business to include artistic clocks.

Unique, personal… Bex loved the thought of it.

A similar piece with a silhouette of his new log house would fit perfectly in Tate's new kitchen. She could commission it, Mel could create it and Tripp would help again because he and Tate were friends. She knew full well that Melody would never take her money. Bex could provide the kitchen design and color of the cabinets, so maybe all of them could go in on the project together.

Housewarming gift: solved.

This landing was as smooth as the last one. Even though it was past Josh's bedtime, it wasn't *too* late, considering two flights, the shopping and dinner. At least she'd be able to sleep in tomorrow, since it was Sunday.

"I'm going to sleep like the dead myself," Tate said, as if reading her mind on the drive back to the Galloway ranch. "This house-building thing was going to be challenging, I knew that going in, but I'm looking forward to being settled again." He sent her a quick smile. "Word of warning—for a vagabond pilot, I'm darned boring. Coffee black. Toast with butter, no jelly. I've eaten all kinds of different food, like I did tonight, but just give me a medium-rare steak, a baked potato and a salad, and I'm happy."

"Word of warning?" Bex looked at him, which wasn't a chore for any woman. "Is that your way of asking me for another date?"

"Not very smooth, but yes."

There was that darned smile again.

"Hmm, I'll have to mull it over," she told him mischievously. "I'll get back to you."

CHAPTER SIX

TATE POURED ANOTHER cup of coffee and went over the plans again. One of the tough decisions he'd have to make was the size of the barn itself. He didn't have the resources to be too extravagant; still, it would be so much easier—and save money—to do it right the first time, rather than adding on later.

He might have to consider asking his father to invest, after all. That would be the more practical route, but he balked at it.

One of the things he wanted to include was a small separate cabin/bunkhouse next to the stables so that eventually, with luck, he could hire staff to help with the horses. Staff who could live right on the ranch. Stalls had to be mucked out, horses would need to be fed, exercised, started or trained, if they were going to be sold as saddle horses. With a few animals he could handle all that, but turning this into a legitimate business meant he'd require help.

The problem was if he so much as mentioned the word *investment* to his father, the man became relentlessly overinvolved. Let him put up one dime, and there'd be spreadsheets and reports and phone calls. All Tate wanted was to live on a serene piece of property with a spectacular view of the Tetons and raise horses and his sons.

It seemed straightforward enough. In theory.

His father's approach to business was probably the correct one, but Tate wasn't out to make a fortune, he just wanted to provide a good life for his children and have a simple existence in a more wholesome environment, rather than a crowded city.

"I need to decide." He ran his fingers through his hair and said it out loud.

"'Bout what?"

He hadn't realized that Adam had wandered into the kitchen, still sleepy and decked out in his Batman pajamas, his hair messy, dark eyes inquiring.

Tate saw a reflection of his own features in his son's small face, and he had to admit that whatever problems he had in this world, they faded away when he looked at his child. "I was wondering if I wanted more coffee or a glass of orange juice. You need to make a big decision, too. Cereal or waffles?"

"Waffles."

Of course the kid chose waffles, since they involved syrup. These were of the toaster variety, but Tate tossed some fresh blueberries on top and handed over a glass of milk. "You guys have fun last night?"

Adam nodded, his mouth full.

"Still want to go fishing?"

Another emphatic nod.

Naturally he'd guessed what the answer would be. "I hope Josh and his dad can go, too." He'd mentioned it to them at the finish line yesterday; there'd been general excitement but no specific reaction to the option of including Greg.

Adam swallowed and washed down his mouthful of waffle with milk. "Josh don't want his dad."

"Doesn't," Tate corrected automatically.

His son stopped eating for a moment to inform him, "He wants Aunt Bex to go instead."

"Fishing?"

That was an interesting picture. She was the athletic type; no one would deny that. Still…he could also clearly remember the slender figure in that black skirt and the graceful curves under the gold sweater.

"She's a girl," Tate pointed out, resting his elbows on the table. The house was small and there was no dining room, just space for a kitchen table. "You want to go fishing with a girl?"

He was joking, but boys were boys, and he sometimes found himself swimming in the dark against a swift current. In other words, he didn't always grasp what they were thinking—or why.

Adam thought about it for a second and nodded again. "She's not really a girl."

Oh, he was dying to hear where *this* was going. And his youngest son was absolutely right; she was every inch a woman, not a girl at all, and Tate was only too aware of it. "How so?"

"She can run a long way."

"Okay, that's true."

"Yeah, she can run as far as you." He popped a few blueberries into his mouth. "You said so."

That stung a little, but male pride wasn't the issue here. He *had* said that as they waited for Bex to cross the finish line. It never ceased to amaze him how children remembered even the most casual of comments. "What I said is that she can go the same distance."

"And it *was* a long way."

"It was, yes."

Adam shrugged his small shoulders. "So that means she can fish, too."

There was a certain logic to that argument, he supposed, at least to a six-year-old boy. *Girl can run as far as a guy, girl can fish just like a guy.*

Maybe she could. He sipped his coffee and considered his response. "I guess I can ask her instead of Josh's father. You're sure that's what Josh meant? Could be he's mad at his father and they need to talk."

"That's what he said. Aunt Bex." Adam polished off his breakfast. "Can I watch TV?"

It was Sunday morning, so Tate nodded. He tried to keep his children's media interaction to a minimum, but cut them some slack on weekends. Since they both read and got good grades—he pushed for both—he allowed lazy Sunday mornings.

Adam went off to the den and Tate heard the television come on. He returned to the architect's plans for another look.

Now, though, he was admittedly distracted.

He'd only met Josh's dad that one afternoon at the ranch, but what Tripp had told him didn't inspire much confidence. He hoped one of *his* children wouldn't choose someone else over him in a situation like this. There was also the issue that *he'd* prefer Bex as the other adult companion.

He didn't know if she could go, or if she'd even agree. She was busy, and the idea might not appeal to her, anyway.

In his experience, some women liked the great outdoors, and some women didn't. That wasn't exactly a profound observation, since the same could be said for men. There were boardrooms and designer suits on the one side, saddles and worn boots on the other, and everything else in between. Personally, he loved to fish, but he also liked a hot shower.

His friend Russ, the cabin's owner, had said, as if it didn't matter much, that the place had hot water from a small heater under the sink, but only enough for washing dishes. The outdoor shower, which pumped water from the lake, was cold; however, you could heat a pail on the stove and pour it in for the final rinse.

Not exactly a four-star resort.

It was only fair to let Bex know what she'd be getting into, but…if he did, she might decline. Since he hadn't been to this cabin himself, he wasn't sure what precise degree of rustic applied. It sounded on the higher end of the spectrum to him—or lower, depending on your perspective. Still, during the summer Bex had participated in chaperoning a trail ride for a group of teenage girls, so obviously she wasn't opposed to camping. If she had time to get away for a few days, maybe the idea would appeal to her.

The prospect of the trip took on a whole new rosy glow.

HADLEIGH WAS IN her quilt shop, draping a new creation over a display rack, when Bex opened the door to the tinkling of the bell. Since she sewed like someone with ten thumbs, Bex always found her friend's talent astonishing. In a philosophical discussion they'd had once over a glass of wine and some pasta dish Melody had whipped up involving garlic, peppers and a sauce made from homegrown tomatoes, they'd all agreed that their different strengths were probably what had kept them friends for so long. Just as Bex had explained to Tate the evening they'd flown to Cheyenne. During their high school days, Melody had been a cheerleader, and Bex a volleyball star. Hadleigh had aced home economics—renamed Family Studies, for some reason. She'd done it so effortlessly, as if she could create beautiful things in her sleep. They'd all muddled through adolescence and then college, a team for the most part, although they hadn't always agreed.

It was definitely time for a team meeting.

On a Sunday, the shop stayed open because during the summer and winter tourist seasons, the town was busy. But autumn was quiet in Mustang Creek. So chances were they'd get some uninterrupted minutes today.

"Mel's bringing lunch," Bex announced as she walked in.

Hadleigh looked hopeful. "Please tell me it involves those turkey burgers from Bad Billie's. I've been craving one all morning. I would've eaten one for breakfast."

"What is it with pregnant women? Can you read each other's minds? Mel said the exact same thing." Bex smiled. "I think your dream is going to come true. How's the armadillo today?"

Tripp had gone with Hadleigh to her first ultrasound, and he'd decided the baby resembled an armadillo, and the term had stuck. He'd always had a unique way of expressing himself.

"He's fine." Hadleigh ran her hand over the curve of her belly. "Moving around, amusing himself by putting various degrees of pressure on my bladder." She glanced at the display window and the sidewalk beyond. "Someone's coming in. Can you watch the front for a minute?"

"Of course." She'd noticed, with mixed pity and envy, how often both Hadleigh and Mel dashed off to the bathroom these days. Maybe she'd be in the same predicament someday.

And maybe not.

When Mel walked through the door a minute later, bag in hand, Bex had just wrapped up a calico-and-cream set of placemats for a very nice middle-aged lady. She'd ordered her purchase online, and Hadleigh was ringing it up on the old-fashioned register.

"Good call on the turkey burger," Bex said after she'd thanked her customer. "H was pining for one."

Mel deposited the bag on the counter. "I know my girl. Billie sent extra pickles, too. Obviously he buys into that pregnancy rumor. I thought it was cute."

"I love his homemade pickles and I'm not pregnant," Bex said, reaching for the bag. "I'll be happy to eat them. You two stole all the cream puffs the other day. Dibs on the pickles."

"I'll lock up for lunch," Hadleigh said. "Let's go to the back room. I can clear enough space for us to eat, and there's bottled water in the minifridge."

The back room always had scraps of material on the floor and various works in progress next to the sewing machines, but there was a small table surrounded by four chairs.

"So, emergency meeting. What's up?" Melody opened her bottle of water and lost no time in getting down to business.

"It's not an emergency," Bex argued. "Well, not really. I just need to talk about something."

"You *said* EM," Haleigh said, referring to their personal shorthand for "emergency meeting." She passed out the food. "Okay, spill."

"Tate called and asked me to go on this fishing trip

with the boys. I need a second—and third opinion—on whether I should. He told his boys that he was willing to invite Greg, too. But…Tate called this morning and said Josh wants me to go instead."

Hadleigh didn't look surprised. "Yeah, it's true. Tripp heard them talking about it last night. Somehow boys think they're whispering, but the truth is, they aren't at *all*. They're worse than deaf old ladies in church. Anyway, Josh isn't interested in his dad going along. He'd rather have you."

"I'm flattered," Bex said, briefly shutting her eyes. "And yet it breaks my heart. Tate's sons adore him. Josh should have that."

"What he needs is a rock." Melody tossed them each a napkin. "And you're his rock right now. When Tara gets it together, he might trust her again. Let's hope… Remember how much trust is involved in being a child? Someone has to feed you, take you to school, pick you up, make you smile now and then. So he wants *you* because you already do all those things for him. Seems logical to me. What's the real question, Bex? I don't think we're talking about Josh at an EM. Of course you'll go. We're talking about Tate Calder, aren't we?"

"He has you tempted, doesn't he?" Hadleigh sent her a knowing look. "Can't say I blame you. I've proven to be susceptible myself with regard to Tripp, which explains the baby bump. What's the problem?"

Their unswerving support meant a lot. "I'm…not ready."

"It's ten years since Will died," Hadleigh reminded her gently. "I understand it might feel disloyal—caring for someone else, I mean—but it isn't." Hadleigh's eyes had turned glassy with tears. "I miss Will, too, Bex, but life goes on. It has to."

Melody stepped in, reaching over to squeeze Bex's hand. "Will loved you. *We* love you, but no one expects you to sit around by yourself for the rest of your life—hence the marriage pact. On that note, no decisions have to be made today, either. Go on the trip for Josh. You'll have fun. And the more time you spend with Tate, the more easily you'll be able to figure out if he *is* the one."

"We've been on one date," Bex retorted. Not including the day they went running together, she added to herself. She picked up her sandwich. "I hope the two of you realize there's an outhouse included in this excursion. When Tate called, I could tell he didn't want to impart that information, but to give him credit, he did."

"Ouch." Hadleigh had recovered, blinking back the tears brought on by the mention of Will's name. "Okay, I concede that's not perfect. If Mel and I were there, we'd be in trouble."

"Our *husbands* would be in trouble," Melody insisted. "If Spence thought for a minute that I was going outside in the middle of the night without him, he'd be wrong. I'd be waking him up every few hours."

Bex stared down at her bracelet and touched the charm Melody had created for her. An airplane, ironically enough. Ironic because Tate hadn't even entered the scene when Mel gave it to her. The tiny charm was supposed to represent the ongoing success of her business, which had expanded within the state and in neighboring states, as well. Mel had joked that she'd probably meet someone on her travels... Which was fine, her friends had said, "as long as you bring him back home." But the way things were turning out, she didn't even have to *leave* home. "Tate's got a lot of history, too," she said, "and while Ben and Adam are great, dealing with Josh is interesting enough. Four males is about three too many."

Hadleigh took a bite of her burger. "So, you're going, then. Good choice."

"I didn't say—"

"I agree, good choice." Melody took a bite of hers, too. "Give Tate a call, Bex, and accept."

Her best friends turned to her expectantly.

She backed down. "Fine, I'll call him. And when I get there, I'll use an outhouse—not that I've got any alternative. Call me when *you* have two six-year-olds with an eight-year-old thrown in free of charge. And don't ask me to help. I suspect I'll be in the mode of never-doing-that-again."

"You'll probably have to take at least one fish off the hook." Hadleigh made a face. "Yuck, I hate that." She tucked into her food, apparently not put off by the memory. "Of course you could make Tate do the honors."

"That part of fishing is not fun." Mel nodded, helping herself to a french fry. "It's those cold mornings that freak me out. Mist drifting over the lake, noises in the woods… I always think it's Bigfoot."

"I'm a believer." Hadleigh's eyes sparkled again, but with laughter now. Her voice dropped to a theatrical whisper. "So if you hear a thump in the middle of the night, don't look outside."

"I'm going to strangle you both," Bex threatened. "And by the way, *all* of these pickles are mine."

CHAPTER SEVEN

IT HAD BEEN a long week. And now Friday had finally arrived. Fishing Friday, as Tate thought of it.

At least the plumbing was finished, and the electricians were nearly done. He was pleased with how the house looked; he particularly liked the two dormers on the second floor and the roomy front porch. The interior was still just a shell full of boxes, and the floors would be the last to go in. He'd also attended three horse sales, and even bought one mare that Tripp was currently boarding for him. There'd been a chili supper at the school and a science project for Ben. Money wasn't an issue yet, but not working bothered him, and he was stressed from chasing after the kids and answering a dozen questions a day on the house construction.

And he couldn't stop thinking about Bex Stuart.

Once she'd accepted his invitation to join them on the fishing trip, he'd made a point of not calling her because he didn't want to seem pushy. Besides, he was still sorting out a few things himself.

He stowed the fishing poles in the bed of the truck and went into the garage to dig out his tackle box and a net, and to find the box labeled Camping Gear. As the male in charge of their little expedition, he wasn't going anywhere without a kerosene lantern, two flashlights with fresh batteries, his fillet knife in case they actually caught a fish or two of legal size, his trusty iron frying pan, and some basics like salt and pepper. Already he'd stowed canned goods—including green beans, corn, chicken noodle and tomato soup, along with a box of crackers, some fruit and a box of cereal— in a plastic container to keep out mice. They'd be able to pick up some groceries; Russ had assured him there was a small store in the nearest town.

Luckily, he had three life vests, since Ben had out- grown his and had a new one, so that was covered as far as Josh was concerned. He was fairly sure Bex didn't have a kid-size one lying around. Maybe her sister would think of it, but he doubted it.

He'd been through an unfortunate marriage. They'd been people with different expectations, different, even contradictory, hope and dreams—to put it mildly. Put- ting it more harshly meant that words like *fraud* and *infidelity* and *dishonesty* would be involved. So he un- derstood that unhappiness could take its toll.

At any rate, back to the practicalities of the moment. Josh had a vest, too, the truck was packed and they were ready to go.

He called Tripp. "About to depart on the grand ad- venture. So what am I forgetting? Help me out. School's over in thirty minutes."

"Poles and tackle?"

"Check."

"Snacks?"

"On it." He had about seven kinds of granola bars, some whole-grain chips and popcorn.

"Beer for you?"

"Who do you think you're talking to?"

"Wine for Bex?"

He swore softly. "Not yet, but thanks for mentioning it. What kind is it she likes again?"

Luckily, Tripp knew. Well, not really. But he went and asked Hadleigh and gave him the name of a California chardonnay. Oh, yeah, sounded familiar now. Wasn't that what she'd had at the restaurant in Cheyenne?

"Sleeping bags, medical emergency kit, extra towels?"

The towels weren't a bad idea. Tate tossed a couple in his bag.

"Don't forget to pack your fortitude."

"My…what?"

"Fortitude. You know, the thing that might make it possible for you to endure a weekend of fishing with a female and three young boys. I have it on excellent authority that Bex isn't thrilled about the outhouse situation."

"Me neither, but at least it's a cabin, not a tent in the woods. Besides, I warned her about this setup. I considered waiting until we got there and letting it all come as a surprise. So I was a nice guy, and I want an engraved plaque congratulating me."

"If you survive this, I'll see that you get your plaque."

"Thanks," he said in an equally sardonic tone. "If I don't return, send out a search party."

"Will do, but I bet she'll know how to cleverly dispose of your body. So I'd recommend you be as charming as possible."

"I'll do my best."

The call ended, he tossed his bag into the truck, went through his mental checklist one final time and headed over to the school. All three boys were waiting; he had to go to the office and sign Josh out since he wasn't a parent. The secretary said, "They've been on the unruly side today. They're so excited about this trip. You might want to brace yourself for the drive."

This was what he liked about Mustang Creek. Yes, people knew what you were doing, and that could be uncomfortable, but they also *cared* about what you were doing. He smiled at Ms. Wainwright, who seemed bossy and overbearing on the surface but, as he'd discovered, was kind beneath that brusque exterior.

"It's very kind of you to invite Joshua." She handed him a slip of paper and peered at him over her glasses. "Becca Stuart is a very pretty young woman, isn't she?"

Word sure got around. Tate merely nodded, then beat a hasty retreat, mumbling, "Have a good weekend."

The boys were still standing with the teacher supervising the children getting on the bus, and he noticed a tightening in his throat as he saw them talking excitedly to each other, backpacks in place, small tennis shoes on their feet, Ben laughing and giving Adam a friendly shove.

No way did he regret turning down that lucrative corporate job in order to move to this small town. He'd missed too much with his children as it was. He walked up and handed the teacher the slip of paper. "I think they're all mine now."

"I recommend a tranquilizer gun," the young man overseeing the process said with humor in his voice. "Aim it at yourself. This trio is bent on conquering the wilderness, one fish at a time. I can't wait to hear their stories next week. I hope you have a net big enough to haul in a whale or two."

"I've heard these guys are more than a little wound up." He put a restraining hand on Adam's shoulder since he could sense he was going to reciprocate that shove from his brother. "I don't have a fillet knife big enough for that job, so all whales are catch and release. Come on, boys, let's go pick up Aunt Bex."

Cheers all around. He could only dream of being so popular.

Once they were in the truck, safely buckled in, backpacks at their feet, he sent her a text just before he pulled out of the school parking lot.

You ready? We're on our way.

Her reply was almost instant.

At the fitness center. See you there.

Bex's gym was on his route out of town. He was grateful—for a number of very obvious reasons—that she'd been willing to take the weekend off. Thanks to expanding her business, Bex's schedule was intense. He hoped that would be his problem someday, since being an entrepreneur was a new experience for him.

It made him nervous, hanging his children's future on a dream, but he also had confidence that he could do whatever it took to bring that dream to life.

But this weekend, anyway, he wasn't going to worry about anything, just kick back and enjoy himself.

BEX SIGNED THE LAST check and closed the ledger, her mind on the time. Payroll was done, and her manager would handle the fitness center. Meanwhile, her need to micromanage her sister's life wasn't helping much at all. Or was it?

She'd given Tara a job at the club, working as a receptionist. Tara seemed to be enjoying the attention—not to mention being relatively free of parental responsibility for the first time in six years. Bex couldn't decide whether she was making a positive difference in her sister's life or just enabling.

Tara hadn't so much as blinked an eye over the fact that Josh wanted *Bex* to go on the fishing trip instead of Greg. Or her. In fact, Tara had agreed to the plan without hesitation. Josh, she'd concluded cheerfully, would be better off with Aunt Bex. Well, Aunt Bex didn't mind, but she wasn't his *mother*.

Sighing, she checked her watch. They'd be there any minute, Tate and the boys. Was she ready?

She had packed what she considered a modest-sized suitcase, and Tate Calder had no business objecting. For a trip like this, she required clean clothes, a couple of different coats for different weather possibilities, and she'd only packed three pairs of shoes.

It was, however, a bit heavier than it looked. She wheeled it outside.

When Tate got out of his truck and approached to grab it, the boys waving from the backseat, Bex told him sternly, "Don't say a word. There's chocolate in there, too. Care to comment?"

"No, ma'am." He hefted it into the back of the truck. It made a solid clunk as it landed.

"We'll be gone for *three* days," she said. She could tell she sounded mildly defensive. And three days was stretching it; they'd arrive at the cabin sometime late afternoon and leave around that time on Sunday.

So, yes. She might have overpacked. A little.

"Remind me not to go on a vacation in Europe with you," he teased.

She sent him a venomous glare. "In your dreams. Now take me to this backwater without a bathroom where I am required to get up at the crack of dawn and put worms on a hook. The truth is, I'm so tired of paperwork, I'm almost excited about roughing it for a while."

"I bought you wine," he offered, "but it's a three-hour drive to get there. So you'll have time to decompress. I'm told the view from the screened porch is really beautiful, day or night."

Bex wished Tate didn't look so boyishly attractive and yet utterly sophisticated at the same time. When he opened her door, she got in and said, "With an outdoor bathroom, it had better be." Then she realized her tone was a bit cranky and relented. "Sorry, I'm not a princess, I promise. All this corporate stuff I'm dealing with has me frazzled. Thanks for getting the wine. That was thoughtful of you. And the porch sounds great."

When he slid into the driver's seat, he said lightly, "You're allowed to be frazzled now and then. Wait until the end of this weekend. I suspect ultimate frazzlization for both of us."

The chatter from the backseat supported that theory.

"Frazzlization is a word?" Bex asked, relaxing for the first time all day.

"It is now. I just invented it." He deftly put the car in drive and they pulled out. "We'll find out if it's dictionary worthy this weekend. Even Ms. Wainwright said the boys were geared up."

She was glad to hear that Josh was excited about something. However, she wasn't happy that Tara had plans to meet with Greg so they could discuss the divorce, but she wasn't her sister's keeper, so she needed to let it go.

"I have to warn you I'm really good at catching fish."

Tate glanced over at her. "Warn me?"

"It isn't a skill," Bex said, shaking her head. "I shouldn't tell you this. I should act like I have some secret expertise, but what happens is I throw in a line, and a fish bites it. Some sort of weird karma. As far as I can tell, I can't *not* catch fish. My father used to stick a pole in my hand and then laugh the entire time. He'd take it back and reel them in. He's always said he's surprised they don't just jump in the boat and land at my feet."

"So, obviously, you're good at it."

"No, you're missing the point. I'm *lucky* at it, that's all. If you want to talk weight training, I'm good at that. When it comes to fishing, there's no skill involved on my part. To be honest, other than sitting in the sun and admiring the scenery, I'm not a real fishing fan. So I'm warning you that once I've got one on the line, you'll have to run the show."

"Hey, you're already the favorite person around these parts, and you'll be even more popular if fish levitate out of the water and land in your lap."

"The favorite?"

"The boys talk about Aunt Bex all the time. They love you, all three of them."

Josh's feelings she understood. She'd known him all his life, and at the moment Tara wasn't what you'd call emotionally available. And, she supposed, Ben and Adam didn't have a mother, so it followed that they might look at her the same way their friend did.

She wasn't even sure about the likelihood of a relationship with Tate, so his sons' apparent adoration was overwhelming. Then again, both Hadleigh and Mel were pregnant and how overwhelming was *that*? She could deal with this.

"I love them right back." She leaned her head back and closed her eyes. "I'm just grateful you're taking me away. I dealt with my share of headaches today. One more phone call and I might have lost it."

The boys had switched on a video in the backseat and were whooping it up. Tate said, "*This* is more peaceful?"

She thought it over. "Um, equally chaotic, but better-quality chaos, let's put it that way. So they're a little loud. I don't mind. If you think the sound of children laughing would ever put me off, you don't know me."

"But I'm *getting* to know you."

He couldn't have said anything more moving.

Oops. Not quite, because he added, "Or should I say *we're* getting to know each other."

They were, and if she had to guess, he wasn't interested in a serious involvement, either.

Bex lightened it up. "Well, I do know your favorite color is brown, so I suppose you're right."

That won her a laugh. "I actually think my favorite color is somewhere between green and gold. You, by the way, have the most beautiful eyes."

She was in trouble, but she'd known that already. "Based on you and Tripp, I'm beginning to think all fly-boys are smooth talkers. How he ever convinced Hadleigh to forgive him for hauling her out of the church at her first wedding is a mystery to me. He was right, mind you, but she was mad as a bee-stung bear at the time."

"Considering her current state, I'd say she forgave him and then some." He signaled to pass a semi as they cleared the exit. "At least both she and Melody seem to be feeling well. It's not like that for every woman when she's carrying a baby."

Bex waited. She expected him to say something about his wife, but he didn't.

They were quite a pair. It wasn't as though she'd talked about Will, either.

The radio was playing quietly; Kenny Chesney, she thought, but the boys were so loud it was impossible to tell for sure. "I think we need a bullhorn to talk to each other," Tate muttered then raised his voice. "Hey, guys, tone it down, please. You don't have to whisper, but keep it under control."

"Sorry, Dad," Adam said.

The relative quiet lasted for about three seconds flat. Bex couldn't help it; she started to laugh at Tate's resigned expression when the volume went back up, and he grinned and shook his head. "My authority works like magic. All I have to do is speak, and they instantly obey, such is my power. There won't be a fish within miles of our boat with this crew on board. Telling them to be quiet is like asking the crowd at a Mardi Gras party to behave."

Bex was just glad to hear Josh having fun. "There's a reason the expression 'boys will be boys' exists."

"I hope you're as cheerful about it on the way home. To change the topic for a minute—I can make hamburgers and spaghetti, but otherwise my cooking abilities aren't impressive. I'm more than willing to prepare either of those difficult culinary delights. If you want anything else, feel free to step in when we pick up groceries. Adam would eat hot dogs three meals a day, but I'm the bad guy who won't allow it. I think he might end up being a lawyer. He has a very compelling argument about potato chips being a viable food group."

"I guess duck confit with roasted pears, maybe an endive salad on the side, is out?" She said it with a straight face.

"Sounds good to me, but I suspect it won't get a lot of enthusiasm from the rest of this group."

"In that case, I'll see what I can do."

CHAPTER EIGHT

THE TRUCK BUMPED along a rutted lane that was barely serviceable, but the small faded sign near the entrance off a dirt road that said Granger told Tate he had the right place.

The term "middle of nowhere" applied.

Although he hadn't really expected anything else, it was damned remote. Nothing but mountains, a lake and a Wyoming tree line with a scattering of ponderosa pines, Douglas fir and aspens. Reliable cell phone service was not an option and hadn't been for about thirty miles.

They bumped along until he was beginning to have his doubts that there even *was* a cabin until he finally spotted it.

Naturally, the first thing they passed was the infamous outhouse. He parked in a relatively flat place near the woodpile, which, thankfully was more than ample. According to the thermostat in his truck, the temperature had dropped fifteen degrees since they'd begun to gain altitude. It was still a pleasant fall day, but he'd be cranking up the woodstove once the sun went down.

"Looks like we're here." He switched off the engine. "You guys carry your own gear."

The cabin itself was modest and quaint, to say the least—log construction with a simple one-story roofline and plain walls. Two small square windows flanked a plain wooden door, and there was no front porch. The structure sat on a hill that plunged down to the crystal water. A series of steps that were really just flat stones embedded in the hillside led down to a small weathered dock, but fortunately there was a hand railing made of pine logs.

The view was, in a word, spectacular.

Even the boys were quiet when they got out of the car. The silence only lasted for a few minutes, but that it happened at all was telling. Bex looked at him, looked at the view again and said, "Okay, you win. I can deal with the outhouse."

Tate nodded. "Russ said it was nice up here. I don't think eloquence is his strong suit. This is a lot better than nice. His grandfather built the place back in the forties as a fishing shack. He owned all the shoreline on this side. On the other side, the state bought the land from a logging company and declared it a state forest. When he said private, he meant it. In fact, I'd say we're the only people around for miles."

Bex agreed. "I bet if you were here when winter decided to arrive, you'd be stuck until next spring."

The rippling water reflected the blue sky, the tree-lined perimeter, the soaring distant peaks already dusted with snow. Adam tugged at his sleeve. "Can we go down to the lake?"

"No. Not until everyone has a life vest on. Give me a few minutes to unpack." Tate ruffled his son's hair. "I know you can swim, but that lake is cold and deep. It isn't at all the same as the local swimming pool. Promise me you won't fool around and try to push one another in. I want your word on it."

"I promise."

Her expression was stricken. "I didn't even *think* about life jackets!"

"I had an extra one. You're covered." He handed her the bag with the vests and towels. "I'll carry in our gear and the groceries. Like I said, the boys can tote their own. This isn't exactly camping, but if I were a betting man, I'd say it's darned close."

"Is there electricity?" She glanced doubtfully at the cabin.

"Generator. We'll be doing our cooking on the gas grill out back. Russ keeps a backup propane tank, and it has a burner."

She wore a fluffy navy sweater with deep pockets, jeans and boots, and somehow managed to look sexier than a swimsuit model posing in the surf. "So everything will be fried or grilled. This is definitely a manly outing. Is it okay if I insist on napkins?"

Tate grinned. "You can sauté stuff on the grill, right? I have a feeling it won't be the same experience as that fancy stove you picked out for my house, but for three days, we'll get along fine. Go ahead with the napkins. I hope you brought some, though, because it didn't occur to me, even though we cavemen actually use them at home."

To his credit, he didn't mention the weight of her suitcase again. He just took it out of the truck. The boys were already at the door, itching to get inside, don their vests and run down to the lake. He remembered being that age, although his father's version of fishing was the deep-sea variety, with expensive guides and charted boats and people strapped into chairs.

He would've preferred something like this a hundred times more.

"I bought some paper napkins when we stopped for groceries in that little town. For tonight, I was thinking along the lines of tortellini soup and grilled garlic bread for dinner. Salad is optional for the boys, but I'll make one and they can choose to eat it or not."

"You won't get any argument from me." He fished the keys out of his pocket. "Now, let's go see just what we're dealing with so we can get the boys on the lake before we have a riot on our hands."

The interior was a reflection of the exterior in that there was a table with two benches that had obviously been made from an old door, a single couch in one corner, and a sideboard that—he hoped—contained enough dishes for five people. The kitchen was so small it hardly fit two people. It had a refrigerator that had to be circa 1940 and also a sink and maybe two feet of counter space. There was a woodstove, of course, and two tiny bedrooms, both sparsely furnished. One with a full-size bed and one with two sets of bunk beds. Not exactly luxury, but better than a tent. The best part was the view from the back windows. They faced the lake, and the sun was setting, the sky growing indigo and crimson, and there was a door to a deck that overlooked the lake.

The unprepossessing front didn't matter. The outhouse really didn't matter, either—to him, anyway. If he was going to spend money on this place, he'd do what Russ had done. Never mind a bathroom. Add a great spacious deck instead.

"Look. Don't miss this."

"Oh…wow." Bex, who was kneeling by Josh, stopped abruptly in the act of buckling his vest.

"I've seen a lot of sunsets in a lot of different places," he said quietly. "Bali. Gibraltar. Greenland… But this is exceptional. I do love Wyoming. It feels like home."

"Aunt Bex, can you help me?" Adam was wrestling with the buckles, sunsets way down on his list of concerns when there was a perfectly good lake a few steps away.

"Yep." She finished with Josh and moved on to Adam. Before Tate could take a step, she shook her head. "I'm on it."

She did seem to have things under control, so Tate went to get her suitcase and the grocery bags. When he was carrying them in he was almost mowed down by three young boys on a mission, bursting out the door at full speed. He put the suitcase in the front bedroom and carried in the food, setting everything on the counter.

Bex peered anxiously out the window. "They'll be okay, right?"

"They just want to look around. They've got life vests and orders not to push each other into the lake. They should be fine. You pour yourself a glass of wine and we'll go sit out on the deck, keep an eye on them. In the next thirty minutes I'm going to fire up the woodstove—it's bound to get a little chilly in here otherwise. I'll start the generator, too."

"You do realize you have to go check and see if there is a rabid badger or something like that living in the outhouse. It looks prehistoric."

"I wasn't aware there were badgers in Wyoming." He said it with a muffled laugh.

"I think they migrate this time of year. Do you suppose there are wineglasses anywhere?"

Tate surveyed the bare-bones interior and wished he'd thought of that when Tripp suggested the wine. "I'm kind of doubting it."

Bex smiled. "Me, too, but quite frankly, despite the facilities and the fact that I might have to swill out of the bottle, I'm glad to be here."

THERE WERE WORSE THINGS than sitting next to Tate Calder, sipping her favorite wine—Hadleigh had had a hand in that, Bex knew it—albeit from a plastic cup. Given how peaceful and pretty the setting was, the hardships were overwhelmed by the positives.

A breeze scented with pine and water swept across the lake. The late afternoon was cool, but she'd dressed for it, and Tate had turned on the grill burner, so her soup was on a low simmer, ready for the pasta at the last minute.

All systems go. Except for her personal life… Nothing organized about that.

She knew one thing, though. They were going to sleep together.

Yep, she knew it, and she knew he did, too. The awareness was there between them, much as she'd like to deny it.

Or maybe she didn't want to deny it at all.

It wasn't going to happen on this trip, not with three pairs of eyes watching their every move, but eventually. Unless he proved to be the worst frog when she kissed him, and she doubted it.

Kissing. They hadn't even done *that* yet.

Josh started yelling and jumping up and down on

the dock. He did have a fish at the end of his line, and obviously no idea what to do with it. But there was a great deal of excitement down below. He yelled, "Aunt Bex, look!"

"I see it!"

Tate got to his feet. "I'll be back. You're handling dinner, so taking fish off the hook can fall to me—with the warning that all three of them need to be doing it on their own by the end of this weekend."

Fine with her. As it was, *she* was trekking to an outhouse. It was hardly a new structure, but not too bad. Trade that for the view—and she still came out ahead.

"Um, I hate to admit this, but I don't take *my* fish off the hook. I believe I've mentioned that." She took another sip of wine and watched him descend the steps, enjoying that view, too. There was something about a man in jeans and a flannel shirt...

The lesson was brief, for the sake of the fish, but she watched as the boys nodded when Tate deftly slid his hand over the fins and extracted the hook, then gently placed the trout back in the water. From this distance, she couldn't hear every word he said, but he did indicate a specific size by holding his palms apart, no doubt explaining how big the fish needed to be for them to keep it.

This was *so* good for Josh.

It was difficult to blame her brother-in-law for the *whole* mess when she knew it was her sister's choice to be with him. And, of course, part of the problem was that he and Tara were a bad fit. Bex had really tried to be positive about the man, but her first impression of Greg had never improved.

Tate came back and sat down next to her in a wooden

chair. "Well, at least we can say that our fishing expedition included catching fish. One fish, anyway."

"Wait until tomorrow morning," she said. "What time are we embarking on this expedition?"

"Dawn."

"Dawn?" she repeated wryly. "Why? You need to tell me again."

"Ms. Stuart, that's when the fish get up."

"Idiots. Why don't they sleep in?"

"I can't answer that." He stretched out his legs. "Why run a marathon?"

He had a point.

After a moment of introspection, she said, "A sense of accomplishment."

"I can only speak for myself, but I agree. I wanted to see if I could do it." He tipped back his beer and took a gulp. "That soup smells fantastic. We need a ten-minute warning for hand-washing and vest removal. Just prying them off the dock could take that long. Hey, look at Ben. I know my son and he'll be immovable until he catches one, too. This is a competition now."

Bex could sympathize. "I'm fairly competitive, too."

"You think?" Tate's tone might have crossed over into irritating, if his smile wasn't so attractive.

There were some things best dealt with once and for all. Yes, she was competitive, and he wasn't forthcoming about his wife, and there was a truckload of unresolved issues between them, but this didn't have to be one of them.

So she set aside her glass, got up and crossed the foot or so that separated their chairs.

She leaned over and braced her hands on the arms

of his chair, noting the startled expression on his face before she kissed him.

She kissed *him*. Mel and Hadleigh would faint if they ever found out, and someday, they almost certainly would. In the end, she usually told them everything.

It was the real deal. Her lips, his lips, and she wasn't shy about the rest of it, either, but neither was he. By the time it was over, she was on his lap and he'd dropped his beer so he could put his arms around her. She'd vaguely heard the clunk as the bottle hit the deck when he pulled her close.

It was the reaction she would've hoped for, if she'd rehearsed this moment in her mind. Which she hadn't...

If she'd thought about the impulse at all, she would never have done it. She'd admit to being competitive, but impulsiveness wasn't typically one of her faults.

"I felt we should get that out of our way," she said, eventually extricating herself from his embrace. Her voice was more than a little off-key. It had been a very nice kiss.

His hold tightened, but then he let her go, although his dark eyes remained intent. "We might need more practice. Let's call this a trial run."

More shouts from the dock. This time it was Adam dancing around. "I think your fish removal services are needed," she said, pointing. "I'll get the soup finished and the garlic bread on."

CHAPTER NINE

DINNER WAS LOUD, but that wasn't unusual. Tate found it reassuring the boys had so much energy; he tried to keep it in check when it really mattered, but he'd long ago come to the conclusion that he wasn't going to be one of those parents ruling with an iron fist. He required order, not a dictatorship. Yes, they got a little rowdy, but that was part of being a kid. He was just grateful that while he was taking Adam's fish off the hook, Ben caught one. All through the meal, his oldest son crowed about the fact that it was bigger than the fish the other two had caught. Adam and Josh didn't argue or object, and peace was preserved.

"Hey, carry your bowls and plates to the sink, please," Tate said when dinner was finished.

"'Kay." Ben motioned to the younger boys. "Let's go." At the last second he remembered his manners—without prompting—and said politely, "Thanks, Aunt Bex. It was good."

The other two chimed in. "Thanks."

The soup *was* a major hit. Adam had declined salad, but didn't say a word about the flecks of parsley in the broth, so Bex was a positive influence because anything green usually meant instant refusal. Oregano on pizza had been known to bring about an impasse. Hadleigh deserved credit for her lasagna, too.

All three boys had taken second helpings, and he didn't blame them. The soup was not only delicious, it was a smart choice, too, since ultimately it was glorified chicken noodle soup—always acceptable to kids.

"You are definitely *the* favorite," he told her when the kids went off to watch a video on his laptop in the bedroom. "Dinner sealed the deal. I'm old news."

The moon had come out, shining on the water. While the generator ran the basic functions like the pump and water heater, he'd lit the kerosene lantern, and the flickering light showed off the golden streaks in Bex's hair. She rested her elbows on the table, laughter in her eyes. "When it comes to dealing with kids, I'm taking lessons from a pro. You aren't old news to me."

That kiss. He wished someone had been filming it, because he wanted to replay it, time and again. Hell, he wanted to *relive* it.

"An amateur at best, but I'm trying."

"You seem to be doing a decent job. I wish my sister would, too. I wish she'd start making some important decisions, I mean." Bex looked pensive. "I don't even want to think about what she's doing tonight. I swear Greg can talk her into anything. Josh does *not* need to be strapped into a roller coaster his entire childhood. Mel calls Greg The Manipulator, and I don't disagree. He's cheated on Tara so often, and she still takes him back. What's wrong with her? How is that okay?"

"My wife was unfaithful."

He hadn't meant to let that slip. Maybe it was the cozy cabin; maybe it was the boys laughing in the other room. Or the uncertainty in his life. Or that memorable kiss. But he'd said it.

Out loud. Even he was surprised.

Bex's initial silence was significant.

Then she said, "Unfaithful...to *you*?"

The incredulity was flattering, the memory painful. He weighed his response. "When I figured it out, she didn't deny it. I'm partially to blame, I guess, since I was never home. If Adam didn't look so much like me, I might have doubts that he's mine. It wouldn't matter, because I'd love him, anyway, but it's part of the reason I walked away from my job. Tripp has exactly the right idea. Money isn't everything. When he told me he was selling out, I really started to think about what I was going to do next."

"You're *not* to blame."

Bex seemed outraged on his behalf.

He didn't talk about this with *anyone*. Why was he talking about it now? Tate sighed and ran his fingers through his hair. "When something goes wrong, it's impossible not to second-guess what you could have done differently. I was gone a lot. When Sandra got sick it was just a virus, or so we both thought. We were right, but it hit her hard. I can't tell you how fast it happened. We'd agreed we were going to file for divorce two weeks before she died from the flu."

"From the *flu*?" Bex stared at him, disbelieving.

He'd had the same reaction.

"Influenza fatality rates are why they have the vaccines. She was a perfectly healthy adult. Never smoked, stayed fit, but it happened, anyway." He'd had it explained to him at the hospital by sympathetic physicians with reasonable voices and a load of statistics. None of it had helped. "Her immune system just...didn't handle it. They don't know why but for some people it's lethal."

"I'm so sorry," she whispered.

He was, too. Not only because he was suddenly widowed, but because his children had been perceptive enough to sense their parents' unrest—and then they were faced with this catastrophic loss. He'd gone over and over in his head what he was going to say about splitting up their family, but he'd never rehearsed having to tell them their mother had died.

"Despite everything, so was I."

"And so you turned down your father's friend's lucrative offer and moved to Mustang Creek instead." Bex rested her chin on her fist.

"There was some soul-searching involved. My sons had lost their mother. I was worried enough about how they'd handle us splitting up, and then...everything changed. I couldn't leave, even with my aunt in charge, for what might be weeks at a time. Money is a necessity, we all know that, but I'd rather do with less and have peace of mind. The job would've entailed flying professionals all over the world. Try to picture me being far away somewhere and getting a message that either Ben or Adam had the slightest sign of a cold."

"I can't imagine."

"Those would be some stranded executives as I made new flight plans and took off at the first sniffle. So let's say I chose my current path as much for me, as for my children. It also made me reassess whether they should grow up in a big city. There are advantages, but at the same time, the dangers are there."

"Spence makes sure Mustang Creek is as safe as any place can be. He can't control people getting the flu, but he keeps the peace."

He didn't doubt that. "Tripp agrees, and that's part of why I moved there."

"I'm glad you did."

He was, too, and it was starting to give him pause. He'd never sworn off women, but he'd decided that commitment was a bad idea. He needed to take into consideration that his sons might get too attached, and then suffer another loss if it didn't work out. Tate stood and took both their bowls. "You cooked. I'll clean up."

She shook her head. "Team effort. Do you want to wash or dry and put away?"

"I'd better wash. You found the dishes and set the table. Nice touch with the leaf arrangement for a centerpiece, by the way. Thoughtful, but you do realize the boys probably didn't even notice."

She'd picked up a few fall leaves and put them in a Mason jar, along with some pinecones and a sprig or two of greenery.

"Mel would have whipped up something a lot more artistic, but I gave it a shot. No, the boys didn't notice, but *you* did."

He didn't really have a reply.

IN THE CORPORATE WORLD, her attempts at flirtation could be filed under: *improvement needed*.

First she'd gone and planted one on Tate Calder without any warning—he'd warmed right up to it, but still... Her idea of a centerpiece had been a jar of leaves because that was romantic all right, and after they'd finished cleaning up, she'd asked him to walk her to the outhouse.

Bex came to the conclusion that, oh, yeah, she was one sexy woman.

In her defense, he'd looked deliciously kissable sitting there on the deck; the leaves were all she could come up with, since it was fall and all the wildflowers were gone; and she didn't want to walk to the outhouse alone because there were bears and mountain lions, and if Mel and Hadleigh were to be believed, maybe even Bigfoot.

The only hot water in the place was from the kitchen sink, so she washed her face there after slipping into her pajamas, which were of the flannel variety and not exactly enticing, but at least practical. The gold-and-green plaid had appealed to her, plus, she had a feeling that once they all fell asleep and the woodstove died down, it might get quite chilly.

She slipped on wooly socks and was about to get into bed when she saw the first one. Yep, the *first* one. A mouse, not a small one, either, scampered across the bed and disappeared between the pillows, followed by a second. Bex was not a stand-on-a-chair kind of girl when it came to rodents, but she backed up about three feet just the same. To make matters worse, she could hear a lot of rustling, and it was definitely coming from the bed.

Outhouse—not perfect. But she'd live. Fishing at dawn in the morning chill. Fine, she'd agreed to that.

Bed filled with mice? No freaking way!

She grabbed her suitcase and wheeled it out—she didn't want mice in there, either—as usual almost slamming into Tate who was locking the front door.

"Whoa, you planning on making a break for it? I warn you, I have the keys to the truck." His gaze sharpened. "Is something wrong?"

"Uh, we have a problem."

"Like what?" He peered down into her face. The moonlight coming through the tall windows was their only illumination. They were both whispering, since the boys had finally fallen asleep. It had taken no little effort to get them to settle down, and there'd been some bickering over who got which bunk until Tate stepped in and assigned beds, telling them they could switch around the next night if they wanted.

"There are mice in my room, *that's* what," she muttered.

He swore softly. "Are you sure? I didn't see any sign of them in the other bedroom. Or the kitchen."

She bristled. "I can recognize a mouse, thank you very much. I can also hear them, and the count is already up to two. Not on the floor, mind you, but *on the bed*. So, yeah, I'm pretty sure. But feel free to go have a look for yourself."

"Give me a minute." He grabbed a flashlight from a shelf by the door. What he-man mouse-conquering feat he was going to perform, she had no idea, but Bex was 100 percent certain she wasn't sleeping in that bed.

He emerged about a minute later, a resigned expression on his face. "I can hear them, too. If you don't object to bunking in with the boys, I'll just sleep on the couch. I've already unrolled my sleeping bag on the lower bed, so you should be warm enough."

And he'd freeze his ass off, not to mention that he was a little tall for the couch. She'd offer to take the couch herself, but not with a rodent-tainted blanket on top of her. "We could share," she suggested against all good judgment—not that anything would happen with three boys in the same room, so it was the practical choice. "I assume you can unzip the bag and we can both use it as a blanket. Mice carry all sorts of diseases and unless there's a hidden cache of blankets somewhere, the only available ones are on that bed."

She couldn't decide whether or not to be flattered at his brief hesitation, but he made up for it by saying, "I'm getting punished for all my past sins, aren't I? My version of getting you into bed didn't include three hooligan fishermen in the same room."

"I do hope you don't snore," she said.

He grinned. "I've never had any complaints, but I suppose it's possible. You?"

She glared at him.

"I'll take that as a no. And I accept your very generous offer." He pretended to ponder the situation. "Let's see, beautiful woman or cold, hard couch? I'd like to think I'm not an idiot, but I occasionally prove myself wrong."

"You just did. Here's some advice. Never ask a woman if she snores. And furthermore, don't tell me if I do. I'd rather snooze in blissful ignorance. Can we go to bed now? I don't know about you, but it's been a long day for me."

"I'll go to bed with you anytime. No need to ask twice."

"It isn't *that* kind of offer."

"I'll remain hopeful."

She glanced down at her pj's. "You'll be able to contain yourself, I'm sure."

He was wearing loose-fitting sweatpants and a gray T-shirt that had a faded Purdue University logo on the front—Tripp had mentioned once that their aviation program was top-notch and had produced a lot of talented pilots and some famous astronauts, as well. Tate had gotten his undergrad degree there. He still managed to look sexy. Meanwhile, she was completely without makeup and wearing an outfit the average grandmother might choose.

That was attractive. "I'm picturing what's underneath."

Whew, they needed to stop this kind of talk right now.

"I'll tell you what. If you meant what you said about fishing at dawn, I need some sleep."

"Me, too."

Was she really going to share a small bunk with him? Apparently so...

The room was dark and quiet except for the boys' breathing and the occasional movement—mice? Oh, surely not in this room! Infuriatingly, after Tate unzipped the sleeping bag and settled in, draping it over both them, she *couldn't* fall asleep. Although, after the day she'd had, she was surprised she didn't pass out in two seconds flat.

Tate wasn't sleeping, either.

It was a small space for two adults, and Bex could tell his breathing hadn't fallen into the rhythm of sleep yet, but the warmth of his body was pleasant, and as they adjusted positions, his arm came around her waist and settled her more firmly against him. He murmured in her ear, "In such close quarters, we're inevitably going to touch each other. Can't be helped. Relax."

He was probably right, but a night in his arms hadn't been in her evening plans, especially with children sleeping peacefully close by. When she thought about being in bed with Tate Calder—and she'd had a fantasy or two—sleep hadn't been part of it.

The warmth of the sleeping bag was like a cocoon, so eventually she found herself drifting off. She vaguely heard one of the boys, probably Ben, since he was in the bunk above them, say something in his sleep.

Even the thought of mice cavorting in the other room couldn't keep her awake.

CHAPTER TEN

MIST ACROSS THE WATER.

The sun was still just a faint glow in the sky, and there'd been a light snow overnight.

As Tate had openly admitted, he wasn't much of a cook, although he could scramble eggs and fry bacon with the best of them. He'd address his mostly sleepless night next to Bex later, but he'd already made coffee and toast when he heard the boys stirring.

Fishing. Dawn. The horizon was lightening.

He'd eased out of bed—at six, according to his waterproof watch—and she was still sound asleep.

Josh was the first one out, wandering into the minuscule kitchen, sleepy-eyed, with his hair messy and, like all boys his age, hungry. Tate passed him a glass of juice, offered strawberry jam on a slice of toast and continued to scramble the eggs.

Ben and Adam weren't far behind, the smell of bacon a guaranteed lure, and they were almost done with breakfast by the time Bex emerged from the bedroom. She was deliciously disheveled—and she was wrong if she thought her plaid pajamas diminished her feminine appeal in any way.

"Morning."

"To me this isn't morning. Don't sound so all-fired

cheerful." Bex squinted at the windows overlooking the lake. "You're sure this is a good time to fish?"

"I'm sure. Dawn and dusk is when they really bite. I hope you don't mind your eggs scrambled. Coffee?"

"Are you kidding? I'll make it a double. Since you already have one and you made breakfast, point me in the right direction and I'll get my own."

He waved the spatula to indicate the appropriate cupboard. He was one of those people who woke up ready to go, which had served him well as a pilot. Bex was evidently the kind of person who took some time to emerge from the sleep cave. As she fumbled for a mug, he prepared a plate for each of them, put in more toast and dismissed the boys. "Go ahead and get dressed. We'll be finished in a few minutes. Jackets and life vests for everyone, got it?"

There was something intimate about sitting across the breakfast table from a person—especially one he'd spent the night with. In a sense, anyway... He'd awakened with the soft weight of her breasts on his forearm and her hair under his cheek. It was part of the reason he'd made such a swift exit.

"I have good news. You don't snore," he informed her as they sat down to their breakfast.

Probably an ill-advised comment. She looked at him balefully over the rim of her mug. "That is *so* reassuring. Thank you. Is that snow I see on the trees and the ground?"

"We're in the mountains." He munched on a piece of bacon. "Happens this time of year at this altitude. It'll melt when the sun comes out."

"I'm hoping you're right on that one."

He almost—almost—mentioned that after the first

circle around the lake, he was taking the boys into town, buying mousetraps and more fish bait—and that there was also a sporting goods store so he could pick up an extra sleeping bag.

But he kept his mouth shut, particularly about the sleeping bag. He'd spotted the store as they drove through but he wasn't sure whether she'd seen it, too. While two adults sharing such a small bed wasn't conducive to sleep, he wouldn't mind a repeat performance. His wife, Sandra, had been enthusiastic enough about sex, but aside from that, she hadn't liked being touched, other than a perfunctory kiss hello or goodbye. But he and Bex had fit together easily, and even without intimate contact, it was far more like he'd imagined marriage.

Two people comfortable with each other.

Companionship and attraction, hand in hand.

After his disillusionment, followed by the tragedy of his sons losing their mother, he'd vowed that he wasn't getting married again. Ever.

"Can you show me how to do this?" Josh, with perplexed irritation in his voice, came into the kitchen, struggling with the straps on his obligatory life vest. "Ben said I did it wrong."

Tate glanced at Bex, since she was still drinking that first cup of coffee, and decided he should handle it. "Here's how it goes. Pay attention to how I fix it, okay? And ignore Ben when he acts all big-brother. It's because he's used to dealing with Adam."

"Okay." Josh let him adjust the straps, watching avidly as he did, and went back into the one useable bedroom.

Tate picked up his cup. Bex hadn't even complained

that the coffee was too strong. He'd been winging it; the cabin only had an ancient coffeepot, and he used those pre-measured cups at home, so he'd dumped in what he'd estimated was the correct amount. His estimate had been a little off.

"Ben is *nice* to him."

He liked the way she defended his oldest. Still... "Ben's enjoying his role as the Supreme Power a little too much. I love my son, but that's just the truth. Besides, all kids need to learn to stand up for themselves. He isn't a bully, but he's aware that he's top dog around here. I don't want him to push either of the younger kids around."

"Here's hoping Tara's also come to the conclusion that she needs to stand up for herself." She lifted her cup in a mock toast. "Unfortunately, she's such a people pleaser. Greg homed in on that as soon as they met. I'm worried about what happens next, but for now I'm going to celebrate outhouses and enjoy worms."

"Don't forget the mice."

"Oh, yeah. The mice."

"And the snow." He was baiting her now.

She knew it, but at least had a sense of humor. "Thanks, and here I was rallying, just waiting for more fun."

"The boys are so excited. That'll make it fun." He got up and took her plate. "Same deal as last night? You wash, I dry and put away?"

She didn't budge from her chair. "I'm fine with the team effort if you'll agree to deal with all the fish."

That sounded easy enough. "Of course."

Only then did she get up.

An hour later, Tate found out exactly what he'd agreed to.

Bex Stuart was like a fishing sorceress if there was such a thing. Once the five of them had piled into the fishing boat—a tight fit, with several seats shared—he set off. They weighed anchor in the middle of the lake, and she cast in the first line.

Instant hit. She raised her brows at him and handed the pole to Ben. "Can you reel it in for me?"

If she hadn't already been the boys' favorite, she sure was now.

The boys caught on quickly. *Aunt Bex tosses out the bait and lets you land the fish.*

They had a grand time, and Tate didn't even get to dip a line in the water, he was so busy. There were some skillet-worthy catches, too, so he put them on a stringer and was glad he'd dug out his fillet knife.

By midmorning they'd caught their limit and he was able to give Bex—and himself—a break, announcing that they needed to head back to town for more ice; they could have lunch there, too, he said—an idea that was generally endorsed.

After he'd docked the boat and the boys raced up the steps, he had to ask her, "How the hell did you do that?"

Her eyes were warm with laughter. "I warned you."

"I'd call you a witch," he murmured, "but I think bewitching is more appropriate."

And then he caught her hand, pulled her toward him and kissed her.

HIS MOUTH WAS WARM, gentle but insistent, and his hands were firm on her shoulders. Bex relaxed into the kiss despite being cold and more than a little damp from the mist. The shiver she felt wasn't related to the weather.

The kiss was good.

Too good.

She was the one to finally break away. A potentially combustible situation was getting more and more volatile with each passing second, and there was nothing they could do about it. Not on this trip, and not when they were back in Mustang Creek, either. He'd always have the boys. She had not only Josh but Tara, too, on her hands. Plus, she had a growing business, and he was building a house, starting his own business, as well...

It was just too complicated.

"*You* kissed *me* the last time. My turn, I guess." Tate's smile was unapologetic. "I find women who can catch a fish every five seconds sexy, what can I say?" They were standing on the dock, visible from the windows if the boys were already inside.

"I wasn't aware that there's a protocol about this. And maybe we should move apart before they see us."

"If you think they haven't picked up on the fact that you and I have some chemistry, you're wrong. I've learned the hard way that they may not say anything, but they know what's going on. And now that we're officially sleeping together, they'll definitely notice."

"We aren't *really* sleeping together." She edged backward.

He stepped forward, and since she had nowhere to go but the cold water, she stopped her retreat. He said, "I could swear that was you in the same bed."

"Where else was I going to sleep? I was tired."

"Bex, we're two consenting adults, and this is our *personal* life. Yours and mine. Just you and me. No one else gets an opinion here, or even needs to know about it."

She looked into his dark eyes and tried to ignore the

way his hair curled against his neck. "You're the one who said even the boys know."

"Yeah, but all they've sensed so far is that we, uh, like each other."

Well, that was one way to put it.

"And it's not like it's going to stay a secret, because you'll tell Hadleigh and Melody. Tripp warned me that there's no such thing as a secret among the three of you."

"Probably," she admitted.

"We've just kissed twice." His smile was slow. "You've kissed me once, and now I've kissed you."

"You keeping some sort of ledger?"

"Sure am. It's your turn next. I'm looking forward to it. Now, I'm going to take the crew into town to do a few errands and grab them some lunch. You can come along, but if you don't want to travel with hungry boys bragging about fish *you* caught, and would rather enjoy some peace and quiet, I understand. If you have a wish list for dinner ingredients, this is the time."

She put her hands on her hips. "What makes you think I'm making dinner?"

"Did I say that?"

"Not in so many words." She paused for a moment, one finger on her chin in exaggerated contemplation. "Oh, wait. You made breakfast and you're taking care of lunch. So…I suppose in all fairness dinner is on me. What if I made tacos? I think the only thing we don't have is tortillas. I assume everyone will eat those? What about Adam?"

"Actually, yes. He loves them. Just leave the lettuce off his. See, you do understand the mysteries of small boys, after all." He sighed philosophically. "There goes our deal. Except for the fish, you don't really need me."

But she was afraid she did.

Saying it out loud was a bad idea; instead she asked, "When are we going to eat the fish we caught?"

"Breakfast tomorrow. And *we* is generous. I didn't even touch my fishing pole."

"Breakfast, huh?" In every old Western she'd ever watched, she remembered the characters frying up trout for breakfast over a campfire. This cabin was an improvement—of sorts—over a bedroll on the ground and stars above, but they'd be having at least one true cowboy meal. "That's definitely on you, then," Bex told him. "Anyway, while you're all gone, I'll take a shower. Perfect timing. I noticed an outdoor one."

"Yeah." He let her walk up the steps first. "I'm kinda sorry I'll miss it, because I would've insisted on guarding you."

"Gee, thanks."

"But yes, at least you wouldn't have the boys running around. I don't know about Josh, but my sons have no problem coming into the bathroom while I'm having a shower to ask me an important question like are we out of peanut butter. Privacy is still an abstract concept to them."

Before he left, she had a favor to ask him. She hesitated, but she trusted Tate, and he was right, there weren't many secrets in her life, anyway. As they gained the top of the hill, she said, "Since there seems to be no signal here, would you mind taking my phone into town and downloading my messages? I don't care about anything related to the business. I told you I'm worried about my sister's meeting with Greg last night, and I want to see if she sent me anything."

"You said she seemed sincere about leaving him this time." He frowned, hands in his jacket pockets as he stood tall in the morning light.

"They have an…interesting relationship."

"What are you going to say to her if she decides not to go through with the divorce?"

His wife had cheated, too, and he'd planned to leave her. Bex wasn't sure how to respond. "It isn't my life," she said after a moment. "Maybe Greg, with all his flaws, is her one and only? I'd never put up with it, especially with Josh in the mix, but she'll have to decide for herself."

"Excellent point. And based on that, the answer is no." He opened the door to the cabin, motioning for her to go in first. "I will *not* take your phone and download the messages. I *will* take the boys into town, I will buy tortillas, but you need to let Tara's mess go for two more days. She's going to do what she's going to do. You need some time off."

Once again, he was right, and it was exasperating.

There were tough decisions to be made, and Tara wasn't the only one making them.

Take her, for instance. Bex was afraid she was falling in love with a man who had a complex past and two children.

But it wasn't a *conscious* choice. To quote him, she was going to do what she was going to do.

Or it might be a done deal already.

CHAPTER ELEVEN

THERE WEREN'T MANY places in Downright, Wyoming, to get something to eat. In the end, Tate took the boys to the local ice-cream parlor on the advice of a checker at the tiny grocery store. The ice-cream place served sandwiches, and…ice cream, which couldn't be had at the cabin. It didn't keep in a cooler, and he'd discovered the old fridge didn't even turn on and was used for storage, undoubtedly against the mice.

The boys raced through their ham-and-Swiss sandwiches to reach the finish line of a hot fudge sundae piled with whipped cream. Tate didn't eat but had a cup of decent coffee, ordered two turkey wraps to go and got the boys into the truck, which wasn't an easy task, due to an excess of energy. They were simply having too much fun.

The hardware store was out of mousetraps.

"The mice are bad this year," the girl at the service desk informed him. "This is when the critters want to come in out of the cold, and we had a warm summer, so there's lots of them. Check with us on Tuesday."

By then they'd be back in Mustang Creek.

"Thanks." So, no mousetraps, and he'd resolutely ignored the display of sleeping bags…

It had turned out to be a sunny day, snow clouds clearing, no mist lingering, and when they pulled in at the cabin, he could hear that Bex had music playing.

Something classical. Vivaldi. He recognized *The Four Seasons*, eminently suitable to this trip. The summer mice, the current fall, the approaching winter and the hope for spring. Four seasons, indeed. And he, too, liked Baroque music, especially Vivaldi, who'd always been his aunt Gina's favorite classical composer. One more thing he and Bex had in common.

"Vests on," he said as the children clambered out. "Aunt Bex and I are going to have lunch, and until then you can run around all you want, but stay where we can see you. Okay?"

"Okay." Ben even helped the other two buckle on their life jackets without grumbling about it and was the first one to head for the steps, the six-year-olds close behind. Tate went inside and set the bags on the counter.

"It was only a semisuccessful trip. I thought I'd get mousetraps, but the hardware store is out, believe it or not. Russ will have to take care of the mouse problems on his own. How was your shower?"

Bex looked soft and fresh, her hair still damp, and although he supposed she might use cosmetics of some kind, he liked the fact that he really couldn't tell. Maybe she darkened her eyelashes a touch, he thought as he watched her empty the grocery bags. She'd put on a pink hooded sweatshirt and her faded jeans and boots, and looked more like a pretty young college student than a professional businesswoman.

She caught him studying her, but it wasn't as though he'd bothered to *hide* his interest. A blush touched her smooth cheeks. "Even with the mice all gone, and who knows how long that would take, no one could sleep in there until the bedding's all cleaned up. I'd vote for a new mattress myself. I don't suppose you thought about buying another sleeping bag?"

"I thought about it," he said with a shrug, trying to appear bland. "But I kinda like the current arrangement."

"Tate Calder!"

"What?" He winked, putting his best effort into a pirate leer, although he probably just ended up looking like an idiot. "Your virtue is safe with me, milady." Then in his regular voice, he said, "Don't think for one minute that I want to get caught doing anything but sleeping in that bunk with you. There'd be questions galore—awkward ones. I'll have that talk with them someday. They're too young right now. Switching to another kind of appetite… I brought our lunch. Shall we go outside and eat on the deck while we keep an eye on them? They're wearing vests, but the potential for some sort of disaster always looms, at least in my experience. Unsupervised for ten minutes is the limit of my faith."

She laughed, which was a good sign. "Thank you for buying tomatoes and oranges. I'm going to get myself a bottled water. You?"

"That would be great."

As he walked out on the deck, he remembered his earlier thought that this kind of comfort—easy and yet respectful, with a sense of humor thrown in—was exactly what marriage should be. What it should offer. Granted, because of the constant and unrequited sexual tension, he couldn't say they were *entirely* comfortable with each other, but…

Maybe he should quit analyzing and admire the blue skies with their hints of horsetail clouds, listen to the boys goofing off on the dock, feel the breeze moving the aspen leaves and forget about the rest of it.

Good advice. Follow it.

They each chose a deck chair and unwrapped their sandwiches. Not as tasty as Bad Billie's—he was becoming a fan of BB's—but delicious just the same. The wraps had survived the thirty-minute trip back and were tasty, and over the course of their lunch, Ben caught his first fish, removing it from the hook with a triumphant flourish of accomplishment. They both applauded, and Ben stood up and took a bow, which made them laugh. "Oh, there's no stopping him now," Tate groaned. "My purpose in this life is gone," he said wryly. "One day, they're sitting in a high chair eating regular food, then comes potty training, the first day of school, and suddenly, they can take their own fish off the hook. I'm a has-been."

"Don't despair. There's always driving, girls and college."

He shuddered. "You're a sadist. Teaching them to drive I can do, college will be a rite of passage for all of us, but girls? I haven't figured them out myself. The boys'll be on their own."

"We aren't that complicated." Bex's eyes sparkled. "Let us have our way, and everything's good."

He observed the rippling water below. "Um, I do have to point out that you all seem to change your minds every five seconds. We need better signals from you— sort of like freeway signs and big arrows."

"Sexist."

"Not at all. Realist."

"I'll consult Mel and Hadleigh and see how *they* feel about your answer."

"If that means Melody won't make those potatoes for me again, don't you dare. I take it back."

"You're as bad as Tripp."

"Come on, no one's that bad."

"True."

He hated to ruin their lighthearted mood, but he'd been thinking about something, trying to figure out his approach, and decided it would be easier just to ask. "You say you're not that complicated," he began. "Which I doubt. I have a simple question for you, although maybe the answer isn't all that simple."

Bex immediately grew wary. He saw it in her eyes. "What?"

"If things hadn't turned out the way they did, if Will had lived, would you and he have been happy?"

OH, THE MAN definitely did not pull punches.

Bex took a deep breath. "It's so hard to say. That was a long time ago, and I was young."

"You still are."

"Sometimes I don't feel like it." She shut her eyes, because that felt less awkward. "I loved him at a different time in my life. I miss Will every single day, but I'm all right." She opened her eyes. "If he'd lived, if we'd been married, I'd be a different person now. In some ways, not in others…" She paused. "We would've changed *each other*, brought out the best in each other. That's how it's supposed to be when you're married, and that's what I believe would have happened. Do you know what I mean?"

He nodded.

She felt she needed to reciprocate with the same kind of question—about happiness. She almost didn't want to ask. "When you were married, were you happy?"

"No." His eyes were shadowed and he stared out at the lake.

"Not even at first?"

"No. My disillusionment began pretty much the day we walked down that aisle."

She'd never claim to be clairvoyant, but she'd sensed there was more to the story than he'd told her before.

Did he want to talk about it? Or not?

She bit her lip then took the plunge. "How so?"

He answered, his expression remote. "I discovered gradually that Sandra hadn't told me the truth about her past in dozens of small ways and later in several very large ones, including the fact that she'd been married twice before and had a child. Her ex-husband had full custody and he was quite a font of information, none of it good, once he tracked her down for failed child-support payments. For one thing, she'd told me she had no family except an infirm grandmother in a nursing home. The truth turned out to be that she was estranged from all of them—parents, a brother and two sisters—after a series of debacles, including stealing credit cards and forging checks. I didn't even know her real birth name. She'd been Michelle Grant and became Sandra Chase. She'd had it legally changed and moved away before they discovered the full extent of the damage."

That was a little startling. "Then why did you stay?"

"She'd gotten pregnant with Ben almost right away, as insurance, I suspect," he said cynically. "So we had a child. She was carrying Adam when it all came to light. I'm not going to divorce my pregnant wife, and besides, quite frankly, I needed someone to take care of the kids. I'd be gone for days and sometimes even weeks at a time."

In other words, he was trapped.

"She doesn't sound like she'd be a good child-care provider to me," Bex muttered, watching the boys, her heart aching.

"Actually, to her credit, in exchange for being able to sit around all day and have a housekeeper come in twice a week, Sandra did take decent care of Ben. To her, that was a fair trade. I did realize quickly enough that I needed to lower the credit limits on her cards and keep a separate household checking account. Everything else was in my name only. I had no idea the problem ran so deep. Some people just can't handle money, or so I told myself over and over."

"Does Tripp know all this? I can't believe Hadleigh didn't tell me."

His smile was faint. "Bex, no one knows this except my aunt, the one you met—she stepped in to help with the boys and came to live with us for a while—and now you. I'm not going to advertise the fact that I married a beautiful, manipulative woman who pretended she cared about me. Who managed to completely fool me. The one thing I don't regret about my so-called marriage is my sons." He rubbed his forehead. "The marriage itself was a mistake I'll never make again but that's what mistakes are for, right? All designed to teach you a lesson."

The unrelenting tone of his voice stopped her from saying anything else. Still, she couldn't help thinking of Tara, wondering if *she'd* finally learn from her mistakes.

Life sometimes isn't what it seems on the surface, she told herself. At first she'd thought that not mentioning his wife meant he mourned her, and then he'd admitted they were on the brink of a divorce and now...

At least between her and Will it was a simple—if devastating—equation and she'd never been betrayed.

Hoots of triumph floated up from the dock, breaking the moment.

"Look." She pointed. "Go, Josh! I think he caught a fish *and* took it off himself."

Tate seemed relieved to change the subject. "That's good news for me, although going up and down those stairs was great cardio."

"As you said, professional fish removal is no longer your purpose on earth."

"I guess I'll have to find a new one."

"I hear raising horses is both satisfying and lucrative."

"Let's hope so. If Tripp's new stallion proves to be a good stud, then acquiring more mares is my next step. I just need the stables completed first." He shrugged. "With Doc Cameron on board, I'm in good shape, but I may have to ask my father if he'll be a silent partner until I can buy him out. I don't want to go small and then have to build again."

She'd seen his family's sprawling house. "Surely he can afford it."

Tate blew out a breath. "Trouble is, *will* he be silent? He's all business, all the time. My grandfather bred and raised horses, so Dad grew up around them, and he probably does know a thing or two, but if his money's on the line, he'll be all too happy to share that knowledge. Often. I can see myself flying out to bring him here about twice a week so he can comanage. Nate Cameron has the skills, but not enough capital to really invest because he's still paying off veterinary school loans. I have the perfect property, and I'll be there to handle the horses, but it makes more sense to build the right facility at the beginning."

"Yeah, I understand what you're saying." When Bex had started her first fitness center, it had been in an older building and there was the process of first getting the business off the ground. Then, once she was making a profit, moving into a newer, more appealing location had added a lot to the stress of the ups and downs of being an entrepreneur. If it hadn't been for an investor with the right connections, she would never have expanded...

"Hold on," Bex said slowly, quelling the twinge that maybe Tate wouldn't thank her down the line, but at least he wouldn't have to ask his father. "I might know someone who could be interested. Um, I can't promise silence, but if you want to launch a business in this area—well, in Wyoming—she's the ticket."

Tate looked dubious. "She? There are plenty of women horse breeders, but—"

That was enough to make Bex clap a hand over her mouth to stifle her laughter. Lettie Arbuckle in a barn. Now *there* was an interesting image. Perfect suit, bag in hand that cost as much as the average compact car...

"She's not a breeder, no. But she has a lot of money and a lot of connections. It doesn't hurt to ask, does it?"

"You don't want to tell me who it is."

"Nope. Not yet." Bex gathered up the wrappings from their sandwiches. "Think we can pry the boys away from the water long enough to go for a hike?"

CHAPTER TWELVE

"WHAT'S THIS?" ADAM ASKED, hunkered down to study a curly frond.

Luckily for him, Tate realized Bex was a flora-and-fauna kind of girl. Oh, all those years of flying and he could practically smell bad weather rolling in, but to him a fern was just a fern. Yet she could unerringly identify every single one.

As a bonus, she bent over to show the underside of the leaf to his son, and he got to admire her backside, as well.

Quite the perk. He didn't pay much attention to the botany lesson.

As usual, she seemed to sense it when he was staring and as usual, he got caught, but what the hell, she already knew he thought she was someone well worth looking at from any available angle. That, however, was one of his favorites.

"I missed that," he said innocently. "Can you show me, too?"

"Calder, don't push me."

Josh, who was collecting pinecones, looked up sharply. Tate noticed it out of the corner of his eye. He said reassuringly, "She was just telling me to stop teasing her, Josh. It's an expression. That's all. She was telling me that if I didn't stop teasing her, she'd start teasing me back."

The kid relaxed. Bex, on the other hand, looked stricken. Their eyes met briefly, and he didn't blame her for the flare of anger in hers, but now was not the time. He said to the boys, "Want me to carry some of those pinecones? I have free pockets. I assume you guys want to hike back and go out in the boat to watch Aunt Bex hook every single fish in the entire lake."

They walked back at a more sedate pace, keeping the boys in sight. Once they'd raced inside the cabin, Bex said in a fierce tone, "I *knew* it. I've never seen a bruise, but Greg's a bully. I'm almost sure he's made at least verbal threats. If Tara wants to put up with it, that's her problem, but not in front of Josh. Can't she see that all their drama, hers and Greg's, is affecting their son? That she's got to make some changes, once and for all?"

He thought about what to say, and then just told the truth. "Bex, you don't get to make that decision. I wish you did, don't get me wrong."

She said a very unladylike word then added bitterly, "I know, but sometimes I just want to shake my sister."

"Hmm, what a coincidence. I want to beat the everloving crap out of your brother-in-law. I doubt either one of those things would change who they are or how they deal with each other."

She looked disgruntled as they walked through a stand of fading ferns, hands deep in her pockets. "Are you always so reasonable?"

"Absolutely not. I sailed right past a display of sleeping bags today so I could sleep in a cramped bed with a fishing sorceress. A bed that's too small for me alone, never mind the two of us. You hogged the covers, by the way."

"I did not." At least she wore a reluctant smile.

Tate wanted very much to kiss Bex on the forehead—and a few other places—just about then, but he didn't. "Josh will be fine. Change makes us all uneasy. I'm a perfect example. Moving my family to Mustang Creek was a leap of faith. But it worked out okay. Otherwise I wouldn't have met you."

"I appreciate your attempt to be charming. If that's what it is. Seriously, though, I'm grateful for your kindness to Josh, for what you represent to him. Stability. That's *so* important now."

"I…" He trailed off when she clasped his arm, turning to look at her inquiringly.

Bex stepped closer, placing one hand on his chest. Immediately, his heart began to speed up. "I believe it's my turn, isn't it? *Now* would be my choice, but you're going to have to help me out. You're a little tall for me to kiss if we're both standing unless you cooperate. The chair was really convenient last time."

"My cooperation should never be in question. Anything for a genuine sorceress."

He bent his head, but didn't kiss her. He let her close that last crucial distance before their lips touched.

It was slow, lingering, exquisite, and he allowed her to control the pace. This was, after all, her kiss, although he couldn't keep himself from circling her waist with both arms and bringing her close. They were both wearing jackets and jeans, but it was still better with her breasts against his chest, her fingers threaded through his hair.

Even dressed as they were, he wondered if she could feel the surge of his arousal. If it hadn't been for the slamming of the screen door, indicating an exodus from the cabin, it might have lasted a lot longer.

Ben yelled to the other two, "Jeez, I *told* you! Kissing."

Caught in the act was better than not participating at all. Somewhat reluctantly he let Bex go. "I predicted there might be speculation among the troops about our relationship. I highly doubt it's more important than fishing, but they *are* paying attention. Now, shall we go and let you work your fishing magic?"

Two hours later, they were definitely having fun but dusk was settling in, the mountains glowing red from the setting sun. She did hook one that was a true beauty, and Tate actually got the joy of landing it because Bex immediately turned to him and mouthed, "This is a big one."

It was a real battle, and he might have kept this massive trout, but it was a beautiful creature and they had enough already. Besides, they'd caught their limit that morning, so this was for the sport of it. The boys were slack jawed with disappointment.

"He's been around a while," he told them. "We'll let him swim in peace for a few more years."

Bex agreed, and eventually they did, too.

He got the joy of cleaning the morning's catch, but the boys were fascinated, although Bex went off to the couch and picked up a book. There wasn't enough room in the little kitchen—and it was generous to even call it that—for all of them.

A romance novel. No bodice-ripping cover, but a man and a woman looking at each other, fully clothed, much the way he and Bex had looked at each other earlier. Horses grazing in the background. He might have to read it himself.

Get some pointers.

Still, after that kiss, he thought he was doing okay.

Adam seemed dubious about fish for tomorrow's breakfast. So Tate played the cowboy card again. "It's what cowboys ate most of the time. Think about it. They couldn't cart around chickens for eggs, and while they had cattle, they weren't going to cut one out of the herd just for a steak since they didn't tow refrigerators behind their horses and the meat would go bad. So trout was easy. Find a stream, catch a few, fry 'em up. Delicious."

All three of them seemed to accept that logic.

They went outside to play on the hillside, and Bex came in just as he was rolling up the last of the newspaper he'd used for cleaning the fish. "You know you pull the cowboy thing pretty often, right?"

"Whatever works. I was their age once. Seems like a long time ago, but I swear I was." He wiped off the counter. There was a fire pit up on the hill; he'd go and burn the newspaper there or every bear within a hundred miles would be knocking on the door.

"I'm going to get started on the tacos and set the table." Bex moved efficiently toward the coolers. "I have a fantastic pinto bean–chili recipe, if I do say so myself. I usually make it from scratch, but I'm winging it this time. I'll put the toppings in separate bowls so the boys can pick and choose what they want on their tacos."

"Shall I pour the cook a glass of wine?"

"I'm on a minivacation, so that works for me, thanks."

It struck him once again that he'd never had a sense of easy camaraderie with a woman before. He and Bex were obviously kindling a growing interest in a sexual relationship; more than that, they thought alike and she valued the same things he did, or that was the impression he had. There was no pretension, either, despite her success, and she was independent without being militant. She didn't *need* him, but she didn't emphasize the point.

He was having fun, the boys were clearly enjoying themselves and yet he had to wonder if this trip was a big mistake.

Absolutely.

But maybe the best mistake he'd ever made.

ONCE THE MEAT was simmering on the grill, Bex added the seasonings and mild salsa, then turned down the burner. Considering the age of the stove inside the cabin, she didn't trust that contraption one bit, so having the gas grill was much better.

Tomatoes chopped, onions ready to go, cheese shredded—she'd cheated and bought the cheese already grated.

There was something about the smoke from a campfire that beckoned, especially in the fall. Since everything was under control, she decided to join the crowd up on the hill, bringing the bag of gourmet popcorn she'd secreted away. She refilled her wineglass, and got a cold beer for Tate, who was managing the wild ones.

While the boys were running around, Tate sat in a camp chair contemplating the fire and occasionally raising his voice a notch or two to tone them down. He had a solid blaze going, and he'd thoughtfully set out a chair for her, too.

Her arrival was greeted with enthusiasm even before she offered them the bag of popcorn, which was promptly whisked away to a decrepit picnic table. There was remarkably little conversation as it was devoured. Tate looked grateful for the beer and cracked it open. "They're wound up tonight, that's for sure. Smart idea to hide the popcorn. If I'd known it was there, it might have mysteriously disappeared."

"You *are* a suspicious character." She settled into her chair. "Good to know my instincts are spot-on. Nice fire."

He glanced up at the sky. It was darkening, shadows gathering under the trees. "Best kind of night for it. Almost no breeze. It isn't as useful as your ability to catch fish, but I have a God-given talent, too. No matter where I sit around a campfire, the smoke blows in my direction. People have actually requested that I not sit next to them. I can change places, and I swear, the wind shifts."

Bex laughed. "What else don't I know about Mr. Tate Calder? I've met your aunt and seen where you grew up, and we don't have to go into your marriage again. Let's see. I'm probably too attached to your kids already. I know you worked with Tripp, and that you attended Purdue University in Indiana, you love horses and living in the country. Tell me a little-known fact."

"Only if this is a reciprocal game."

She took a sip and hid a smile behind her wineglass when a wisp from the fire curled his way. "Deal."

"I was born in the Azores. My father was in the air force before he started his company." He reached over and picked up another small log from a pile next to his chair after waving away the smoke. "Your turn. What don't I know about Becca Stuart?"

That was an easy one. "I can play a pipe organ. One of those big ones with six keyboards, the foot pedals and the different stops, the kind they have in a big church. Yep, I can do that."

Tate did seem intrigued. "Whoa, before we go on with the game, you'll have to explain that to me."

"My grandfather was an organist, and my mother didn't have the knack for music, but when I took piano lessons, I showed promise. She got it into her head that I needed organ lessons, mostly I guess, to please him. FYI, there's only one place to practice and that's in a big echoing, empty church, because no one has *that* instrument sitting in the living room. I was twelve. Walking through the dark sanctuary terrified me. I toughed it out for a couple of years but then got into sports, and she finally dropped it. I did stick with the piano. I minored in music at college."

"You'll have to play for me sometime. I wondered about the Vivaldi."

"Your turn now."

He sipped his beer. "I started a novel when I was in college. I've been thinking about it for all these years. If I can find any spare minutes between being a single parent and everything else I've got going on, I might try my hand at it again."

"Things are going to settle down when you start breeding horses?"

"No." He flashed that smile. "Fantasy, right?"

She thought it over and couldn't refrain from provoking him, just a little. "No, I don't think so. You're the sensitive type. You could write a novel in the wee hours, hunched over the keyboard—"

"I am *not* sensitive."

She couldn't help grinning at that.

Luckily, he was a good sport. "Okay, I fell for that one. It's your turn again."

"I love Thai food."

"I already know that."

I could be in love with you. She wasn't going to say it.

"Then I guess I don't have much else that's interesting in my deep dark past. I met Hadleigh and Mel before we were old enough for school. We've been fast friends ever since. They're like my true sisters."

His gaze strayed to Josh, sitting on the picnic table bench, legs swinging as he munched popcorn. "You're not close to your sister? You've been worrying about her all weekend."

She loved her sister. That was different.

"We're total opposites." She ran her fingers through her hair, letting it fall back around her face. "Yes, I've been worrying about what she's going to do next. Not quite the same as being *close* to her."

He stretched out his long legs and dangled the beer bottle in one hand. "Men are simple. Either you like someone or you don't. We don't spend a lot of time on introspection when it comes to that kind of thing. We shoot from the hip. Nope, don't like him. Then we move on."

"You're imparting this information as if I haven't learned about the behavior of the adult human male."

Since she couldn't get phone or text messages, the situation with Tara—or more accurately, not knowing what the situation was—made her nervous. She got up. "I'd better go check on dinner. The way those kids inhaled that popcorn tells me they're seriously hungry."

CHAPTER THIRTEEN

THE TACOS WERE the hit he thought they'd be—they were delicious—and Tate listened contentedly to the laughter and general mayhem during the meal. Bex wasn't the only one who'd been holding out on the boys with that popcorn of hers. He'd bought the video game both boys had been begging for, instead of saving it for Christmas, and it was worth it to see the excitement on all three faces when he handed it over. "The game system's hooked up on my laptop, but you'll have to take turns playing. And when we say pajamas on, teeth brushed and lights out, I don't want any argument. Are we clear?"

"Clear!"

"Well, we'll never see them again," Bex observed drily as they ran for the bedroom. "So much for my favorite-person status. Show-off!"

He leveled a look at her as he rejoined her at the table. "I wasn't the one keeping a secret stash of popcorn in my back pocket."

"It was in my suitcase, actually."

"I was speaking figuratively, which you know, and it's a damn good thing the mice didn't figure it out."

"Why do you suppose I hauled my suitcase out of the bedroom so fast?"

"Quick thinking on your part, and I'm impressed that you didn't scream, by the way."

"I'm not the screaming type."

"Hey, now you ruined the surprise. I was hoping to find that out firsthand."

She choked on her drink, and he was probably lucky she didn't toss the rest of it at him, but apparently she wasn't the tossing type, either. She wiped her shirt with her napkin. "Damn you, Tate."

"I'm sorry. Who could resist that?"

She didn't respond, just rolled her eyes.

"I was being sincere, but we've both determined it won't be on this trip." He tried to sound as casual as possible.

"Don't be too confident, flyboy."

"Isn't that what everyone expects from a pilot? We know where we're going—and how to get there?"

Bex gave an exasperated sigh. "I'm done with the sexual innuendo. Want to play a card game?"

"Strip poker?" He did his best to keep a straight face.

"Watch it or I'll kick your ass. At cards, I mean."

"I'm sorry. Okay, truce. Yes, to the cards. I feel like I'm at camp, anyway. The boys are hogging my computer, so we'll have to entertain ourselves the old-tech way. Let me put another log in the woodstove first."

Before he returned, he got another beer from the cooler since he'd only had two the entire evening, and he wasn't driving anywhere, so why not.

She was sitting at the table, a battered pack of cards in front of her. Her eyes sparkled. "I found these in a drawer while looking for a potholder."

He sat down and inquired cautiously. "And?"

"I used to play this with my grandmother when I was little."

He twisted the cap off his bottle. This was obviously not going to be any kind of poker. "Play what?"

"Old Maid."

Tate registered that. "Old Maid?"

She looked endearingly excited. "You know it." She tapped the deck. "These are exactly like the cards she had."

"I actually don't know that game. But enlighten me. What are the rules?"

"We deal the cards and if you have a pair you lay it down. Otherwise you get to pick from the other person's hand. The Old Maid's in there and she doesn't have a match. The trick is not to pick that one. If you're stuck with her, you lose."

"So, if I don't have that card, I know you do."

"That's the beauty of it. I have it and want you to pick it, but you don't want to end up with it. Then if you do pick it, I'll know you have it and I don't want it back."

"That sounds confusing."

"It's not, but it *is* fun, trust me. Sort of a race against the clock."

Ben was, of course, the first one to come out of the bedroom, just in time to see him get the Old Maid card. Maybe he was drawn by Bex's laughter. The other boys followed him minutes later.

They'd abandoned the expensive video game, which was fine with Tate, and Aunt Bex once again ruled the day as all three boys joined in. The game really was simple, despite her convoluted explanation—simple enough that even Adam and Josh could play. Tate had to hand it to her; sitting around the table with all of them playing a game together was a lot better than having the boys glued to a video game.

Ben grinned at him. "Dad, I think you're going to be the Old Maid again."

"How do you know if I have it?"

Bex was oh, so helpful. "I can tell from the look on your face."

"What kind of look?"

"Like maybe you have the Old Maid card."

All the boys thought it was very funny. He did have it again, in fact, but that was beside the point. "I do not."

"He's bluffing," Bex told the crowd at the table. "Let's take him down."

His turncoat sons had no problem with that, and as it turned out, he was as unlucky with Old Maid as Bex was lucky with fishing.

Tate had the dismal feeling that he was going to walk away from this weekend with a new nickname and it was going to include the words *old* and *maid*. When all the tooth-brushing was done and the boys were settled in their bunks, he went back to the table, where Bex was sipping her wine and reading her book. He returned her mischievous smile with a sour one. "You must've cheated," he told her.

"Explain how." She looked suspiciously innocent.

She also looked too beautiful for his peace of mind. It didn't help that the cabin was relatively dark, with just the lantern's glow; outside, the lake shimmered with re-flected moonlight. All of it the perfect atmosphere for a romantic moment.

And speaking of romantic moments… It was *his* turn.

"I think I need a consolation prize. Something to soothe my injured male pride."

Bex leaned her elbows on the table. "Is that so?"

"Absolutely. My ego is very fragile."

She made a sound of derision that could even be described as a snort. "Yeah, there's nothing like being good-looking and successful with two adorable kids to make a man feel bad about himself. And let's not forget I know Tripp, so I'm well aware that pilots don't have fragile egos."

"Good-looking, huh? Go on. I'm listening and starting to feel a little better."

"You're impossible." She shook her head but was laughing.

Shared humor was part of the connection between them. Maybe another part was that they both had sorrow in their pasts, his from a marriage that had been based on deception, and hers from the destruction of her youthful dream and the grief of a catastrophic loss.

But they did make each other laugh.

He'd met women since he'd become single again, plenty of them, some of whom just liked the way he looked, some who found his job sexy, some who ran the other way when they discovered that he came with a built-in family. He'd slept with a few, but had always felt dissatisfied. Physical release did not equal emotional happiness, and he yearned for that.

He asked her, "Would you mind coming over here? I think a kiss would lift my spirits."

IT WAS A BAD IDEA, no question, but she wanted the same thing.

Bex listened for a minute, realized the not-so-quiet whispering from the bedroom had died into silence, which meant the boys were probably asleep after a long day and a late night.

Kissing Tate. Again. Oh, yeah. Bad idea.

She decided that maybe bad was the new good.

Tate had scooted back his chair, and she settled in his lap and put her hands on his shoulders.

If he thought *she* was going to kiss *him*, he had another think coming. Earlier he'd insisted she do it, and turnabout was, as they said, fair play.

He flashed that smile and she could tell that he knew exactly what it was doing to her. "Is there a rule in this game you invented that specifies *where* I can kiss you?" he asked.

"I invented it?" She stroked the line of his jaw. He had a hint of beard already and she liked it. "What did you have in mind, cowboy?"

He nuzzled her neck. "North of the border, since there are small children in the house. I'm fairly sure no one's going to come out and want a drink of water, but I've been wrong before. South's in our future, too. Not tonight, though. I was thinking *here*." His thumb grazed her nipple, and even through her shirt and bra, it felt incredible.

Tate was obviously aware of her reaction. "I won't take off your shirt," he promised, already undoing the buttons. "Someday, when we can catch some time alone… For now, I just want to give you a good-night kiss. I could easily explain that away, because it's recorded history in their brains that I like to kiss you, but anything else might require a discussion I am not equipped to handle."

He unclasped her bra and the warm exhalation of his breath across her skin was enough to make her restlessly shift position. "Tate."

The path of his tongue downward over her collarbone and then the upper curve of her breast was so beguiling, she dropped her head and shut her eyes. When he gently kissed her nipple, she made a small sound of pleasure.

He held her in place and continued what he was doing until she gasped and pushed at his shoulders. "I think this kiss is over." A moment later she added, "My turn again."

It was probably ill advised but she kissed him hard and hot on the mouth, and he responded the same way, and they were both breathless when they were through. She immediately slid off his lap. Things were a little out of control and they still had to share a very narrow bunk.

"We need some space."

He didn't disagree. "I might go for a quick walk."

Bex laughed weakly. "It's cold out."

"That might help."

"I'll go put on my flannel pajamas."

He stood up. "Just button them all the way to the neck and be snoring when I get back. Some drool would be good, too."

"I don't—"

"Well, start, if you have any regard for me at all."

Once he'd stalked outside, she had to stifle a burst of laughter. He didn't even take his coat, but she was a bit overheated, too.

Bex changed her clothes and swiftly completed her own nightly ritual, then crawled into the bunk. Tate was gone for a decent interval and when he came in, she heard him check the woodstove and lock the front door, but he didn't come to bed. Eventually she couldn't stand it and went into the living room.

Shirtless, he lay on the couch, his legs hanging over one

end, and while the room wasn't officially cold, it would be in another hour or so. "Tate, what are you doing?"

"Sleeping."

"Obviously not. You're going to freeze to death. Why—"

"I'm in love with you."

Speechless, she stared at him. He had a very nice muscular chest, toned abs and she could tell he worked out because his biceps were defined… What *did he just say?*

He kept his eyes closed. "I've been worried that this was going to happen ever since I met you. I had this bad feeling. You know, like when you think you're getting food poisoning."

He really knew how to sweet-talk a girl.

Bex wasn't sure how to respond and came up with, "I thought love was supposed to be a good feeling. Where does food poisoning come into it?"

"I mean that feverish, shaky…sense of foreboding. You're right, love *is* a good feeling. It's falling in love that's the problem."

"You're going to have to explain that one to me." She sat down next to him, although there was barely enough room to keep her balance.

"I love Ben and Adam."

"Of course. I love them, too."

He opened one eye. "Don't make this worse, Bex."

She was starting to get annoyed. "You don't want me to love your sons?"

"Anyone would love them. Hmm, well, not all the time, I do have to say that. They have their moments. I'm just saying that *falling* in love is like plummeting off a cliff and not knowing what's at the bottom. Could be a deep pool down there, but it could be jagged rocks.

I've landed on those rocks before. It wasn't a pleasant experience."

"You can drown in the pool, too." She caressed his shoulder, and his muscles tensed. "There isn't a safe way to fall." She paused. "That's why they call it *falling*."

His gaze was searching, holding hers, both his eyes open now. "I didn't expect this, expect *you*."

"Don't sound so resentful."

"How come I get the sense you're laughing at me?"

"Because I am."

He had the grace to laugh, too, and he grabbed her wrist to pull her on top of him. "There've been studies that prove sexual frustration makes adult males act like they have nonfunctioning brains. I'm not inventing that."

She kissed him lightly. "You don't have to produce the literature. I believe you."

"So what do we do now?"

"Get some sleep?"

"In that little bunk next to you? Seems unlikely to me."

"You can keep me warm."

He said huskily, "You have no idea."

He was wrong; she certainly *did* have an idea.

"Now, walk me to the outhouse?" She got to her feet.

He grinned. "Okay, that's it. Keep saying sexy things like that. Maybe it'll work and I can catch a few winks, after all."

CHAPTER FOURTEEN

HOW HE EVEN got a lick of sleep was a mystery to him, but Tate managed to make it to dawn, coming awake with an acute awareness that Bex was spooned against him. He eased away, went outside to answer nature's call, then came back in to wash up and start a pot of coffee.

He was getting to know the ancient, grumpy pot. His coffee was decent this time, he decided later as he watched the sun rise over the lake, the water gilded to a dozen different shades. He could hear an elk bugle in the distance, and another returning the favor, and that made him smile. The trees gradually took shape and definition. He'd been able to stir the coals in the wood-stove enough to get it going again without too much effort, so the cabin felt cozy.

Life was good.

Except for one little thing.

No, one giant thing. He'd told Bex he loved her. Where did that leave him now? Leave *them*?

Despite himself, he felt at peace with telling her about his feelings for her.

He wouldn't trade anything in his life—the boys, his new business, his new home—but he was used to being on his own, and Bex Stuart had changed all that.

When he heard stirring in the bedroom, he went

into the kitchen and got out the battered iron skillet he'd found in one of the cupboards. He got to work, dredging the trout in a light dusting of cornmeal and seasoned flour before heading to the grill on the deck to start frying it.

Since he wasn't positive the trout was going to go over with the young fishermen, no matter how eager they'd been to catch it, he also made toast.

Bex emerged onto the deck, and he saw that she had a mug. "Morning," he said. "I think the coffee's okay this time."

"Thank you." She took a sip and nodded. "Good, or maybe my standards have adjusted."

"I'll accept the backhanded compliment and point out that big girls go to the bathroom by themselves when it's light out."

"Like I need an Old Maid to protect me."

The boys thought the banter was pretty funny.

"I hear the bears are hungry in the morning," he shot back, but she blithely waved a hand as she walked down the steps.

"If she screams, I'm not going after her," he said to the group at large. No one believed him, since he wasn't serious, anyway. If Bex needed him to rescue her, he'd be there with a knife clenched between his teeth, ready for battle.

Ben muttered, "Yeah, right, Dad."

"Maybe if she screams loudly enough. Anyone want toast?"

Two did, one didn't. He also made some for the adults in the cabin, and tried to ignore that she'd been gone for at least fifteen minutes.

When he went to the front door, he saw Bex at the top

of the hill, checking her phone. He'd had a signal now and then, but service was notoriously unreliable; it was better to assume that you were simply out of range. She must've found a sweet spot. She was sitting at the old picnic table, sending a message, and she looked upset, but her issues with her sister weren't his business. Still, he wanted to be the shoulder she could cry on—except he didn't want her to cry at all.

So he went to her. "I made toast," he said, and once again felt like idiot.

She gave a little hiccup of a laugh and responded, "Toast is exactly what I need. Toast and trout? That's an interesting combo for sure."

"Bex."

She stood and practically flew into his arms. He almost staggered backward. "Tara's going back to Greg. I *knew* it would happen."

He held her close, searching for the right thing to say. It was a special type of torture when someone you loved was making an obvious mistake and you couldn't do anything about it. "So we circle the wagons and wait."

"I *hate* this. He makes her so unhappy."

"It's a bad decision, you and I both know it. All we can do is wait for the next time she realizes it and be ready."

"Tate, she's going to drag Josh back into that mess."

"And there's nothing you can do about it," he pointed out with a long sigh. "I know it's hard, but Tara and Greg are Josh's parents, and as long as he isn't being abused or neglected, it isn't your place—or mine—to get involved."

In typical Bex fashion, she took a deep breath, straightened her spine and stepped away from the rickety table. In the morning sunshine, wearing her plaid pajamas, hair still tousled, she looked about sixteen. "Okay, minibreakdown over. I'm not going to tell Josh and spoil this last day. Tara has to be the one to let him know." She blinked a couple of times. "He doesn't talk about whatever is going on—Josh, I mean. So maybe he'll be perfectly happy to move home."

Tate doubted it. He'd seen the kid's face when his father pulled up to the Galloway ranch. Not to mention that he preferred to have his aunt come along on the fishing trip rather than his dad. Nope, this probably wouldn't make Josh happy. He sighed again. "For the moment the best thing you can do is try to act cheerful as you go back in to eat your gourmet toast or he'll know something's up."

She forced a smile. "How's this?"

"Like a clown with a stomachache. Try again."

Bex narrowed her eyes. "Watch it, Calder. I feel like punching someone in the nose, and you're awfully handy."

He held up his hands in mock surrender. "You can't hit the man who slaved over a hot toaster for you and threw in a trout for good measure."

Her next smile was a lot more genuine. "I suppose you have a point there."

"After breakfast we'll go out in the boat for a couple of hours. Then we'll pack up and close the cabin, maybe have a late lunch at the sandwich-and-ice-cream place in that little town."

"I wish we could just stay here, but escapism solves nothing."

Once upon a time, he'd been in avoidance mode himself, grateful for the charter flights that took him far from home, far from the reality of his marriage. Bex was right, though; running away never fixed the problem. Still, it was only human, wanting to walk—or fly—in the opposite direction now and then.

"It doesn't," Tate agreed. He took her elbow and guided her back toward the cabin. "You can handle this, Bex."

She was quiet for a few minutes, thoughtful. When she spoke she caught him off guard, as she so often did. "Are you really in love with me?" she asked.

He pretended to consider. "With the woman who just threatened to punch me in the nose? With the woman who disdains toast as a side dish to fried trout? Hmm, I might need to rethink this."

SHE LIKED TATE's sense of humor.

He was very easy to be with, but there were some demons cavorting around in his past, and she knew they could leap into the present at any time.

"I was joking," she said. "About punching you in the nose."

He looked so attractive first thing in the morning, his hair disheveled just enough that he could sling a coat over his shoulder and pose for a magazine cover. "I figured that."

Why was she being so tentative? Three simple words. *I love you.* He'd said that. Why couldn't she? "I would never actually hit you." And why was she belaboring this…this silly remark?

"Like I said, I wasn't all that worried. Not that I don't think you could pack a mean punch, but let's face it, Bex, you're just too nice."

I am not too nice.

"Look, I've already apologized for calling you sensitive, so let's drop it. There's no need to call me *nice* to get back at me."

"That's an insult?"

"The way you said it, yes."

Why was it so hard for her to tell him she felt the same thing he did?

"Tate, I'm—"

He saved her. "Letting your breakfast get cold. We can talk about this later."

That might be better, once she felt more centered. More grounded. But...she couldn't leave it unfinished.

She took his hand. "I'm involved, too. In whatever's going on between us."

He swung around and his fingers curled briefly around hers. "Bex, if I didn't think you were, I wouldn't be here. Look, the boys have been alone and unsupervised a little too long for my peace of mind. The cabin could be on fire for all I know."

True enough.

The trout proved to be a hit, which surprised both of them. It was mild and flaky, and he'd cooked it plain except for some melted butter. The boys cleaned their plates, although the toast came in a sad second. Afterward there was an eager fishing party ready to go.

Bex pulled her hair into a ponytail, put on her worn jeans and slipped on a sweatshirt. The noisy launch of the boat went more smoothly this time, and she wished once again that they were staying a few extra days. She stood in front of the cloudy mirror in the bedroom, which made her face look as though she'd acquired a second set of cheekbones. Staring into it for a long moment, she asked out loud, "What are you doing?"

The mirror didn't answer.

So much for fairy tales.

So much for fishing, as well, apparently, because no sooner were they out in the middle of the lake, than gray clouds rolled in and it started to sprinkle. The boys were undeterred at first, but it was a chilly fall rain, and when the wind rose, even Ben was willing to concede that being wet and cold took the fun out of the whole experience.

They were all subdued as they began the process of packing up, and Bex predicted that someone—she hoped it wasn't her or Josh—would be taking home a mouse in their luggage. Against strict orders there'd been in-room snacking, judging by the granola bar wrapper she found on the floor.

After all the sweeping and washing had been done, and Tate had cleaned out the woodstove, he locked up, remarking, "I wouldn't mind having a place like this. That might sound ridiculous if you're going to live on a ranch in a brand-new log home with a wonderful view of the mountains, but having my very own outhouse, now, that would be *sweet*."

Bex gave him her coldest glare. "Let's not forget the outdoor shower. As for me, I'm looking forward to a long, hot soak in a real bathtub. I might even go so far as to indulge in a glass of wine while I bathe. Oh, and some soft music would be lovely, too."

There was a brief, pulsing silence. Then, his voice husky, Tate asked, "Can I join you?"

"If Tara's already moved out, you're invited," she said recklessly.

He opened the truck's passenger door and ushered her in. "That's an invitation I wouldn't pass up for a million bucks. Now dare we hope that fishing despair can be cured by burgers and hot fudge sundaes? Listen to

Ben and Adam arguing over who's going to sit where. I'm just going to let them figure it out."

Josh, the peacekeeper, offered to sit in the middle, solving the problem.

He would.

She really loved him.

And if Tara had indeed gone home, Bex knew she was the one who'd have to explain why they were dropping him off there instead of going directly to her house. It wasn't a conversation she wanted to have and would definitely be post–ice cream.

She sent her sister a text as soon as she had a decent signal that wouldn't cut out at any second.

On our way back.

If she hadn't been securely buckled in, the reply would've made her fall out of her seat.

I'm in Denver.

She looked over at Tate, driving them down the winding tree-lined roads. He understood the expression on her face to the extent that he said, "I take it something's happened and we can't talk about it now."

"You could say that," she muttered, punching in a reply.

Tara, what the hell?

I changed my mind. I couldn't do it. I caught a flight this morning. Without Greg. I need to move away. I have a friend here who can get me a job.

What about Josh?

Can you keep him?

She'd prefer it.
Beyond a question, yes.

Of course. Is Greg going to give me trouble?

I don't think so.

That wasn't reassuring, either. Bex stared at her phone. What were her rights? As far as she knew, she didn't have any.

Quietly, hoping the boys wouldn't hear, she asked Tate, "Could we stay with you tonight?"

He didn't even blink. "Of course."

"Just for tonight," she reiterated.

"As long as you need."

"I'd ask Hadleigh or Mel, but I think Josh would be better off with Ben and Adam around. I'll explain later."

They were speaking in hushed voices.

"What happened?"

"Tara is in Colorado."

"What?" He navigated the slick road. Pines flashed by, lonely sentinels. "What? Just like that?"

"I'm afraid so."

"She has a lot of faith in you."

That was kind of him. He could've mentioned how irresponsible it was to go off to another state without your child, but didn't. Bex didn't know whether to applaud Tara's decision or not. If she'd taken Josh, things would be so much worse.

"This way, he can stay in the same school," she said.

"Bex, you do realize that Greg could show up and claim the boy at any time?"

She nodded grimly. "I have to sort this out, get some advice. Greg can be unpredictable, and I'll feel safer if we stay with you."

"There's no way I'd let you stay alone, anyway." Tate sounded serious, dangerously so. "I still think your sister is out of her mind."

Bex agreed on that score, but something else had occurred to her. "It's just possible that Tara's done the best thing for everyone," she mused. "By accident, probably, but—"

Tate's phone beeped and he handed it over. "Can you see who that is, please? This isn't a good place to pull over."

She checked the ID. "I believe it's your father."

He groaned. "Not now."

"According to his text, he's in Mustang Creek."

CHAPTER FIFTEEN

WITH BEX BUNKING at his place—a development he hadn't expected, or not yet, anyway—Tate was glad he'd cleaned the bathroom just before they'd left on the fishing trip.

As a rule, he kept the house reasonably tidy, but things were usually in a state of controlled chaos. This time luck was in his favor; there were no dishes in the sink, the floor had been swept and he'd done a quick dusting. So the place was respectable, or as respectable as it ever got.

The rented bungalow was small, with three tiny bedrooms, a single bathroom and a modest, dated kitchen. As temporary accommodation, it suited a bachelor with two young children just fine, especially since it had a fenced backyard where the boys could play. The majority of his furniture was in storage and what he had here didn't exactly fit the place. His big couch overwhelmed the dainty living room, while his television took up most of one wall—but it was a short-term arrangement. And, a real plus, they were close enough to the school that the boys could walk. When they moved out to the ranch, he'd have to drive them.

He couldn't wait to move into their brand-new log house. The interior finishes were all that remained to be done, and then the contractor could start on the barn and stables.

"It's okay. Josh and I can just stay here," Bex had said when they pulled up to her house. She was clearly having second thoughts. Previously she'd planned to drop off her laundry and pick up some clean clothes and a few personal items. "We'll be fine."

"Like hell you're staying here," he'd told her bluntly. "Until we find out how your brother-in-law reacts to Tara leaving town, I'm your new shadow."

She'd frowned slightly. "What about your father?"

"He has a room at that fancy lodge at the edge of town. Much more his style than a modest house on Aspen Street. Even in Kirkland he didn't stay with us. Fact is, he's never had a lot of time for noisy young boys. Grab a dress. Unless you're vehemently opposed, we're meeting Dad for dinner."

"I don't know if Josh has anything appropriate to wear. Why don't I stay with the boys?"

"He's the same size as Adam, so we'll work it out."

Tate carried Bex's suitcase as far as her front porch, but she stopped him there. He didn't ask questions, didn't want to crowd her.

Ten or fifteen minutes later, when she emerged carrying a canvas gym bag, the expression on her face told him something had happened. "I'll tell you later," she said very quietly when she got back in the truck.

Practically a repeat of their earlier conversation in the truck. He drove away, assuming it wasn't going to be great news.

It wasn't.

When they got to his place and the boys had vanished into their rooms, she told him, "Greg left me about a dozen messages asking why Tara wasn't answering her phone or returning his texts."

"Nice of her to make you explain it to him."

She shook her head. "This might sound strange, but I'm happier about her taking off this way than I was when I thought they were getting back together. She can't say no to him, so she removed herself from the situation. It's the smartest thing she's done in a long time."

He found it incomprehensible that Tara could leave her child, but at least Josh was safe with Bex. Tripp had said Greg wasn't a truly bad guy, just not a truly good one. He reminded Tate of Sandra—self-centered and unfaithful. There should be a law against it. There wasn't, though, and Bex was probably right; if Tara could be so easily persuaded to go back to Greg, then getting the hell out of Dodge was the best alternative.

He pointed down the hall. "I use that bedroom as an office. There's a daybed in there, and that's where I'll sleep. You can stay in my room. There's a shortage of bubble bath in this male household, so I hope you brought your own. Otherwise, help yourself."

At the moment her eyes looked very gold. She gave what he could only describe as a sultry look, but that kind of language wasn't his area of expertise. "We could just share the bed. It isn't like it hasn't happened before, and I feel confident your bed is bigger than a bottom bunk."

It was. King-size, took up the entire space, and without three small boys in the same room, he had a feeling things might get out of control.

In a really good way.

"That's up to you."

"Hmm, then my vote is we share. I'm going to take my bath."

Leaving him with the image of her naked…

Last thing he needed.

He went to call his father. "I hope you don't mind, but there'll be five of us joining you. My friend Bex and her nephew are coming along."

"The pretty little brunette? Ah, I see. What does she do again? Teach fitness classes?"

This was the big problem with his father. Everything was measured in terms of financial and career success. Tate was tempted just to say yes so she could be judged on the merits of her personality and her warmth, but the truth would come out, anyway. "She owns a chain of fitness centers, actually. What time is the reservation?"

"A chain?"

He could tell that Bex had gone from pretty brunette to a much higher status.

"Yes. What time?"

"Seven. I'll make sure we have a big enough table."

"We'll be there."

He unsuccessfully tried to ignore the fact that the water in the bathroom had stopped running.

If he lurked in the hall, he could probably hear the slight splash as she moved, but he wasn't programmed to lurk, so he went into the living room and switched on a football game instead.

His phone rang. Tripp. "The Seahawks are losing."

"I see that."

"How was the trip?"

"Great."

No, even better than that...

"Hadleigh said Bex sent her a text that she's going to stay with you tonight. Do we have a problem?"

Tripp would automatically go into full big-brother mode if it involved Bex; Tate was well aware of that.

"We just don't *want* a problem," he explained and told him about Tara's sudden departure. "Greg could go to the school anytime he likes and pick him up, so this is just a stopgap solution to let him cool off. It sounds as though Tara agreed to move back home, then changed her mind at the last minute. She up and left town without letting him know. Getting away from him isn't a bad decision in some ways, but Bex shouldn't be the one who has to tell the little guy about it." He paused. "I doubt he has any idea where she is at the moment, but this is Mustang Creek, so he could figure it out easily enough. If he does show up, at least I'll be here."

Tripp said slowly, "I don't think he'd touch her. I promise you there'd be a nasty argument, though. He knows Bex doesn't approve of how he's handled his relationship with her sister, and I can't say I approve of it, either. There are damned few people in this town who don't think Tara Stuart married badly. Here's hoping she finds the backbone to call him and tell him she's gone for good so Bex is off the hook. Tara's a good person, but she's a pushover. If the meek really do inherit the earth, she'll get a fair chunk of it."

"That's the impression I have of her." Tate sighed. "Not once in three days did Josh even mention his dad. He hasn't asked why they're staying here tonight, either. The fishing trip and hanging out with my boys was fun, I get that, but usually kids want to go back to their own rooms, their routines, their family life. He's attached himself to Bex like a limpet."

"You ought to talk to Spence. His mother just dumped him with his aunt when he was a kid and only recently got in touch with him again. He's always maintained he was better off with his aunt, anyway, so he adjusted, like kids do."

Hard to argue, since Tate suspected that was true of Josh, as well. Not only that, he was convinced that his sons were better off without their mother's influence, too. Maybe Sandra wouldn't have instilled her lack of ethics in them, but you could never be sure. In the divorce proceedings, he'd planned to fight for full custody, and given her past, his lawyer said he would've won easily.

Tate changed the subject. "My dad's in town. I can't wait to find out what that's about."

Tripp had met his father plenty of times before, when he'd used the charter service. "I've told you all along he's got to be itching to invest. His father bred and sold horses. You're doomed to lots of advice and criticism. Why not take his money and build that bigger barn and better stable?"

Sound advice, perhaps, but the problem was, he didn't want to ask. "If he offers, I'll consider it. Bex knows someone she thinks might be interested."

"Who would…" Then Tripp started laughing. Or would you call it chortling? "I bet I know who it is. Lettie Arbuckle. Yeah, Mrs. A. probably will want to invest, but then you'd need to choose between the devil you know and the one you don't."

Hardly great news. A smaller barn seemed better all the time. He replied wryly, "I'll take that into consideration."

BEX ADJUSTED THE HEM of her skirt, looked critically in the mirror and decided she was doing okay.

Nice black-and-white dress, stylish but comfortable black suede shoes...

Now she needed to get Josh ready.

She was waiting for him to ask her about Tara, both dreading it and worried he *wouldn't* ask.

He seemed happy enough, and that was the most important thing, but surely a child should be eager to go home. Either he was and he was covering it up, or he wasn't. Which was worse?

Covering it up, she decided, looking at her image again but not really seeing it. Maybe she needed to talk to Ben and find out if Josh had said anything to him and Adam. She had no idea how to do that, though. He was only eight, and he shouldn't have to deal with an adult question like that. Besides, he was Tate's child, not hers. No, she couldn't put Ben on the spot.

One problem at a time. First step was to see if Josh had something decent to wear to dinner at Mustang Creek's fanciest restaurant—and, if not, if he could borrow an outfit from Adam.

She'd put a few of his clothes in her bag, but the choices had been limited; a lot of his stuff was still at Greg's place. However, he had clean jeans, which would do, and a pullover shirt that would work. Okay, problem solved once she got hold of an iron. She let Tate supervise the baths, which meant he directed them into the bathroom in sequence, told them he expected shampoo and soap to be used and handed out towels.

Very efficient.

It was cute to see Josh respond to him in exactly the same way as Ben and Adam, and if she didn't have Tate in her corner, she wasn't sure quite *what* she'd be doing right now.

Sitting in the living room on an outrageously large sofa, she tried calling Tara again.

She'd had no success with the last few attempts, but this time her sister answered.

Yes, she was in Denver.

No, she hadn't talked to Greg yet. She knew she was putting it off.

What about Josh?

"Greg won't push for that." Tara sounded confident. "He'll let you keep him."

Good news and bad news for everyone involved. Bex hated the idea of letting Josh go with his father, but she was also trying to picture suddenly raising a six-year-old. Even though Tara was going through a rough time, her son should come first.

"Everything okay?" Tate looked fantastic in dark slacks and a gray shirt, his brown hair still damp, since he'd gone last in the shower sequence.

And yet…the concern in his eyes moved her more than anything else.

"I just talked to my sister." She dropped her phone in her purse. "I think Josh will be staying with me. She swears Greg won't want to deal with him on his own."

Tate nodded. "Bex, I know you're sitting there agonizing over how to tell him that, but if I had to call it, this is really what he wants. You're safety and security to him, and he's out of the war zone. He gets to play with Ben and Adam, go to school as usual, and not deal with all the acrimony."

"I *have* to talk to him about it."

One hip propped against the counter, Tate asked, "Has he given you any indication he's ready for that?"

"He's six. He doesn't know what he's ready for."

"You want to fix his world, and I'd like to do the same, but we can't, and he'll deal with it." His voice was calm and reassuring. "We all do at the end of the day. I guarantee that with you to support him, with me and all our friends, he'll cope." Then he grimaced. "Oh, man, we should probably go. My apologies if the conversation tonight gets uncomfortable. My father's not renowned for his tact."

There spoke another abandoned boy. Maybe not in a factual sense, but his emotional distance from his father was very evident.

A boy who'd definitely grown up into one hell of an attractive man. She moved closer. "Okay, I'll forgive him in advance if you'll kiss me. Do it now while we have two seconds of privacy."

He did a spectacular job of complying with that request, and his arms only loosened when they heard the boys laughing. "You just ruined my lip gloss."

"I hope so, or I didn't do it right."

"Let me go repair the damage while you get the boys in order."

"It's a deal."

The surreal quality of the weekend continued as they all got back in Tate's truck. Bex felt as if she'd gone from independent businesswoman, single and busy with her life and friends, to being in a relationship and becoming surrogate mother to three small boys.

After getting Josh dressed and ready, she'd helped the other two pick out shirts and tied their shoes. At least she could say they all looked clean and neat, hair combed. The usual wrangling over seats didn't occur. Josh automatically climbed into the middle again.

The lodge was a replica of the grand ski hotels but

on a Mustang Creek scale, with a hint of Swiss chalet, and was definitely the most expensive place in the area. At this time of year, the parking lot was only half full, and when Tate parked next to a sleek vehicle with an impressive pedigree, he commented, "I see my father drove here. He must really have something to say. Let's get this over with."

CHAPTER SIXTEEN

TATE HAD TO ADMIT he was apprehensive about the evening. Ridiculous? Yep. He was a grown man, and he was hardly a failure.

But Tripp was right; his father had some sort of agenda.

They were seated at a big round table next to a window with a view of the Tetons. The boys sat there, feet dangling, remarkably subdued. His father, formal as always, wore the usual tailored suit, and Bex was stunning in her fitted dress. Even before the drinks were delivered—red wine for the adults, lemonade for the boys—his father hinted at why he'd decided to make the lengthy drive over.

"I want to go look at the ranch tomorrow. How are you planning out this whole venture?"

Yes, he definitely wanted to get a hands-on interest. The question was whether to decline or accept.

"If you'd like to look it over, that's fine." Tate's response was cautious. "I'm trying to decide on the size of the barn now that the house is close to completion."

A waitress came by to take their order. All three of the boys chose chicken fingers and french fries. Bex asked for the special, a duck breast with a red wine and plum sauce, and he did, too. His father predictably ordered a steak and then immediately returned to the conversation.

"I suppose, since you've chosen to go in this direction, we should make sure it's a success."

The hint of disapproval was still there, but Tate ignored it. When he'd elected to play soccer instead of football in high school, they'd had this same conversation. Switching from chemical engineering to aviation in college hadn't met with approval at first, either, but few things did in his experience, so he'd found a balance between annoyance and amusement, and accepted that this was his father. It was how he operated, and Tate's self-esteem no longer suffered when his judgment was questioned.

He just hoped Bex could weather the storm known as Randolph Calder. There were times it required a life vest, a rain slicker and tying yourself to the mast.

She said with endearing loyalty, "It's a beautiful piece of property, and the house is going to be gorgeous. Plenty of room for the horses, and a great place to raise the boys."

His father transferred his attention to her. Tate took a hearty sip of wine—he was limiting himself to one glass—and braced himself for the coming lecture.

"Breeding horses is not an occupation, it's a lifestyle," he began. "They require constant care. It's not a matter of just showing up for work. The mares drop foals at all hours, and only some are viable as riding stock. There are stud fees and vet visits. A contagious illness, if it isn't caught quickly, can wipe out a stable. I'm not even going to go into how often they need to be fed, have their stalls mucked out and so on. Plus, training needs to be done by someone who really has a handle on it. You can't sell an ill-mannered horse."

Bex didn't blink. Her eyes, green in the restaurant's

lighting, shone. "Tate knows all that. He has the stud and the vet lined up, and his only concern is how much to put into building the stables and the barn. As he says, it's so much more cost-effective to build what you need from the beginning rather than adding on later."

That was a challenge if he'd ever heard one. He didn't need her to fight his battles for him. And yet, he was touched by the effort.

He intervened before his father could respond. "I've done my homework, Dad," he said mildly.

"We'll see."

Bex bristled, but then she must have noticed his half smile and relaxed. Their silent communication felt natural, and Tate hoped for a similar kind of physical communion later.

She was the one who'd suggested they sleep in the same bed tonight, but this time in privacy, with a door that locked and no one else in the room. Very little, in his estimation, that could ruin this night.

Wrong.

"Bex Stuart."

The woman who stopped at their table was petite, gray haired and well dressed in a dark green suit that had not been purchased in Mustang Creek. New York City, more likely. She was in her late sixties, he guessed, and she had quite a commanding presence. She said very clearly, "I got your message. Is this the young man who needs an investor in his new business?"

Tate rose politely. "Uh, Tate Calder, ma'am. You must be Mrs. Arbuckle."

Bex probably wondered how he'd known the name, but he assumed she'd figure it out. Good thing Tripp had warned him.

The devil you know...

His father rose, too, but Mrs. Arbuckle ignored him as she surveyed the table. "Those two must be yours. Handsome children. I'll come by tomorrow and we can talk."

After she'd walked away to join a group of ladies at another table, Bex cleared her throat. "She's actually very nice, but she's always abrupt. I love Mrs. A. She can be an acquired taste, though."

"We've met before," Tate's father said in an acid tone.

Of course they had. It made sense because they were probably both in the same tax bracket and same social level. And in the state of Wyoming, with its population of well under a million, that meant they occasionally bumped into each other. He refrained from pointing this out and said, "Bex knows her and thought she might be helpful."

"You wouldn't ask *me* first?"

Now, that was a volatile question. Tate strove for a politic answer that was also honest. "You seemed to disapprove of the idea in the first place. Why would I?"

His frankness didn't defuse the situation. The arrival of the bread, however, did help, providing a distraction; the basket was being passed around, butter distributed, and noises of appreciation resounded. Tate was aware that his father wasn't mollified, but he didn't care anymore.

Oh, he cared about his father. Pleasing him was less important than it used to be, though. A *lot* less important.

Now Bex's eyes looked like warm gold. She handed him the basket. "Have a roll. Otherwise the sharks will come cruising in again and you'll lose your chance."

If he wasn't already in love with her, he would have

tumbled off that cliff right then and there. It was clear that while she wanted to keep the peace, she was in his corner. Tate took a roll, and it was delicious.

"You can't let Lettie Arbuckle invest."

"Because?"

"She'll meddle." His father was testy.

So will you.

Tate assumed that Bex wouldn't have recommended Lettie if *she'd* experienced any problems or the woman had interfered in her business. He didn't want to discuss it further, though, not over dinner. He was aware that, much as they might seem to ignore it, the children were aware of the subtle argument at the table, so this just wasn't the time. "I'd like you to come tomorrow and tell me what you think." And that was the end of the conversation.

DINNER WAS BOTH better and worse than Bex had expected it to be.

She found Tate's father an interesting combination of suave and overbearing. No question he thought he knew it all, but she sensed that he was decent underneath, and that mattered.

A relief, really, since she'd been worried she wouldn't like him.

She answered all of Mr. Calder's questions as candidly as possible. His father was interested in her business and that didn't surprise her, because she'd dealt with dozens of people like him. It was the language he knew, and he spoke it well.

He and Tate, on the other hand, might have been living on different planets.

If Tate didn't think he was sensitive, he was so wrong.

She'd fallen for the way he loved his sons and the way he treated Josh.

He'd have to stop arguing about the whole "sensitive" thing. There was nothing wrong with it, and she was exactly the woman to prove that to him.

It was the magic of the marriage pact.

Bex had never seen so clearly how this wasn't just about her, Mel and Hadleigh; it was also about the men who needed them.

"I'd ask why you're staring at me," he said in a low voice when their dinner was being served, "but I'm afraid the answer involves my father. Everything okay?"

She jingled the little charms on her bracelet and said, her smile slow, "I think it is."

He saw the gesture, and his look was questioning, but at that moment Adam spilled ketchup on his shirt in one of the inevitable minor disasters associated with young boys. Tate needed to do cleanup and assure his son that accidents happened, so they trooped off to the bathroom. When they'd left, Tate's father asked her, "So how did the two of you meet?"

She thought about Tripp and Hadleigh's wedding and the party they'd thrown when they got back from their honeymoon. "Through shameless matchmaking by one of my best friends."

He chuckled. "I see. Seems to be working."

Cautiously, because she wasn't sure how Tate would feel about this conversation, she said, "We're getting along so far."

Randolph Calder glanced at Ben and hesitated, as if he wanted to say something about Tate's wife, but refrained. Instead he muttered, "Tate's made a decision or two I haven't agreed with, but I suppose that's unavoidable. What do you think about this horse-breeding business? You're from here, right? I don't feel that Mustang Creek's big enough to support it. Where's the market?"

All business, all the time was how Tate had described his father.

At least she knew the answer. "There are a lot of ranchers who need working horses, but he mainly wants to target the tourism trade in this area. Trail rides and camping packages require good-natured, well-broken stock. There's a market around here."

"That's interesting. What about the property? Is there a place for a hotel like this place?"

"A hotel?"

"I assume if Lettie Arbuckle's interested, there's going to be a hotel. She owns half of them in the state. If he was planning to do that, he should've asked me."

Oh, no. Bex didn't have the impression that was what Tate wanted at all.

"I...I think he just wants to raise horses."

"A hotel would be more profitable. This was about my only choice of a place to stay around here. I'm not always on board with Lettie's ideas, but I believe this one could be a success. A lodge on a working ranch with the view around here? That could be a solid decision."

With relief she saw Tate coming back with Adam, who seemed to feel the need to skip between the tables. "I'm not sure how many acres he bought," she was able to say hastily. "You'll have to ask him."

"Problem solved," Tate informed them as he sat down, but his gaze went from her to his father and back to her. "What did I miss?"

"Here's the dessert menu." Bex handed it over, evading the question.

He knew she was doing it, too; she could tell from his resigned expression.

They split the chocolate-fudge tunnel cake. The boys had the usual ice cream, and Tate's father drank coffee and a snifter of expensive cognac.

It wasn't until they were in the truck, driving back to his rental house, that he said, "Just tell me. What did he say?"

"This could be my fault, Tate."

"What could be your fault? Now you're making me nervous. You'll have to clarify."

"Can I first say that I had no idea your father knew Mrs. A.?"

"Okay, but that disclaimer does not fill me with joy, Bex. Why would it matter, other than that they seem to dislike each other and both might want to invest? Tripp already gave me a heads-up that Mrs. Arbuckle is a force to be reckoned with. I haven't made a decision yet, but whatever I end up doing, I have to include Doc Cameron, since he's part of this."

"Your father mentioned a hotel."

"No."

Unequivocal. Not up for discussion.

"I'm just telling you what he said to me." She sank a little lower in her seat. "You know, he has a point. We *could* use another nice hotel around here. Right now the pickin's are sparse if you want to stay somewhere that isn't a chain, and we don't even have very many of those."

"I want my log house, my corral and pasture and a stable and barn. That's it. I want to look at the Tetons, not the silhouette of a hotel."

Bex nodded. "I agree. But there's no reason that either your father or Mrs A. couldn't buy some land and put a lodge on it. That could help your business, because you could rent them the horses for trail rides and such. They might still invest in your stable and barn if you presented it that way. See which one makes the better offer. Both of them are coming over tomorrow."

It took a minute, but he grinned. "You're very sexy when you move into business mode. But then, you're sexy all the time, so it goes without saying."

"Thank you for the compliment, but…thoughts?"

He checked the rearview mirror. "We have some sleepy boys on our hands, this dilemma will still be around tomorrow and right now I'm concentrating on the fact that you decided we should both sleep in the same bed."

She was concentrating on that, too.

CHAPTER SEVENTEEN

On a scale of one to ten, the evening had been about a seven, considering that his father was involved. Between hotel schemes and ketchup spills, there'd been a few glitches, but Tate could wash the shirt and say no to the hotel idea, so all in all, it was a success.

His father liked Bex.

That was good, anyway.

There was no middle ground with him. He liked you or he didn't, and usually it was obvious either way. Bex was beautiful and successful, so her popularity with his critical parent was no surprise.

Tate was drawn to her for entirely different reasons. Well, maybe not *entirely*. But aside from the undeniable attraction he felt for her was something deeper.

She had an undefinable quality he wouldn't even try to analyze, at least not tonight.

Tonight he was focused on one thing. The fact that she was sexy as hell.

Definite thumbs-up there. The boys were all worn out from the long day, so getting teeth brushed and pajamas on wasn't met with the usual resistance. Adam was asleep before he'd left the bedroom, and Josh looked zoned out, too, lying on the blow-up mattress on the floor. Ben managed to say good-night, but it was sleepy and halfhearted.

Bex was lounging on the couch, shoes off, ankles crossed, relaxed. "You did that so well, getting those kids to bed. How about a lesson?"

There was no way he could resist going over and scooping her into his arms. "I have an ulterior motive tonight, so I pulled out all the stops. Now can I put *you* to bed? I'm hoping that's an offer you can't refuse."

"I'm about to nod off." She gave a fake yawn.

"Well, let's see if I can keep you awake for a little while, anyway." He carried her down the hall to his room in what he had to admit was a theatrical gesture, but Bex was laughing, and he grinned back when he deposited her on the bed.

The first thing he did was shut the door. Then he unbuttoned his shirt and tossed it on a chair. "Can I tell you how much I'm looking forward to sleeping with you again?"

"I thought that bunk was fairly comfortable," she lied.

"Maybe if you aren't over six feet tall." He sat down and yanked off his boots. "But I have to say there were some perks, namely you. I've mentioned that I have a serious crush on you, right?" It was more than that, of course...

She shimmied out of her dress by lifting the skirt and pulling it off over her head. Beneath she wore a scanty black bra and even scantier panties.

He could no longer swallow, his mouth went so dry.

"I was hoping to see that expression on your face," she said in a low voice. "I don't normally dress like this. Remember my plaid flannel pj's?"

"You looked hot in those, too," he told her, and that was the truth. Still, she looked even sexier with her loose shimmering hair and all that bare skin. "But this is a little better. Take it all off?"

"Same goes for you, cowboy. All or nothing."

He'd never shucked off his pants so quickly. If someone had been timing him, he would've set the world record.

Bex unfastened her bra and slid the panties down her long legs. He figured it was a good sign that he didn't expire on the spot—it meant he had a healthy heart. He'd stopped at the local drugstore earlier and bought a box of condoms, although it had been quite a while. He wasn't celibate by any means, but fleeting encounters only satisfied one urge and left him feeling cheated, and he really wanted this.

Wanted *her*.

"You want this, too, right?" He settled next to her, and touched her nipple. "I won't pressure you."

In answer she rolled on top of him. Bare breasts to bare chest, and her smile could have tipped the earth onto a different axis. "I want this."

"I'm just—"

"Overthinking it." She kissed him, her lips lingering softly on his. "Just make love to me."

He had to ask. Thanks to Tripp, he knew about Will, and he had some sense of what had happened in her past, but he doubted even Melody and Hadleigh knew every detail. He touched her cheek, "I feel stupid asking this, but you aren't a virgin, are you?"

"I'm almost thirty."

"That isn't an answer."

Typical Bex, she came right back at him. "Would it make a difference?"

"It might slow the pace."

She shook her head then, her eyes luminous. "No. Will and I had a week before he shipped out again. He

wouldn't touch me until I was eighteen, and I understood that since he was older, and…and he was a man
of honor. We waited, but that was a memorable week.
He didn't come home again."

"No one else?"

"Nope. I've dated, of course, but wasn't ever interested enough for this." She touched him and he groaned.

Pretty damn close to a virgin. Tate rested his forehead against hers. "I'm sorry you lost him but I'm glad
I found you."

"We're in complete agreement, then."

He threaded his fingers through her hair, the silky
feel of it familiar after those two long nights sharing
that bunk. He kissed her and she kissed him back with
fervor, and then he reversed their positions, rolling over
as he began to explore her body, listening to the cadence
of her breathing as it changed with each caress, every
touch of his mouth and hands. Her spine arched as he
kissed his way down her rib cage and stomach, and
when he kissed her intimately her response was intense.

He rolled on the condom with hands that weren't
steady, and the press of her hands told him she did want
this as much as he did. He entered her and began to
move, her hips lifting naturally to the rhythm.

She surrendered first, and the tightening of her inner
muscles brought his release. The pleasure was overwhelming.

"Hmm." Bex stroked the base of his spine. "I think
I might want to do that again sometime."

He laughed, the sound a bit strangled. "I just hope
I start to breathe again sometime. Maybe next year."

Her grin was pure Bex, saucy and teasing. "I hope it
doesn't take you that long to recover, cowboy."

HER GRANDMOTHER USED to have an old expression she was fond of trotting out. It went, "If you cross a flooding river while it's still raining, you're going to have a hard time crossing back."

Bex had already come to the conclusion that sleeping with Tate was plunging into that current.

He was a considerate lover, no question. Her pleasure before his, but he wasn't going to slight himself, either, and in the floating aftermath of the third time, she decided that if it was a mistake, at least it was an enjoyable one.

However, outside the bedroom, they had some problems that weren't going away. She had Tara's mess to deal with, and her business, which took up a great deal of her time. He wasn't even currently employed on an official basis, but about to embark on a brand-new venture. Add the well-being of three children, and it was just plain complicated.

Still cradled by his left arm, Bex slid her hand over his bare chest. "So tell me how you're going to handle tomorrow's visitors."

"Jeez, you know how to ruin the mood." His dark eyes held wry amusement as he turned his head to look at her. "The question involves hotels and horses and two possible investors who don't like each other."

"That certainly sums it up."

"This answer will impress you. I have no idea."

"Want some thoughts?"

"Only if you don't tell me I should consider the devil I know or the devil I don't."

That was true enough. Bex frowned. "I stand by my earlier suggestion that if your father decides a hotel is a sound business decision, let him buy the land and lease the horses from you. That seems logical to me. Pitch it to Mrs. A., as well." She added, "Mrs. A. has been willing to trust me with her investment. No meddling at all. That's been my experience, anyway."

He nodded.

"You could see which one would be willing to fund the bigger stable."

"Or I could build a smaller one I can afford myself, and keep them both out of my hair."

He had a point, but...

"Then you'd have to build another stable in the near future," she said. "God willing and the creek don't rise."

Her grandmother's sayings must *really* be on her mind.

He was quiet except for a long sigh. "I know," he said finally. "That's both a plus and a minus. If the business goes well, it's exactly what I'd have to do, and that's another outlay of cash. I've been arguing with myself. I've talked to Tripp. I've asked Doc Cameron, and everyone thinks a bigger stable is the way to go—they say not to wait—but I like to do things on my own."

"I've gathered that." It wasn't as if she didn't understand. That was her, too. She made her own way, but she also relied on Hadleigh and Mel—all three of them relied on each other. For that matter, Tripp and Spence would be there for her in a heartbeat. And there was also the matter of Mrs. A's very generous investment. While complete independence was appealing in theory, the reality was a little different.

It was nice to have some backup.

"Let's just see how it goes." He kissed her temple, his body beginning to relax in a way she knew signaled sleep. "I'm too tired to worry about it right now."

She wished sleep would come as easily to her.

It didn't.

So she eased out of his embrace, got up and slipped on her T-shirt and shorts. Then she went into the living room with her phone, taking a quick peek through the boys' door. All three were sleeping peacefully. Her throat tightened as she looked at Josh, with one fist curled under his little chin, his pajamas patterned with dinosaurs.

She hoped Tara knew Greg as well as she claimed, and there wasn't a looming battle she couldn't win.

Tate had what could be the largest couch ever made. She propped up a pillow and when she'd accessed her email, she sent both Hadleigh and Melody a message.

Kind of a significant evening in Bex-land. I could use some girl time soon. Shopping? Lunch?

Mel was obviously awake, because she answered immediately.

I have the worst heartburn and I believe the baby is deliberately sitting on my bladder. What's up?

Tate.

Oh, is that a double entendre?

Mel!

I was joking.

Talk soon?

Date.

It wasn't as though she'd give details. But there'd been an ongoing conversation among the three of them about the fact that she had no social life or romantic involvement. Her friends knew she'd loved Will, but both of them encouraged an interest in Tate.

They would both be so happy for her. Over the moon. She hit Send, smiling.

Tate was a light sleeper, probably due to being a single father, because when she went back to bed, he woke instantly, pulling her close. "Everything okay?" he murmured.

"Better than."

"That's the answer I wanted." His eyes drifted closed again.

"I'm not ready for a serious relationship," she whispered into the dark. Not that she didn't *want* one. She did—with him. But her remark was an attempt to persuade herself, on both a practical and an emotional level, that this was too fast, too soon.

"You got that straight."

Damn, he wasn't asleep, after all.

Bex jabbed him in the chest. "What does that mean?"

He rubbed the spot. "Hey, I was trying to be agreeable."

She nestled against his shoulder. "This is a terrible time for us to get involved. Neither of us *has* the actual time."

"Yep."

"Maybe we could just sleep together now and then." His chest was solid and warm.

"Now and then? I'd go for more often than that. If tonight didn't do it, maybe I need to read up on it so I can try again."

"You could teach classes," Bex said sarcastically, "so stop with the false modesty."

Finally, she was the one getting sleepy. She yawned. "Bex, things will work themselves out."

She put her arm around his waist and settled in. "Funny, that's what I was going to tell you about tomorrow."

His face was shadowed. "Oh, yeah. Mrs. A., as you call her, and my father? I'd rather be a professional fish-from-the-hook remover."

"That reminds me. We should take the boys fishing again. Could we choose one of those fly-in places that fix all the food and have real bathrooms?"

"Aren't *you* the princess? Hey, except for the outhouse, that one wasn't bad."

"I tend to avoid them, so I've got a very short list for comparison."

Still, she'd go there again, outhouse or not. The boys had *loved* the place.

And there was no way she'd ever forget that it was where Tate had told her he loved her.

THE NEXT MORNING, school preparation was the usual chaos. Tate told Ben that he was in charge of getting everyone there, but then changed his mind and drove them all. He sat in his truck, watching them walk through the front door of the building.

Sandra had always said he was overprotective, and it might be true...

He wanted them to be independent, but he also wanted them to be safe. Josh was part of the equation now, and against his better judgment, he was becoming attached.

Even if Greg didn't step in, once Tara was settled in Denver, she'd want her son back.

Bex had gone off to the fitness center and he needed to be at the ranch, so after he saw the boys inside the school, he headed over to the property.

Everything was routine, with trucks all over the place. The driveway would need to be graded when the construction was finished, he noted to himself, because of the ruts.

Unfortunately, before he'd even parked, he saw that not only was his father there, but a very expensive car he didn't recognize was, too.

He checked his watch. Barely nine in the morning.

If it wasn't for the reflected glow of last night, he'd be even more on edge. Tate got out, slamming the door, prepared to be cordial. He did whip out his phone and quickly called Cameron. "Operation Stable is about to begin. How many stalls do you think we need again? I have the potential investors and contractor right here."

"Twice as many as we originally planned if you can pull it off. Aside from my regular practice, I can take care of that many horses—with some help. And I have a friend who's moving here from Idaho. He's also a vet, Jaxon Locke, and he's good. Hell or high water, he's coming to Mustang Creek. So we're covered. He'd be willing to step in on a day-to-day basis until he gets settled. After that, we'll need to hire some hands."

Twice as big?

That was ambitious. No, Tate couldn't do that on his own.

Where were Mrs. Arbuckle and his father? Probably killing each other somewhere. He should get going. "I'll let you know how this turns out," he said tersely.

"Good luck."

His contractor stopped him in the driveway. "Sorry, but they just went on in. When I tried to talk to them, they ignored me and just walked through the door."

"That's not surprising," Tate responded. Then he raked his fingers through his hair. "If we did a stable twice the size, what's the timeline?"

Bill brightened. "Seriously?"

"Think about a bid."

"Numbers are already running through my mind."

Tate found his father and Mrs. A. in his kitchen, arguing.

Over what, he wasn't sure.

The kitchen looked damned good. The counter Bex had picked out was perfect, and the contrast to the floor and the cabinets really set it off.

He and Ben and Adam should be able to move in by mid-October. For the first time since he'd taken on this project, he inhaled an easy breath. They could've stayed in Kirkland and done just fine, lived comfortably in the house he owned there, but he wanted a different life. This was it.

He expected his new life to be an improvement over the old one.

Especially if Becca Stuart was going to be part of it.

"Hello." He leaned against the cabinets and tried to intervene. "Sorry I'm late to the party but the boys needed to be dropped off at school. So, good morning. What do you think of the house?"

"How many bedrooms?" his father asked abruptly. This morning he wore an expensive sweater and tailor-made slacks, his hair was, as always, immaculately groomed.

Mrs. Arbuckle hardly came up to his shoulder, but she exuded the same powerful aura and she, too, was overdressed in her designer suit and silk scarf, carrying a leather handbag with an impressive logo even Tate recognized.

He felt a little grubby in his faded jeans and denim shirt, although both were clean, and he'd actually polished his boots a few days ago. "Four bedrooms," he said in response to the question. "Three bathrooms. Right now the living room looks like you could land a plane in it, but there's going to be an office at one end with a view of the paddocks and pasture. They haven't framed it in yet."

"Ha, I guess that means I was correct when I informed you that my son would have his office in the house." His father's smile was meant to irritate.

It worked, judging by Mrs. A.'s scowl.

"Well," Tate said in a mild tone, "we plan on there being one in the stables, as well, where we can keep the bloodstock books and other records, like veterinary notes."

"So, you see, Randolph, you can wipe that superior smirk off your face." Lettie Arbuckle sniffed elegantly. Tate had read that description in books and inwardly laughed, but he'd never seen it in person. "Bex told me he was a bright young man," she went on, "so of course I assumed he'd put an office in the stables. He must take after his mother's side of the family."

That was what they were arguing over? This was going to be a comfortable morning. Tate needed to go and get the original plans out of his truck but he was afraid to leave them alone.

And *Randolph*, was it? They'd met before, which had

already been established. Tate had the impression now that they'd disagreed in the past. It could be political, since they were both involved in campaign funding and charity work, but he didn't want the details of whatever had inspired such acrimony.

"It's a beautiful morning. Do you want to walk out and see the site? My partner thinks we should build twice as many stalls as we originally intended, if we can find the capital to do so. In addition to an office, I'd like to have an apartment attached. With that many horses, a stable manager could live there full-time. I have no qualms about running the business, but I'm going to have to hire some hands."

"That sounds well thought-out to me."

"He gets that from *my* side of the family," his father snapped.

Mrs. A. placed her hand on Tate's arm and acted as if his father hadn't even spoken. "Lead the way."

He noticed she was wearing at least two-inch heels, thought of the rutted driveway and decided he might just have landed in hell.

HADLEIGH'S KITCHEN WAS WARM and the tea delicious, and since both of her best friends were addicted to the lemon-cream pastries now, Bex was welcomed with open arms.

"I brought chocolate doughnuts, too," she remarked as they all sat down.

Hadleigh waved a hand. "Take them for the boys. I can't believe I'm saying this, but I'm off chocolate. How is that possible? Remember college? That was practically my whole diet, other than an apple here and there. This baby does not like chocolate."

Melody shuddered. "I'm suddenly so opposed to anything with tomato in it that I can't even have ketchup. I love tomatoes, but not right now. Let's talk about maternity jeans instead. I'm thinking I might wear them all the time, even after the baby comes. Takes comfy to a whole new level."

Considering that Mel was naturally slender, Bex laughed. Today, she was gorgeous in a pink smocked top.

Hadleigh laughed, too, and nodded. "I know what you mean." She turned to Bex. "Now, tell us about the fishing trip. And we need an update on Tara. Not to mention your message last night."

Mel chimed in, licking some cream off her fingers, "We're really boring these days, so we have to live through you. I went to bed at eight-thirty last night. Seriously!"

Bex lifted her hand and pointed at the third charm on her bracelet. "I'm thinking…"

"He's the one. *The One?*" Mel looked delighted. "Perfect! Airplane charm. Pilot man."

Hadleigh's smile was equally genuine. "I'm really glad, Bex. You deserve to be happy. The minute I met Tate Calder I thought of you. He seems so great. You have a lot of things in common, too."

They'd both suffered losses, but their stories were not the same. What he'd gone through and what she had were very different experiences. She wasn't sure which was worse.

"He *is* great. Considerate. Smart—"

"Good-looking. Like, really hot." Mel was her usual forthright self. "That doesn't hurt. I'm just sayin'…"

Bex couldn't agree more. Up close and personal, he

was even better. "Tara is in Denver. Josh is here, and she promises me Greg will stay out of the picture once he figures out she's gone for good."

"That leaves you holding the bag, doesn't it?" Hadleigh's brow furrowed. "She's asking a lot of you."

"I adore Josh. I don't mind."

"You might later," Mel observed, her gaze holding concern. "I'm worried about that."

"I'll *never* regret taking care of him."

"Jeez, I know *that*, but will you regret giving him back?"

Now that was a poignant question. Bex bit into one of the chocolate doughnuts. "How can I possibly answer? It's not up to me."

"Yeah, but it just seems wrong for you not to have a say in this. For you and Josh to be subjected to the whims of two irresponsible people."

Bex's eyes filled with tears. She was a dreamer, but she was a realist, too. "I keep waiting for life to be fair, and it just isn't working out."

Hadleigh had a way of getting to the point without saying it directly. "Two boys? Maybe three? I'm worried about one small baby. Dump three on me and I'd be a goner."

That was all.

Mel was more straightforward. "Josh *would* be better off with you. Spence would totally back me up. His aunt is one of the best people on this earth. But no one can ask that of another person who isn't willing."

"I'm willing enough." She sighed. "Could it *be* more complicated?"

"It could." Hadleigh smiled. "You could have two really pregnant bridesmaids, be marrying the father of two boys, caring for your nephew while your sister's in the middle of a divorce, and trying to expand your business."

"He hasn't brought the subject up at all."

"Marriage?"

"Yep, that's the one."

She would never explain the details of what had happened with his wife, not even to Hadleigh and Mel, not without his permission. It wasn't her story to tell. And the fact that he'd confided in her and almost no one else made her feel privileged. And trusted—a trust she would never abuse. But she did add, "His first marriage was unhappy."

With typical loyalty, Hadleigh said, "You're not her. Tripp wasn't happy the first time around, either." As if that solved the problem.

Bex doubted Tripp had had quite the same experience of finding out that his wife had been married before, was a thief who'd betrayed her family, changed her name and had a child—and never mentioned any of those tidbits of information. "All I'm saying is that he has no problem saying the word *love*, but *marriage* doesn't seem to be in his vocabulary."

Mel pursed her lips, looking thoughtful. "It's early days yet. Spence wasn't exactly rushing me to the altar, either. It took a while before he jumped on that train. Don't sell Tate short, Bex." She paused delicately. "Have you... I mean...you know."

Bex had to laugh at the idea of two pregnant women dancing around the subject of sex. She widened her eyes. "I guess I don't get the question. No, I don't know. What?"

Melody pointed the last bite of her lemon pastry directly at her. "If this wasn't so good, I'd throw it at you."

Hadleigh said, "I feel like I'm at a slumber party. *Did he kiss you? Was it good? Are you going on a second date?* If anyone at this table giggles, I'm not going to answer for the consequences. We aren't sixteen anymore. So are you sleeping with him or not?"

"Yes."

"Good?"

"Double yes." The night before it had been a triple yes.

"See how simple that was?" Hadleigh gave Melody a significant look, and then they all burst out laughing.

Bex glanced at the clock. "I should probably check my messages and then go out to the house to see how it all went. I didn't realize when I asked Mrs. A. if she might want to invest that she knew Tate's father and that they don't like each other. I swear I was trying to help Tate and Doc Cameron, but we all know that the road to hell is paved with good intentions. I'm guessing that he's on that very road this morning. I'm feeling guilty about it, but I'm not sure why."

"Tripp thinks it's hilarious. That man can have a questionable sense of humor, though. He predicts a bidding war that will become part of Wyoming history." Hadleigh got up hastily. "Excuse me, but if I start laughing again, there could be trouble. I don't think I've gone to the bathroom in the past fifteen minutes. A record for me right now."

"It is," Mel confirmed. Then she got up, too. "I have something for you. Do you want to see the clock?"

CHAPTER EIGHTEEN

TODAY HADN'T BEEN the most auspicious day of his life.

On the one hand, both his father and Mrs. A. were willing to invest in the larger stable. On the other hand, the bidding war was out of control.

Or his control, anyway.

It was the dream of any person trying to start up a business, and a nightmare in the making.

When they'd driven away, Tate had been extremely relieved. If, in some alternate universe, he'd remotely imagined them getting along, he'd have suggested they both invest, but that sounded like a catastrophe he wanted no part of.

To his consternation, *they'd* suggested it. During an acrimonious argument that didn't even include him, they'd hammered out the details, and every single time he'd attempted to say anything, he was shot down so he finally gave up.

It was going to be quite a stable.

Nate Cameron and his contractor were thrilled. He was the one who'd be mopping up the blood, so he wasn't nearly as excited.

When his phone rang, he was more than grateful to see Bex's number pop up. She asked, "How did it go?"

"I'm fairly sure I'm not going to survive this."

"That good, huh?"

"I hear the laughter in your voice. You'll pay for that."

"I want to hear the details first."

"You'll get them tonight. I want to have dinner at home. The two of us. A glass of wine, a normal conversation and maybe even some civility. Possible?"

"What about the boys? Don't you mean the five of us?"

He sighed. He'd thought the kids could have their dinner first, then disappear quietly to do their homework. Not too likely—another alternate universe idea. "Okay, you're right. Five. Two isn't possible," he conceded. "What kind of wine goes with hamburgers? The kids can have juice."

"Wine with hamburgers? Red, I guess. Did your father leave already?"

He'd pick out a suitable merlot. "His mission to complicate my life was apparently accomplished. Yes, he took off. I was afraid he and Mrs. Arbuckle were going to drag race each other down the driveway."

"I'd love to have seen that."

"Will you and Josh spend the night again?" Until he knew Tara had informed Greg of her plans, he was going to remain worried. He'd been trying all day to figure out how to camp out in front of Bex's front door with two children sleeping in his truck if she said no.

"I appreciate the concern. Greg hasn't contacted me yet."

"Is that a yes?"

"I called the school. He hasn't said anything to them, either. Maybe Tara actually knows him better than I thought. He isn't interested in Josh, and Josh isn't interested in him." Her voice broke. Just a fraction. "It makes me so sad, Tate."

"I know." He really did. It made him sad, too, at least for Josh. And angry. At Greg. He also noticed that she hadn't answered his question.

"I'll bring a salad. And maybe some mac and cheese."

"Adam won't leap up and down about the first, but I know that won't surprise you. The second offering he'll go for because that's his all-time favorite food. Ben and Josh will eat both."

"If I was going through this alone—"

"You'd manage fine, but we're good together."

He could hardly believe he'd just said that...but he had. And he'd meant it, too.

To gloss over his response—and what it revealed about his feelings—he moved on. "Here's an idea. Do you want to have dinner at the ranch house tonight? Not everything's done, but there are working bathrooms now and the kitchen is almost finished. The boys can run around outside."

Wasn't that the point of it all? To give them an upbringing that included space and horses and vivid blue skies with snow-capped mountains in the distance. No traffic, virtually no crime and the freedom to run and play.

"That sounds perfect. Um, has the kitchen been painted yet?"

He found that an interesting question. "They were working on it when I left. Why?"

"No reason. What time do you want us to come out?"

"I'll pick the boys up from school, including Josh. Whenever you're ready is fine. We'll be there. I want to go over the new plans with the contractor now that the game has changed. By the way, my father didn't say anything about hotels. He was too busy arguing with Lettie Arbuckle. So at least I dodged that conversation. Maybe we should have champagne with our burgers to celebrate the event."

"I'll buy some." Bex laughed. "After all, it's supposed to go with everything."

When the call ended, Tate rubbed his forehead and propped his elbows on his desk. His rocky relationship with his father always made him consider how he dealt with his sons. Loving someone didn't necessarily lead to a perfect relationship. In fact, as he knew from experience, there was no such thing, even though Tripp and Spence had ended up in marriages that were as close to perfect as marriage got. People were individual, and they handled life's joys and problems in their own unique ways. Accepting that someone else's way might not be yours wasn't easy. Especially if you disapproved of the other person's approach.

Look at Bex and her sister, for instance.

That neither of Josh's parents was taking care of him was beyond the scope of Tate's imagination, but then, maybe they knew Bex would be better at it than either of them. At this particular time, anyway.

The three boys came out of the school together, and when they saw him, ran with flattering eagerness in his direction.

No, he was mistaken. Bex had also arrived and was holding a magic cookie box, which they could see from a distance. His boys dashed past him as if he didn't exist.

Turning, he had to say, "That's not playing fair, you know."

Unabashedly, she grinned. "I left work early today and I'd already stopped off at the bakery so Hadleigh and Mel could get their fix. I would've told you on the phone, but—"

"This was more fun."

"You bet." Her eyes held that sparkle he found so captivating. She wore a little red cap patterned with snowflakes; it matched her sweater. The boys milled around her, and several of their friends joined in as she passed out cookies.

"That is purchased popularity," he informed her, hands in his pockets. "Shameless bribery."

"I don't deny or defend my actions."

"Doesn't matter. The truth is, *I* love you for you."

"I'd offer you a cookie but I seem to be fresh out." She displayed the empty box.

The word *love* made her uncomfortable. He saw that. The word *marriage* made *him* want to run. "That seems to be the case," he said drily. "Will you take the boys, while I stop at the grocery store? I need supplies for our ranch picnic."

Adam didn't need to be asked twice. He grabbed her hand and announced, "I want to go with Aunt Bex."

Obviously, Tate needed to think ahead and buy cookies so he could stay in favor, too.

DINNER WAS LIKE a continuation of their fishing vacation, with the boys bickering but getting along, running amok and tossing a baseball around, their boundless energy reminding Bex of cherished childhood days.

Adam even ate some of her salad. Tate declared it an official miracle.

"You've seen him," he said with clear disbelief as they cleared the dishes from the counter. "If there's green included, he's just going to balk. I've tried everything. How did you do it?"

"Apparently, my special powers aren't confined to fishing." Bex raised her brows. "I just asked him to eat it."

"I've started believing in those powers." Tate dropped the last paper plate in the trash bag he'd brought. He looked at her meaningfully. "Especially after last night."

There was no denying they'd been hungry for each other. Bex felt her cheeks warm. He wasn't shy in bed, but she hadn't been, either. She looked right back at him. "It was…nice."

What a dumb thing to say! The knowing gleam in his eyes flustered her even more. "Nice?"

"Okay, *very* nice."

"I'll take that bet and raise it to *extremely* nice."

"This isn't a game of poker."

"I'm the Old Maid champion, please don't forget. You aren't even in my league."

"You lost every time, Calder."

"Not last night."

"I want to see the stable plans," she declared, skirting the subject. "I'm dying to see what the war between your father and Mrs. A. produced."

He crossed his arms and shook his head. "I think we ended up with a small airport, a strip mall and five hundred stalls or so. I might as well not have been in the room. They were tossing around numbers like confetti at midnight on New Year's Eve."

She wiped off the counter with a damp paper towel. "There are worse problems to have than rich people throwing money at you."

"True, but I've got some reservations about those two playing well with each other. I want to run a business, not be a mediator. Not that either of them listens to me, anyway."

"Did you ask your father what their problem is?"

"No, never had a minute alone with him. If I had to guess. it would be a mutual bullheaded determination to have their way—but I'm just the person who stood there for an hour or so, trying to get a word in edgewise.

Shall we take our wine out to the front porch? We don't have any chairs but we can sit on the steps."

"In a minute? I have something to give you first. Well, we all do, Hadleigh, Tripp, Mel and Spence, too. It seems fitting that you should get a housewarming present after your first dinner in this house." She removed a wrapped gift from her oversize bag, which she'd propped up against the wall, and set it on the counter.

"Not necessary. Thank you." He did look intrigued.

"My idea. Mel and Tripp get all the credit, though."

"All Tripp can do is fly a plane and ride a horse."

"Oh, he's got a few more skills than that."

When Tate seemed about to continue their mock argument, she nudged his arm. "Just open it, okay?"

It seemed a little selfish to be the only one to see his expression when he unwrapped the gift, but she didn't care. He held up the clock—face glowing with astonishment and gratitude—and it was exactly the reaction she'd wanted.

"It's the house." He traced the outline over the glass.

"Yep."

"And the mountains."

She nodded.

"Bex." His voice was hushed.

"All I did was suggest it to Mel. The one she made for Spence was so beautiful I thought you might like one, too."

"I *more* than like it."

He did. That was very obvious. Tate said, "I'm not even going to guess where you want me to hang it. You choose."

"It's your kitchen."

"Doesn't matter. You choose."

She found the perfect spot, above the nook for a table and chairs. There was a bay window and the clock was the right size to fit just above it. Bex pointed. "I'd put it there."

She'd almost said: *If this was my house, I'd put it there.*

Tate caught her around the waist, his mouth warm as it pressed against hers. He murmured, "Thank you."

"You're welcome." She kissed him back.

"I bet there is a hammer around here somewhere and a stray nail or two. I'll put it up tonight. Did Tripp really help make it?"

She nodded. "Mel did the design, of course, but he cut out the metal. I keep telling her she needs to add the custom clocks to her business, but she's busy as it is. Maybe she needs an assistant. I do think clocks like this would be in demand."

"I do, too."

"Dad! Dad. Come and see! This is *really* cool." Ben was trying to whisper, not quite pulling it off. "You've got to come out and see."

Two moose stood at the edge of the pasture. The boys were entranced, quiet for once, just watching as the giant animals grazed. Bex saw that Tate was no less focused.

Minutes later, he turned to her. "This is exactly why I moved here," he murmured.

"It's wonderful."

"Oh, yes, it is." But he was looking at her.

CHAPTER NINETEEN

TATE SIGNED THE BILL of sale and wrote the check. Tripp slapped him on the shoulder as they walked out of the livestock barn. "That mare was a bargain. Clean lines and just the right age." He was pretty distracted these days.

He hadn't really seen Bex in two weeks. *Two weeks*.

Well, he'd *seen* her, but they hadn't been together.

She was busy, and he knew that, and he picked up Josh when he got Adam and Ben. She'd decided to move home, so he only saw her briefly and in passing.

He understood that the rental didn't have enough room for all of them. Not only that, she was used to her independence, her nephew was an unexpected responsibility and she was very involved with expanding her business, but...two weeks?

It wasn't as if *he* was free, either—not very often, anyway. The house was all but done. He was going to have furniture delivered today, and they could move in soon. He'd given notice to the rental management company to terminate the lease, the plans for the stable and barn had been altered to match the demands of his warring investors and he should feel that his life was on target.

Not so.

He and Tripp walked out to the truck. "I appreciate

you coming along. I thought that horse was worth the price. Thanks for confirming it and for keeping her until the stable's finished."

"No problem."

"Hey, is Hadleigh at the shop today? I need to talk to her for a minute."

"About Bex?"

He doubted Tripp wanted to hear about his feelings, so he kept it simple. "Yeah."

"She's avoiding you."

"Tell me something I don't know." He paused, his keys in his hand. "Obviously, your wife has mentioned it. Do you mind telling me *why* Bex is doing this?"

"I would, but I didn't ask. Hadleigh said Bex wasn't talking about you, and that's about all I heard."

"I could swear everything was going well."

Tripp shook his head. "If you're asking for insights into the female psyche, you've come to the wrong guy. When they're pregnant, it's even more mystifying."

That wasn't his current problem. Three times their first night together, and three condoms. They'd been careful. He just needed to talk to her and find out what was going on. Maybe Bex really was just busy.

Whenever she swung by to pick up Josh, she got the heck out of there as quickly and efficiently as possible. He was glad Greg wasn't causing her problems, but he missed her.

Hadleigh heard the shop-door bell and came out front. Her smile was warm but there was a cautious light in her eyes. "Hi, Tate."

The shop was small and cozy. He hadn't been in lately; he saw that the merchandise was geared toward fall and the holidays at the moment, the quilt colors mostly oranges, dark greens and reds. A maple leaf–patterned one caught his eye and he knew what he was going to buy his Aunt Gina for Christmas.

One problem solved. On to the next.

"Hi, Hadleigh. So, what's up with Bex?"

That might be a little too straightforward, but school was getting out in fifteen minutes, and he had to be there.

Hadleigh leaned on the counter and to his relief didn't pretend not to know what he was talking about. "If you want my opinion, she doesn't like being in love again. It scares her, makes her feel like the safe, solid world she's struggled to rebuild is sitting on quicksand."

In love? Had Bex actually said that? Or was it just Hadleigh's description? He remembered what he'd told Bex about the difference between being *in love* versus *loving* someone—and how being in love reminded him of tottering on the edge of a cliff. So he should understand her fears. But…things had changed. He'd become used to the comfort and companionship he'd found with her, and he wanted more of it.

He sighed in frustration.

Hadleigh's expression was sympathetic. "She obviously needed some space. I know her, and Mel and I have always said that of the three of us, she's the one who has to have everything clear and logical. For instance, she's happy Tara is going to leave her disaster of a marriage, but she can't really grasp her sister leaving Josh with someone else, even her, and even if it's better for him. I mean, Tara's right, since she's sleeping on a couch in a friend's apartment, and staying that far away from Greg is a good idea all around—but I know Bex can't quite comprehend it. She could never do it herself."

He couldn't, either. No way would he ever leave Ben and Adam with someone else, even Aunt Gina, and just take off the way Tara had.

"I don't want to push, but couldn't Bex at least talk to me?"

"She will eventually." Hadleigh watched him for a moment, her expression thoughtful. "I don't think she knows what you want from this relationship, Tate. She isn't the only one not talking as far as I can tell."

That was a valid point. He wished he could deny it.

"I want her in my life."

"Great. On what terms?"

He saw Hadleigh touch her charm bracelet, something he'd seen Bex do often enough. He'd asked about the piece—she and Melody and Hadleigh all had duplicates, he's noticed—and Bex had explained, in somewhat oblique terms, that the charms represented the accomplishment of a goal the three of them shared.

"That bracelet," he said with a nod toward Hadleigh's wrist. "It's beautiful."

She blushed ever so slightly. "Yes," she agreed with a nod of her own. "Melody made one for each of us."

"That's meaningful," Tate mused quietly.

"Yes," Hadleigh said again.

That was when his intuition kicked in, and he knew what that mysterious common goal was—Hadleigh and Melody were both fairly recent brides, and they were both expecting babies. Each charm symbolized a marriage, the start of a new family.

The bracelets were their way of celebrating both the hope and the fulfillment of a dream.

Well, he definitely wanted more children. That was one of *his* dreams.

But marriage was another matter. It wasn't something he felt ready to attempt again now, if ever. For reasons that had nothing to do with Bex.

"I'm not sure."

"Then you'd better forgive her for not being sure, either."

Okay, that made sense.

"I have to pick up the boys from school. I've given her space, like you said, but now I'm afraid it's creating a distance between us. When she comes to get Josh, should I make her discuss this, or still back off?"

Hadleigh's mouth twitched. "You've been extremely patient. With Bex, the direct approach is the best bet. Oh, and by the way, you didn't hear that from me."

"Exactly the advice I wanted," he said, pointing at the display. "I want that quilt. My aunt will love it. Here's my credit card—you can give it back to me later. Gotta run."

"Good luck."

"I'm hoping I won't need it."

"Oh," she said, "you will."

BEX WAS RUNNING LATE, but there was nothing new about that. Balancing the demands on her time was hard, and balancing her personal life with work was even harder.

Staying away from Tate had been so difficult. Almost impossible, in fact, and she had to remind herself why she was doing it.

She was *so* attracted to him, which was precisely why she'd needed to step back. She felt no regret about making love with him; in any event it had happened, and she couldn't wish it away. But because of her past—

and his—she was still trying to figure out a few things. To find some clarity. At least that was the plan.

That plan wasn't working.

He was outside, raking leaves, when she pulled in to collect Josh. The boys weren't exactly helping, since they were leaping through the piles, scattering leaves everywhere. She knew he'd be moving very soon, so he wouldn't be able to drive Josh to school, and that was minor, but another issue she'd have to resolve.

Just her luck, he looked great in a gray sweatshirt with the sleeves pushed up to his elbows, and the usual faded jeans. When did Tate *not* look great?

"Hello." She got out and closed the driver's door.

He leaned on the rake, watching her closely. "Hello, back. Can we talk? As you see, the boys are having fun, so I'll have to do this yard all over again, but I won't mind it if we could just…*talk*."

It wasn't as if she hadn't sensed that he was unhappy with the sudden and unexplained distance between them. However, she hadn't expected such a direct request.

"We can." She wasn't prepared for this conversation. She knew what he was going to ask; what she didn't know was how she'd answer.

"So what do you think is going to happen next?" he began.

"I'll take Josh home. I'm making spaghetti."

He gave her the look she deserved. "We aren't exactly strangers. Can't I get a straight answer from you, please?"

"The answer is…I don't know."

"You're running scared, then?"

"You haven't told me what you want, either, or what *you* think should happen next."

"Fair enough," he said with a shrug that was probably meant to seem nonchalant. "I want you in my life. In my bed. I love you. And I'm not the only one who misses you. The boys have been pestering me half to death about Aunt Bex." He paused. "I wasn't planning to ask this yet, but when we move to the ranch, would you consider moving in, too? With Josh, of course. In some ways, it's your house as much as mine, since you picked out all the important stuff."

Bex wasn't entirely taken off guard. She'd had a feeling this question was coming, but she had a very mixed reaction. When Spence had asked Melody to move in with him before they got married, Bex was the one to say, *Don't settle for less than everything.*

Because that's what the pact means.

Back when they'd made the pact, she hadn't counted on being in the same position as Melody, with even more complicated circumstances. Tate was a package deal. She loved Ben and Adam, now diving gleefully into piles of brilliant leaves with Josh, but being the instant mother to one child was hard enough. Three?

She'd really missed him, too. It had taken a lot of resolve to stay away while she thought it all over. She still hadn't found the clarity she was searching for, the certainty she needed, but the moment was *here*.

Tate expected a response. He deserved one, since he'd crawled out on a shaky limb and risked a question that could be met with rejection.

Mel was going to give her hell for this. Hadleigh would have an opinion, too, since she always did.

"We could try it." The words just came out.

Decision made.

"Josh would love it," she added.

Tate's slow smile was worthy of Hollywood. "I was kind of hoping you'd love it, too."

It was impossible not to throw in a smart-ass comment to deflect the panic. This was a giant step. "The kitchen counter *does* look good. And there's that six-burner stove. I fell in love with it the minute I saw it. I'm really moving in with your kitchen."

"At the moment I'm thinking it was worth every penny." He lowered his voice. "I haven't kissed you in two weeks. Not that I've been counting the days or anything."

He seemed so elated, and that made her happy, too. His happiness deepened her own, and solidified her decision.

"Well, a man with a rake is hard to resist."

"Oh, yeah?" He strode over and took her in his arms, dropping the rake at one point. She didn't notice.

Their kiss was swift because they were standing in the driveway on a residential street with children playing nearby, but it was still satisfying.

They broke apart when Josh ran over to hand her a piece of paper. "This is a note from my teacher. I'm not 'sposed to forget."

He dashed off and she looked at it apprehensively.

Tate correctly interpreted her expression. "Parent-teacher conferences. No big deal. That time of year. You walk in and they explain how the kid's doing in class, address any concerns and you get his report card. Just like when we were in school—only we're on the other side now."

"Oh, okay." That was a relief, although she had no

real idea how Josh was doing in school. Tara hadn't said. He was just in the first grade, after all.

"Their teacher's very helpful. She'll let you know if anything's going on with Josh. He seems well-adjusted to me, all things considered, and if there *was* a problem, you would've heard by now. I'm going to bet he's doing okay."

"I don't want Greg involved, but I don't understand how he can just walk away. I don't even know if the school will talk to me about Josh. I have no official status." She stared at him. "I should've made Tara sign something, giving me temporary custody."

Tate shook his head. "Don't worry. This is Mustang Creek they know exactly where he's living and who's taking care of him. His teacher will talk to you." He took her hand and squeezed it lightly. "This isn't as hard as it seems."

"You've been doing it longer," she muttered.

"That's true, and it's never really easy. I'm not going to pretend it is. But if you make a mistake, and we all do, then dump ballast and adjust."

"Like a hot-air balloon? There's an interesting analogy."

She turned and motioned to Josh. "I'll ask him if this—moving in here, I mean—is what he wants. It seems to me that the one thing that hasn't happened is anyone asking Josh anything. I know what his answer will be, but he should have a say."

"I couldn't agree more."

He was obviously sincere, and she appreciated his vote of confidence.

Tate would definitely have to start over when it came

to the yard. By the time she got Josh into the car, there were leaves everywhere.

Bex waited a few minutes, and once they'd pulled onto the street, she simply asked, "Do you want to move out to the ranch with Ben, Adam and Tate?"

"And with you?"

"And with me," she confirmed. "Of course."

"Yep." He grinned and she noticed one of his front teeth was missing. She almost ran the stop sign before turning onto Main. "What *happened*? Are you hurt?"

"My tooth was loose. It fell out. Don't worry, Aunt Bex, it's in my pocket. We can put it under my pillow."

Now she was the tooth fairy?

Not a big deal, maybe, but it was yet another new role in a season of change.

CHAPTER TWENTY

ON MOVING DAY, Tate was grateful for the assistance—and the muscle—of Tripp and Spence. The three of them dealt with the heavier furniture, while Bex, Hadleigh and Melody had no trouble directing them. They'd indicate where a particular piece should go, change their minds, arguing in a sisterly way and then eventually settle on a final destination.

The men all looked at each other whenever a new arrangement was requested and obligingly moved stuff around.

Personally, as long as he had a couch and a place with a view of the mountains, a television nearby, and a side table where he could set down a beer or a cup of coffee, he was content. But having some feminine input was not a bad thing.

When he'd approved the plans for his house, he'd had a picture in mind, but the reality was even better. The river-stone fireplace was a masterpiece, and he could picture snowy winter nights with a cozy fire and Bex in his arms.

She was in the kitchen now, and he could hear her laugh and Melody's laugh in return, as the boys ran past the window after Muggles, Harley and Ridley, and it felt like...home. Much more so than the big suburban house he'd shared with Sandra.

He dusted off his hands as they set down the last box. "Thanks, guys."

Spence glanced around at the high beams and log walls. "Hey, this turned out great."

"Yeah," Tripp said, nodding. "The location's perfect for raising horses and kids."

"I hope so." Tate took a drink from his bottle of water and wiped his brow. "This is where I'm planning to live forever. Wandering the globe is a learning experience, but I'm ready to just stay put."

"I know exactly what you mean."

Tate was sure he did. After being a pilot, plus a stint in the military, Tripp had returned to Mustang Creek. The kind of experience he'd had made you value the comfort and contentment of *home*.

Spence started to say something but was interrupted by shrieks from the front of the house. Alarmed, they all rushed to the door, Tate getting there first and yanking it open, only to realize—with immense relief—that the noise was a sign of joy, not fear. Mrs. Arbuckle's signature car was parked next to their trucks, like a royal personage in a row of peasants. She stood beside it, dressed fashionably as usual in a wool skirt and jacket, seemingly oblivious to the fact that six canines were romping around her two hundred–dollar shoes.

Not to mention the three ecstatic boys in the melee.

Mrs. A. spotted Tate, who'd stopped dead in the middle of the front porch, and imperiously waved him toward the crowd, announcing, "I brought you a house-warming gift. Eight weeks old, and they have all their shots."

Three puppies. The boys were in heaven.

Both Tripp and Spence were laughing. He could hear them guffawing away behind him.

Eight weeks old? They seemed pretty big to him. One of them was enthusiastically licking Adam's face, Ben was holding another one and Josh was on the ground, giggling, letting the third one crawl all over him. He'd intended to get a dog. A. Dog. Not three monster puppies.

Since he had yet to speak, because he couldn't think of a thing to say, Mrs. A. fixed him with a steely look. "Rescue puppies. Lab mix. All males. Every working ranch needs a few dogs."

"Lab mixed with what?" he finally managed to ask in a strangled voice. "Great Dane?"

She airily dismissed that. "I'm not sure. They're from the same litter. I'm on the committee for the Humane Society, and when they were brought in, I thought of you. There's lots of room here, plus the children. They'll be happy."

Maybe so, but would *he* be happy?

Bex would probably run the other way as fast as possible now, and he couldn't blame her. The boys were enough of a handful as it was…

As usual, he was completely wrong.

"Oh, how cute." She and Hadleigh and Melody had come outside, drawn by all the ruckus, and Bex brushed past him to go and pet them all, including the adult dogs, Harley, Muggles and Ridley.

"They are," Hadleigh squealed. "So sweet."

"Adorable," Melody said.

He couldn't possibly say no. Not to the boys, not to Mrs. A. and certainly not to Bex, if she was okay with the idea. Although he had a sinking feeling that *he* was going to be taking care of the animals and cleaning up after them during the necessary process of getting them house-trained...

Small price to pay. Everyone seemed thrilled.

Especially Tripp and Spence, who were still laughing.

He actually thanked Lettie Arbuckle, agreed with her suggestion that he drive into town to pick up three doggie beds and corralled the animals as she drove off.

Then he was stuck with three puppies rolling in the leaves with three boys, and three more dogs running around, a half-furnished house and five adults watching him try to control the chaos until they all pitched in, carried the squirming puppies inside and whistled for their dogs.

Melody had made sloppy joes for dinner. Instant hit with the boys—and with the new members of his household, the ones he hadn't known he was going to have. Boys were messy. Puppies happily took care of the problem.

Spence and Tripp, cold beers in hand, made the most of it.

"I'm thinking they're part Saint Bernard," Spence said.

"I don't think so... Could be boxer."

"Too big for boxer." Spence tilted his head as one of the puppies ran past. "Irish wolfhound?"

Melody punched him on the shoulder. "Stop that."

He caught her hand and kissed it. "Honey, I'm kidding, and Tate knows it, but those are going to be big dogs. He knows that, too."

"Maybe we should take one."

"You do remember that we have three cats plus a dog

already, don't you? And which puppy would you take away from which child?"

The boys were busy talking about names through mouthfuls of their dinner. Three boys and three puppies. What a zoo.

Melody narrowed her eyes. "You are so rarely right, but I do concede that point, Spencer Hogan."

"There's a first time for everything."

He turned suddenly, to see the alarm on Bex's face. "We'll work that out," he said reassuringly and slipped an arm around her waist. He knew she had to be thinking about Josh and the puppy.

"Tara won't let him have a dog."

"We can keep his dog, and he can come visit him. Mrs. A. is right about one thing—there's lots of room here for them to run."

"You sure are taking this in stride." Bex leaned into him and briefly rested her head on his shoulder.

"Do I have a choice? They're so excited. Look at Adam, eating his green beans without an argument so they can take their dogs out to play. I'm going to bet Mrs. A. will be considered the best-dressed fairy godmother in Bliss County by three of the people in this room."

BEX WAS WELL AWARE of Hadleigh and Mel exchanging smug smiles over Tate's casual—and public—embrace.

She said stoutly, "I think *every* person in this room can say that about Mrs. A., even you. All her friends buy Hadleigh's quilts, she commissions pieces from Melody, she certainly helped me out with my business contacts and the list goes on. Let's not forget your dream stable. I'll admit her tactics can be high-handed, but she means well."

His smile was rueful. "That's why she and my father don't get along. They're exactly alike. He'll move heaven and earth to get you to do what *he* thinks is best for you. It's against my principles to lie, but I might omit the truth about who delivered the dogs and just say we got them from the Humane Society. If he gets wind that his archenemy was the benefactor who made the boys so happy, he'll try and go her one better. I shudder to imagine it. Pet giraffes, maybe? Rhinos?"

She laughed. "That would be interesting. For now, I think cleanup duty is in order and we can free the beasts, all of them, into the wild so the adults can eat." It was true; there was a bit of napkin work to be done on three little faces, plus strict orders for them to go in and wash their hands, and then a whirlwind of boys and dogs hit the door at full speed.

Bex and Hadleigh set the table for six. Tate had explained that he'd sold the formal dining room set from his previous house and bought the rustic farmhouse-style table instead, with seating for eight, because it matched the house so much better. He'd made a good decision. It looked perfect in the space, and she'd picked out the low burnished-copper light fixture above it and the high-backed chairs.

Bex hadn't given him puppies as a housewarming gift. Besides the clock, which was a joint gift, she'd chosen something else. In anticipation that it might not occur to a male, she'd bought cloth placemats and napkins and brought her favorite set of plates from home, plus matching soup bowls.

She hadn't told Hadleigh and Mel yet that she intended to leave the dishes there…

Not sharing such critical information was unprecedented. And it wasn't as though they weren't going to find out soon enough. When they'd made the pact, she hadn't realized she'd be so afraid of falling in love again.

But now she had—and she suspected she wasn't fooling Hadleigh and Mel.

She set down a plate and said as casually as possible while she arranged the silverware, "Tate wants me to move in."

"Not surprised. Mel and I figured that one out." Hadleigh handed her a napkin for the place setting.

Suspicion confirmed.

"It'll be so good for Josh," Bex said.

Hadleigh raised her brows. "So you *are* thinking about it. Yes, it'll be good for Josh. What about Becca Stuart?"

She flushed and didn't mention that she'd already agreed. "I…it's just happening so fast."

"You've known each other for months. Remember me, the one who introduced you? Tripp's discerning about his friends, so I knew Tate was a good guy before you ever met him."

"You're going to take the credit if this works out, aren't you?"

Hadleigh grinned. "Damn straight." Then her expression changed and her hand went to her stomach. "Ooh… just felt the baby move. He must be hungry. I'm getting the signal. *Lady, I could use some grub.*"

"He?"

"Just a guess."

Bex had to laugh. "Alpha males have daughters, too."

"And protect them like rabid wolves," Melody remarked as she carried in the salad bowl and bread.

"If I know Tripp," Hadleigh said, "that's going to be the case."

"Would you have it any other way?"

"No."

"Okay, listen up," Bex told them. "The menu today is vegetable-beef soup, Bex-style, salad and garlic bread. I figured hearty for the men and healthy for the pregnant women. When Mel offered up sloppy joes for the kids, I jumped on it."

Hadleigh grinned. "If you suppose I haven't sampled the soup, you've lost your mind. Any pot simmering on the stove is fair game. It's really good, by the way."

"That's just like when we were in college. You haven't changed. Starting on dinner before it was served."

"Just making sure it's good enough for everyone else."

Bex laughed again and hugged her. "Always thinking of others."

"You bet." Hadleigh hugged back and whispered, "I'm so happy for you."

It was premature to assume anything, but the marriage charm might be working. "We'll see how it goes."

"Am I missing something?" Melody set the salad and bread on the table.

"She's moving in with Tate."

Bex wasn't sure she wanted that announcement made —in front of such an audience—since naturally the men had followed the food, but at this point, she was resigned.

"You are?" Melody's delight was quickly replaced by amusement. "Welcome to instant motherhood—times three. You can give Hadleigh and me pointers. We'll need advice."

If Spence *and* Tate hadn't been standing right there, Mel might have said that Bex had told her not to settle for less than marriage, but this was a different story.

Bex resolutely changed the subject. "I hope everyone's hungry. I couldn't find a soup tureen, so carry your bowl to the stove."

Tripp turned to Tate. "You don't know where your soup tureen is?"

"That's not the problem. I don't know *what* a soup tureen is." Tate sent Bex his special smile.

Spence was just as helpful. "I think it holds soup."

Three female glares fixed on the men in the room. They grabbed their bowls and moved swiftly toward the kitchen.

Hadleigh muttered, "It's a wonder we put up with them."

"Their idea of humor is kind of questionable," Bex said.

"But they come in handy now and then." Mel took a piece of bread. "Like if you need a picture hung or air put in a tire."

"Nice body heat, too." Hadleigh was magnanimous. "Being with Tripp is like having a personal furnace."

Bex asked poignantly, "Am I making the right decision?"

"Yes," they said in unison.

"What about the *marriage* part of the marriage pact?" Bex couldn't keep herself from asking.

"That'll come," Hadleigh said confidently.

"Yeah," Mel told her. "He's going to want it all. Just as much as you do."

Except that Bex wasn't entirely sure she did...

NIGHTFALL WAS A BLUR of indigo blues over the tips of the peaks.

She'd been basically moved in for a week. The house still wasn't completely put together, but it was taking shape.

Bex ran her fingers over the cool marble counter after she'd finished the postdinner cleanup. "We made a good choice when we bought this."

"*You* made a good choice." Tate lounged in the doorway, one broad shoulder propped against the entry. "It looks great, and so does the clock. Take a bow."

Mel had definitely made a statement.

With an old spittoon, no less. That was what Tripp had used for the numerals and the outline of the house. Melody had found it, handed it over and he'd made it happen.

Bex loved the result. The old man who'd made the frame had used slender broken branches of alder, spruce and aspen.

"I want to see the foundation for the stable." She'd had a busy week at work, and adjusting to living with four males and three rowdy puppies was an interesting experience. She hadn't had a chance to check out the progress. The contractor Tate had hired had his crews there early every morning, and that added to the general chaos.

What had happened to her well-ordered life?

Oh, yeah, one handsome pilot with an irresistible smile, that was what.

"Good idea." Tate nodded. "I want to talk to you while we walk over to the pasture."

Uh-oh.

He looked uncomfortable, too, and as they crossed

the front porch, and Bex felt a hint of warning when he held the door for her. She took a peek at his expression a second time.

Something was up.

Good news? Or bad? Had he changed his mind about her being there? One week in, did he feel it wasn't working?

Tate was usually so self-assured, but she was getting a very odd feeling. Two scenarios instantly raced through her mind. He wanted to break it off, or he was going to propose. Hadleigh and Mel had predicted that the latter was going to happen any day.

She hoped not. She loved him, but he'd made his position on marriage fairly clear. For Hadleigh and Melody, the pact and the charm had been a blessing; for her, it might turn out to be a curse.

The very last time she'd seen Will, he'd asked her to marry him. She understood Tate's fear of marriage, which was based on his experience. Her fear was irrational; she knew that on an intellectual level. When the three of them had made the pact, she hadn't even realized that particular fear existed. But it did. And it had emerged, full-blown, since she'd fallen in love with Tate.

Bex took a deep, calming breath and reminded herself that she'd faced worse than this, but her heart was breaking. Nothing could be worse than learning about Will's death. And yet, she was terrified that what she had with Tate would not survive the realities and the demands of marriage. At one point, she'd believed that marriage—to him—was what she wanted. Now…she just didn't know, but she was afraid to take the chance.

"She's gorgeous, isn't she?"

Her frantic introspection was broken when Tate pointed at a filly grazing a few feet away. It was no lie to agree, which gave Bex a chance to regroup. The animal had sleek lines and wonderful markings, plus she came up to the fence at once, begging for attention, nudging Bex's arm until Tate grinned and handed over a carrot he extracted from his pocket. "I think she likes you."

She stroked the animal's silky nose. "I like her right back. When did you get her?"

"I bought her two weeks ago but the rancher brought her over today now that the fence is up and they installed the gate."

While one crew worked away on the foundation of the stable, another one had been fencing the grazing area.

Tate said, "Name her."

Startled, she turned to him. "Really?"

"Please don't make it Trixie." His teasing smile made her relax a little. Maybe the horse was what he wanted to talk about.

"That never crossed my mind."

"I bought her from an old rancher who just bred them, but never named the foals before sale. He said he ended up feeling too attached. She needs a name."

Bex thought it over. "Um, how about Flora? My grandmother's name."

"I like that. Flora it is."

He was looking at her very intently, and she doubted the horse's name was why they were there. Bex had never been keen on surprises, so she asked bluntly, "What did you want to talk to me about? Tate, we know each other pretty well—"

"Intimately. In fact, this has been the best week of my life, hands down." His slow smile reassured her, and by the same token, made her more anxious. "I hope you're as happy as I am."

Okay, they weren't about to break up. She hadn't *really* thought so, but please, not the other. Yes, she was happy.

Don't spoil it.

His next words, however, weren't reassuring. "I have an important question and, of course, you can say yes or no. I want you to say yes, but be aware that a no won't ruin what we have now."

She should take off her jacket, because a hot flush of panic had spread over her skin.

The hard truth was that she wasn't ready. Tate was everything a woman could want and more...sexy and, despite his denial, sensitive. A good father. Make that a *great* father. Josh was becoming more outgoing every day, and he'd settled in with a happiness she'd never seen in him before. Friends who were like brothers, puppies, horses and someone like Tate playing the role of dad—what was there *not* to like about the situation? She felt the same way.

So leave it alone.

She squared her shoulders and faced him. "Well, don't leave me on the edge of my seat."

Tate lifted his brows. "You nervous?"

"No." Flora nudged her shoulder again, and Bex thought about vaulting onto her back and riding off into the sunset.

"You're *acting* nervous."

"*You're* acting nervous, and maybe that's making me nervous. Could you just ask?"

"Yes, ma'am." He took off his hat and ruffled his hair, his dark eyes serious. "Here goes."

That made her stomach do a flip-flop.

Then the game changed.

"I want more children."

Bex did a double take.

"With you."

What?

He went on, speaking slowly. "You love Josh so much, but when the divorce gets settled, either Tara or Greg is going to take him from you. I wondered if you'd consider having a baby. With me."

Not exactly a marriage proposal.

But what he'd just asked her—to have his baby but not to marry him?

It was a little hard to absorb.

Bex said nothing. Her vocal cords seemed to have gone on vacation.

Tate went on, reading who-knew-what in her expression. "In case I wasn't clear about it, I mean together. You and me. My child, your child... You know I'd be there every step of the way. That's not in question, is it? I hope you know me better than that. I'm the one *asking*, remember? I'll be at the ranch so I could be the caregiver a lot of the time... You might have noticed, I'm kind of used to that. And you could bring the baby to work." He looked at her, his expression half serious, half humorous. "Am I rambling? Am I making sense?"

She still couldn't speak.

He touched her chin, tilting her face up so their eyes met. "Bex?"

She was relieved that she didn't have to say yes or no to marriage at the moment, but a *baby*?

She thought of Hadleigh and Mel. She did want children, but she wasn't ready, any more than she was ready for a marriage proposal.

MAYBE HE WAS acting like a fool.

Wouldn't be the first time.

His moratorium on marriage was part of a past life, and perhaps he should just get down on bended knee.

But no one else, not even Tripp, understood that when Sandra got pregnant, he'd been denied the simple joy of impending fatherhood because of all the flotsam that had risen to the surface about her past. With Ben he'd suspected, but with Adam, he'd *known* what a mistake he'd made. And while he would sacrifice anything for them, he wanted a different kind of experience if he had a third chance at fatherhood.

None of that—his poor judgment as a much younger man—had anything to do with Bex or his relationship with her.

"I realize the usual sequence is to get married first, but—"

He stopped short. Now *there* was the most tactless thing he could say. He tried to start over and give it a better shot. "I meant—"

"Tate, be quiet."

He stopped talking. She was looking at the mountains, her expression unreadable. The mare had begun to graze nearby, the sound of it soothing.

He had no doubt that he was supposed to spend the rest of his life with this woman.

So he waited.

She didn't speak for an excruciatingly long minute. "I know what you meant. You had a really bad experience the first time and don't want to try again. But… don't you think that whenever you get into a car and drive away—or a plane—I'm going to be petrified that you'll have a fatal accident? I care, too, and I don't *want* to care. I can't go through that again."

"We're good together, and not just in bed." His smile was obviously intended to be persuasive. "Though I admit to a great fondness for that part of our relationship. We enjoy the same things, very rarely disagree, give each other space and quite frankly, we've already proven that we make a good team when it comes to parenting."

The charms on her bracelet caught the fading light as she lifted a hand to sweep back her hair.

"We both have a lot going on in our lives right now," she said with the hint of a tremor in her voice. Her cheeks held a hint of pink from the brisk autumn breeze.

"Do you think that'll change?" He shook his head. "There's never that perfect time, that perfect day, when you say to yourself everything's settled, and I have time for a baby. It just doesn't exist."

Her smile was tremulous. "And here I thought maybe you wanted to break it off."

He frowned. Was that the cause of the apprehensive look on her face earlier? "Why the hell would I want to do that?"

The way you rejected even the idea of any kind of commitment, you idiot.

"We could always decide to get married later. Plenty of couples go that route."

"Not usually in Mustang Creek." She averted her face and looked at the Tetons instead. "Sure, everyone knows I'm living here, so the fact that we're sleeping together isn't a secret. But a baby is different."

He leaned a shoulder against the fence and experienced a twinge of anger—though not at her. His first marriage wasn't the total problem. The words *prenuptial agreement* were the least romantic in the world. They translated to: *I don't really trust that this will work out.* The odds of success weren't all that wonderful to begin with, when it came to marriage. Luckily, Bex was successful in her own right, so she should probably ask *him* to do the same thing. But his trust fund was in the millions and when he'd balked at asking Sandra to sign one, his father had threatened to eliminate it. All that money didn't mean much to him—he could make his own way and always had—but finally he'd caved and informed her she'd have to agree for the sake of any children they might have.

She'd haggled over it, and that almost made him back out of the wedding; it was the first warning bell. But because he was in love with that perfect body and seductive smile, he'd told himself he would've been insulted, too.

The hell of it was his father had been dead-on right.

Tate wasn't a coward, or he sure didn't think so, but he didn't want to have that argument with his father again. He didn't want to ask Bex to sign one, and the thought of that painful visit from the lawyers—his father's lawyers had come to the house—with all the paperwork made him sick to his stomach.

Bex was nothing like Sandra. She was honest and giving and warm. Still, his father would force him to do it if they were to get married. Because of Ben and Adam he would, but it would be like injecting poison into a vein.

A marriage proposal might ruin everything.

He couldn't let that happen. He loved her, his sons loved her and as much as he didn't want to ask her to sign a prenup, he also didn't want to explain why. His thoughts circled around and around.

His first marriage had been to a woman he couldn't trust, although of course he hadn't initially known that. He *did* trust Bex and hated to suggest, via a prenup, that he didn't. Yet he couldn't risk losing his sons' inheritance, either. No, to him, status quo was the best and safest option. Especially when the status quo was so…satisfying. "I didn't expect you to agree without taking some time to reflect." He said the words quietly. "I love you, so I want you to be happy. I think we *are* happy now. Maybe that explains my fear of changing anything."

Her eyes looked pure gold in the light. "Tate, you don't think a baby would change everything?"

She was right; what he'd meant, though, was that *marriage* would change what they had.

The card he wanted to play was to point out that if they managed to get pregnant fairly soon, she and Mel and Hadleigh would all have children close in age, kids who could play together, but he figured that had already crossed her mind.

He'd also made a conscious decision not to have this conversation while they were in bed. It wasn't fair to try to persuade her that way, and he refused to do it.

"Children are the most incredible thing that can happen to two people." He straightened but didn't reach for her, though he wanted to. Badly. "Yes, they do change everything, but—granted, I can only speak for myself—in the best possible way. I'm hoping for a girl," he added.

She smacked him on the shoulder. "That was a lowdown tactic right there."

At least there was laughter in her eyes.

He pulled her to him and kissed her lightly. "I'm just asking you to consider it."

"If you think I'm not going to have this stuck in my mind, you're really selling me short. I mean, most women wouldn't file this in the category of *don't forget to scrub the kitchen floor, pay the electric bill and, oh, by the way, we're out of milk.*"

He kissed her again and murmured against her lips, "I hope not."

CHAPTER TWENTY-ONE

LONG DAY...VERY long day, and the last thing Bex needed was to run into Greg as she was locking up the fitness center. Her manager had gone home sick, and she'd stayed for the duration, twelve hours, and wanted nothing more than to go home.

At least she was out on the sidewalk and not inside alone. Her brother-in-law had a grim look on his face.

He didn't offer a greeting, but she didn't expect one. His shoulders were hunched under his jacket. "I want to know exactly where she is, Bex. Don't put me off."

She stood there, trying to figure out how to handle it. "Are you threatening me?"

"Maybe. Not physically—don't worry about that. Your friend Spencer Hogan would have me in jail in a heartbeat if I did. I could take Josh. He's my son."

A light rain had started to fall, more a mist than anything, and she put up her hood. "You haven't been too interested in him so far," she said as her throat tightened. "What's different now?"

"I got a letter from her damned lawyer, that's what."

Good to know. Tara called every couple of days to check on Josh, but Bex hadn't been convinced she'd go through with the divorce. She looked Greg in the eye. "If you'd been faithful to her, you wouldn't be standing here on a wet sidewalk having this conversation with

230   THE MARRIAGE SEASON

me. This is *your* fault, and if you care for your son at all, you'll leave him alone. I will do this much—I'll talk to Tara and relay the message that you want to speak to her. What happens after that is up to the two of you."

She'd lent Tara the money for legal assistance. It had better be worth it.

"Okay. I just need to talk to her."

Bex was afraid Tara would give in to him again… but she'd keep her word and give her sister the message. "I'll tell her."

"If she doesn't call me within two days, Josh is coming back to live with me."

When he walked away, she felt a wash of relief. Bex practically ran to her car, slid in—double-checking the locks—and negotiated the main drag of Mustang Creek, pretty much on autopilot.

She called Tate via her hands-free phone in the car. "I'm finally headed back. You have Josh, right?"

"Of course. They're all out in the yard with Ace, Joker and King. What's going on? You sound upset."

She loved the names the boys had chosen. They'd come up with them during another game of Old Maid—the night after Mrs. A. dropped off the pups—after chortling happily that Tate was, once again, the Old Maid. "Not really upset," she replied. "I ran into Greg. This is a small town, so I knew it would happen."

She couldn't restrain a small sob.

"I assume that means she filed," Tate said.

"She did."

"That's progress."

Bex braked for a light. "He's going to use Josh to try and get her back. He said he'd take him, and I'm so afraid he will. I agreed to call Tara, tell her she has to talk to him. Was that a mistake?"

"No," Tate said firmly. "This is their problem, but Josh needs to come first with *both* of them. If you think it makes sense, we can fly him out to Denver at any time. By law, Tara has to tell Greg where he is, even though he hasn't made any effort to see his son."

She didn't want to take Josh to Denver, but it was a generous offer. Josh would be better off with Tara than Greg—that wasn't in question. But her sister needed to get her life in order first.

"Thank you. I'll be home soon. Then we can talk about all of this."

"I hope spaghetti is okay. One of my limited number of specialties, remember? Don't expect gourmet or anything. Oh," he added, "the boys have had carrot sticks and cheese to tide them over."

It *was* a lot later than she'd intended. She appreciated that he'd waited so he could eat with her. Was this what it was like to be married? Shared responsibilities and the privilege of relying on someone else to pick up the slack when you couldn't?

"Spaghetti sounds just fine to me."

When she'd driven down the rutted lane, the puppies rushed out, dashing around in greeting, followed by the three boys trying to corral them. As she got out of the car, three pairs of muddy front paws left marks all over her tailored slacks. The dogs leaped around in joy until she was laughing, and she would've sworn that was impossible after her stressful day.

Ben did try to control the pack. "No!" he shouted.

Tate was much more effective when he came out and

whistled. "Down," he ordered in a deceptively calm voice.

The puppies all sat obediently, apparently contrite. Bex brushed at her pants then gave up. She wanted to put on jeans, anyway. As she went up the steps, she asked, "How *do* you do that?"

"They know I mean it. I poured you a glass of wine." He fixed the boys with a pointed look. "In fifteen minutes, it's bath time. You're muddy and it's getting colder by the minute. I don't care who goes first, but take off your shoes before you come inside and wipe off the dogs' paws."

He was such a natural at being in charge, and tonight she was going to let him handle all the chaos.

"I'm going to change. The wine's a wonderful idea." She hurried to the bedroom; most of her clothes were still at her place, so it only took a minute to choose comfortable jeans plus her favorite gray shirt from her suitcase. There were so many decisions she still had to make. One of them was what to do with her house if she stayed at the ranch permanently. She wouldn't sell it, but maybe rent it out? She stopped over regularly to pick up clothes and other personal things, check the locks and so on.

She was looking forward to relaxing, but it seemed that every single time she and Tate sat down, there was a puppy or child incident, and then relaxation went out the window.

Still, she had to acknowledge that she was really experiencing family life, and it felt…right.

When she joined him in the kitchen, Tate said with humor in his voice, "You do realize that they'll all come piling in the minute we sit down to eat, and they'll have a million questions. Then someone won't be able to find something he can't live without, and wet puppies will race around the entire time. A Tate Calder version of a romantic evening."

She picked up her glass of wine. "I like the sound of that. This wasn't the best day of my life. There've been worse, but there sure have been better. Hmm, that sauce smells great. What did you do?"

"Opened a jar and poured the contents into a pan." He grinned. "I do admit to splurging on the good stuff to impress you. Plus, there's my secret ingredient. Nothing like Italian sausage to win a girl's heart, right?"

"That'll do it every time. Throw in garlic bread and I'm yours for life."

"I was kind of hoping that was true, anyway." He poured the drained pasta into the sauce and his tone was casual, but his body language was not.

Then she did it. She just said it. "Yes to the baby."

TATE WAS SURE his hearing was faulty.

She'd said yes.

He stared at Bex, who looked tempting in just about anything. This evening it was jeans and a plain shirt that somehow managed to emphasize how fantasy-perfect her breasts were—at least in *his* fantasies. *She said yes.* He was at a loss for words.

Since the initial discussion, she'd said nothing about it.

"You're dripping sauce on the floor," she pointed out, and he glanced down to discover that the spoon in his hand was no longer over the pot.

He set it on the counter, ignoring the mess it made.

"Since I brought it up, you haven't been interested in talking about it."

"I haven't had time to talk," she said reasonably, "and besides, you must know me well enough by now to figure out I was thinking about it. There's a stipulation, though. Do *not* ask me to marry you."

He gazed at her in puzzlement. He couldn't help feeling confused, since he knew those charms signified marriage and commitment; not only that, she never took her bracelet off. After his relationship with Sandra he'd sworn off marriage—which wasn't exactly a secret—and yet, this threw him.

The sauce bubbled away merrily. He spoke slowly, weighing his response. "I don't understand why that's your position, since you agreed to move in here and now we're going to try to expand our family. But if that's what you want, I'm fine with it. Clarification would help, though. I'm not prying—your feelings are your feelings—but I do want to hear your reasons."

She took a sip of merlot before answering. "You proposed to Sandra and it was a disaster, correct?"

What an understatement. "Aside from Ben and Adam, yes, it was." He felt he needed some of that wine himself for this conversation. He reached for a glass.

She crossed her arms under those tempting breasts. "Will proposed to me, and that ended up being an entirely different kind of disaster. I mean it, I do *not* want a proposal."

So he'd fallen in love with the only woman on the planet who didn't want a ring and a proposal on bended knee?

"You're superstitious," he said. "Because of what happened to Will."

"I guess so."

It was ironic, since he'd told himself over and over that he didn't want to get married again, that now that he might actually change his mind, he didn't have that option. She seemed dead serious, too, straight up Bex-style. He had to acknowledge that *his* reasons for being marriage shy were also based on past fears and a degree of superstition. Because Bex wasn't Sandra.

"Just putting my cards on the table. Take it or leave it, Old Maid."

The touch of levity helped. "That's downright mean. I'm still convinced you cheat."

"Prove it." Bex got out a couple of plates from one of the cupboards. She knew her way around the kitchen better than he did. "Now, please give me some pasta before I faint. Lunch was an apple at one o'clock."

Predictably, the crowd swarmed in right then, and not one of the boys remembered to wipe a single puppy paw, so the floor was immediately a mess. He could yell, but it wouldn't solve the problem and besides, all six of them had come in on time and on command, so that alone was a victory. The muddy paws were just fallout.

"Told you," he said to Bex, scooping out spaghetti and sauce for each boy and ignoring the mayhem. "It never fails. If there's a football game I want to watch, someone needs help with his homework. If I get an important phone call, suddenly they both need to talk to me. The night I desperately need sleep, they start running a fever."

"But you want more kids." Her eyes had turned a soft gold.

"Yes," he said simply. "Mind bringing in the garlic bread?"

He could have added: *more children, yes, but only with you*.

She didn't want him to propose. He *should* be relieved.

He wasn't. That shook him up a little.

The three boys ate rapidly, if sloppily, and eschewed the grated Parmesan, which Bex added liberally to her spaghetti. Then they mumbled requests to be "'scused" and disappeared, leaving the two of them to finish their meal.

The sound of running water from the bathroom down the hall diminished some of the romantic ambiance, such as it was. So did the puppies circling the table, not begging, just hopeful and romping around. One of the children was actually taking a bath without prompting. That worked for him. Casually picking up his fork, he asked, "What precisely did Greg say?"

"He reminded me that Josh is his son." Bex stopped eating and sighed. "If I believed he really wanted to be a good father, I'd feel differently about this. To be fair, maybe he does—but he's nothing like you."

As a compliment that ranked right up there. She wasn't trying to flatter him, either. She was just ruminating, twirling pasta around on her plate.

He was touched by that.

But he had to say, "Bex, you knew this was coming."

Her eyes glistened as she nodded. "I know."

One of the puppies—he thought it was Ace but they all looked alike, so he couldn't be sure—tried to crawl onto her lap in sympathy. Usually the dogs seemed to stick to their allotted boys. His must be the one in the bathtub. She absently patted the puppy's head.

"Josh is resilient," he said.

"I don't want him to *have* to be, but I don't want my sister to go back to Greg, either."

"I'd guess he's bluffing."

The spaghetti was good. No wonder the boys had devoured it. Tate took a bite and washed it down with a sip of wine. "I've met his type before. He won't last more than a day or two, and then soccer practice and laundry will get to him."

"So speaks a man with experience."

"Oh, it got to me, too." He couldn't be less than honest. "It's a lot of work. I get tired and exasperated at times and have to remind myself that it isn't an easy journey, but worth it."

"I'm more worried Greg won't *let* him play soccer and won't do his laundry. He refused to pay for his lunch ticket, Tate."

She was really worried. He could see it in her strained expression.

There was suddenly some dispute in the bathroom, probably Ben and Adam. In his experience, Josh didn't cause dissension. He started to get up to mediate.

"No."

"No, what?"

Bex said, "Sit down. I'll handle this one. I need the practice. I can't be nice Aunt Bex all the time if we live together."

She did well; they listened long enough not to resume the controversy until they hit the bedroom, where the grumbling gradually reduced in volume and then subsided completely. The puppies also disappeared to their beds, which he'd insisted be left on the floor in an effort to keep the animals off the furniture. He'd already caught one of them snuggled up with Adam when he checked on everyone before he went to bed last night, and he'd just let it go with a sense of the inevitable. Boys and puppies… Yeah, the dogs were going to sleep on the beds eventually. Who was he fooling?

When Bex came back to the table, he did notice that she took quite a long sip from her glass. He kept a straight face but she saw him, anyway.

"I've never thought," she said defensively, "that it's easy to have kids."

"No." The shimmer of her hair made him want to run his fingers through it. Speaking in a slightly husky tone, he said, "Why don't we finish dinner, and then, when we're sure the kids are asleep, let's go make another one."

CHAPTER TWENTY-TWO

She wasn't sure what attracted her more.

The fact that Tate openly admitted he wanted more kids or that she could tell the situation with Josh bothered him as much as it did her.

Oh, he was definitely sexy, which was, of course, what had attracted her in the first place, but there was a lot more to him than that. How a man looked and how he acted were two very diverse parts of who he was. Tate won on both scores.

His bedroom was typically male. King-size four-poster bed made of walnut. Besides that, Tate had only a single dresser, plus a small nightstand with a book on it and a plain bronze reading lamp. She was interested to see that the book—the old-fashioned print kind—was a hardcover history of the Civil War. The closet was a walk-in and huge, so she'd give him points for planning ahead. There was more than enough room for her clothes. All he seemed to have, other than a few suits, were jeans, shirts and cowboy boots.

Overall, there was no clutter in his room, and nothing unnecessary, which seemed somehow typical of him.

The house was almost disturbingly like her dream house. The rustic comfort, the sweeping view, the land, the children and horses and dogs—the entire package.

Plus Tate.

Was she really going to do this? A *baby*?

He undid the buttons on his shirt. "Just an observation, but you're wearing entirely too much clothing."

She *was* going to do it.

Bex pulled off her top. "Better?"

He sat down and tugged off his boots, his gaze intent. "Oh, yeah. Keep going."

She unfastened her bra. "Like this?"

"Exactly like that." She removed it, conscious of him watching, and then unfastened her jeans and slipped out of them. By the time they tumbled onto the bed, entwined and kissing, she was just about ready for what was going to happen next.

Or so she thought.

It wasn't that he touched her differently, but it *felt* different. His fingers still traced her breasts with the same reverence, his mouth caressed her neck, but there was a heightened sense of awareness between them that she wasn't entirely prepared for. A sense that a life-altering decision had been made. And yet she knew that if she changed her mind, he'd accept it.

Tate lifted his head and looked at her as their positions shifted, and she could feel him hard and ready. "Are you having second thoughts? You're so tense. What's wrong? Talk to me."

There was a lock of hair hanging over his forehead, and she smoothed it back. "Just a small reality check. This is like jumping out of a plane and hoping the parachute opens."

"I'll be right beside you, holding your hand, as we float down together."

If she didn't think he meant that, she wouldn't be with him. "I know."

"This is mutual, right?"

"The baby decision or the moment?" She kissed him, putting her arms around his neck. "Or both?"

"I've never been in love before." He said it against her mouth, so quietly she almost didn't hear it. "I thought so, for a little while, anyway, but I was wrong. It never felt like this."

She felt the same wonder, although she *had* been in love. How many people experienced it more than once in a lifetime? Then she told him what he already knew. "I love you, too."

His smile was tender. "I guessed maybe you did. The clues pointed that way, even if you never said it."

When she didn't speak, he added, "You didn't have to. I understand."

Her arms tightened around his neck. "Make love to me."

"I think I can go along with that."

He did, his eyes closing, and Bex gasped his name at the sensation as he joined their bodies.

She'd learned a lot in the past weeks.

About her body, about the sexual rhythm of a man and a woman—or at least of her and Tate. She'd started to recognize the way he breathed as he got closer to release, the lowering of his lashes, how the sudden heat prickled across his skin just before his control evaporated.

He knew her even better. He knew when she wanted him to move faster, how to lift her just the right distance as she was about to climax, that a wicked whisper in her ear made the experience more vivid.

She came first, going wild in his arms. She heard him make a low sound, and then he was there with her, saying her name loudly enough that she was glad the door was solid wood and firmly shut.

Catching their breath, neither of them spoke until he finally murmured, "I'm hoping that didn't work and we have to try it again."

Bex laughed and bit his shoulder playfully. "Maybe. But only if you're on your best behavior."

"Or worst?" He licked her nipple.

Her sensitized body responded. "Quit that."

"Never." His thumb rubbed along her lower lip. "You make me happy. I don't think I've ever said that to another person."

She looked into his eyes. "You make me happy *again*. I didn't think I'd ever say that. I was content with my life. It was good, peaceful—"

Someone knocked on the door. "Hey, Dad."

"Just a second! Hold that thought." Tate scrambled for his discarded jeans and muttered, "It isn't peaceful now."

Bex drew the sheet up to her chin and suppressed a laugh. "Nope."

"Don't expect any improvements. I'll solve the current problem and be right back. That's all we can do, take it one situation at a time."

"I took care of the one during dinner, so it *is* your turn."

He glanced at her over his shoulder. "Be here and still be naked?"

"I have no other plans at the moment." She said it breezily. "Have fun. I have a feeling this might involve Ace, Joker or King."

"I have the same feeling." He stalked over and

yanked the door open, but said patiently, "Okay, here I am. What's going on?"

"Why was your door locked?" Ben sounded peevish, cute in his Batman pajamas.

"Never mind why. Just give me the bad news."

"I think one of the dogs might have…well…"

"Show me where."

Bex dissolved in laughter once the door shut behind him, but at least she waited until he'd left.

Step one. She'd finally been able to say it. *I love you*.

Naked, yes.

Awake, no.

Tate went back to his bedroom, hoping for a repeat performance, but Bex was sound asleep, her respiration soft and slow.

He slid in beside her, listened to her breathing in the dark.

Crossing his arms behind his head, he told himself how damn lucky he was right now. Sure, the boys were a handful and he just cleaned up an unattractive mess on his brand-new floor with an apologetic puppy watching. His father and Mrs. A. were going to meddle and feud with each other, there was still a month or two of construction to be finished…

But he felt very lucky.

Bex was in his life.

Sleeping next to him, she turned over with a small sigh, and as much as he wanted to kiss her awake, she'd looked really tired when she'd walked in the door.

No proposal.

He sensed that she really meant it. Lying there in the dark, he thought about it. While a part of him was convinced he didn't want to get married again, was afraid to…there was another part that felt very differently now.

Her hand was under her cheek, and he reached over and touched the tiny airplane charm on her bracelet. He'd never looked at it closely and only now realized what it was. *An airplane.* Which was a coincidence, no doubt—but somehow it proved to him that this was meant to be. *They* were meant to be.

He wasn't going to ask her to sign a piece of paper that reduced their relationship to dollars and cents. She'd forbidden him to propose, much as he now wanted to, so he needed a way around this dilemma. There had to be one.

He lay there and thought about it some more.

As he drifted off, he wondered if there was something he could do he hadn't considered before.

Maybe.

Oh, hell, worth a try, anyway.

BEX POURED ORANGE JUICE into three glasses and passed them out. Toast made, cereal distributed and children munching, as were the puppies, all at their bowls. None of them were quiet, none of it was dainty, but it was under control.

She could do this.

Tate was still asleep.

That surprised her because he normally got up at daybreak and prepared breakfast for the boys. Maybe they were all settling into a new routine, with her sharing responsibility for the three boys, and she liked the idea of that.

The construction crews started to arrive. She could hear the trucks pulling in and the sound of slamming doors. Flora was in the pasture, ears pricked forward, and from the window, Bex watched her move warily to the north end.

"Good morning." Tate wandered out, rubbing his face. "I overslept. I never do that. What time is it, anyway?"

She made him a cup of coffee with, as usual, cream, no sugar. "About seven. Maybe you needed the extra sleep."

"I have to go feed Flora, take the boys to school, pick up more hay so I can bring over the horses Tripp's keeping for me. Then I want to see if I can get a solid timeline on the stable and barn."

"The boys are doing fine. Have your coffee first." She leaned on the counter. "I've got an idea." She spoke in a low voice, since this wasn't a conversation she wanted the boys to hear.

He paused in the act of taking his first sip. "Uh-oh. When a woman says that I get nervous."

"Don't be funny." She sent him her most lethal look.

"My apologies." He did seem contrite, except for the smile. "So, what's your idea?"

"My current manager constantly calls in. I don't want to fire her, but I don't want to work twelve-hour days like yesterday, either. I could move her to another position, offer Tara the job and she could rent my house if she agrees to move back to Mustang Creek. Thoughts? I doubt she's happy in Denver away from Josh. Actually, I know for a fact she's not."

The constant stream of emails was evidence enough. Tara knew Josh was safe with her, but she missed her child and her friends.

"I wouldn't be happy at all in her situation."

There was a reason she'd fallen in love with Tate

Calder. Well, quite a few, actually, but that was one of them. He understood how her sister must be feeling, understood the importance of family.

He drank some coffee, his lean body braced against the counter. "It sounds perfect, except for Greg. If she comes back here, what's he going to do?"

She played with her hair, something she did when she was thinking; it had been pointed out before, but she couldn't stop herself. "I'm inclined to go with the idea that a united front, a decent job and a house will make a big difference. If she doesn't need Greg, it's over. She had the courage to leave. I think she has the courage to come back."

"United front?"

"Hadleigh, Mel and me. We can get her back on her feet. And we can help her deal with any problems Greg might cause."

"You sound confident."

"We can make things happen."

His eyes held amusement. "I don't doubt that. And you wouldn't lose Josh."

Bex had to admit that had entered her plans. "You have to acknowledge that is one nice kid."

"Agreed. He has a pretty nice aunt, too."

"I'm attached to him."

"I'm attached to him *and* his aunt."

It was impossible to suppress a laugh. "So? Your opinion?"

"I think it would be best for everyone all around. But Bex, it might not turn out the way you want."

Her fear exactly. She glanced at the clock as it ticked off the minutes, the hands moving along the numerals and the image of the house. "He's happy at school. Mustang Creek is his home. I don't want him to lose that."

"We could fly out today to pick her up in Denver if she can't get a reasonably priced flight," he suggested. "Or if there's any other way I could help, let me know."

He already *had* helped. Immeasurably. She studied him as he leaned against the counter. "How come I always have this distrustful feeling that you're too good to be true?"

Tate laughed, choking on his coffee. He wiped his mouth with the back of his hand. "Don't do that to me again. Okay, full disclosure. There *are* some things I neglected to tell you. I don't dust. If it was left to me, this entire planet would just be coated with the stuff, so that chore will fall to you. I didn't mention that on purpose in case it scared you off. I do laundry, but no sorting is involved. If you have, uh, delicate items that require special care, my advice is not to put them in the basket because they'll go in with red athletic socks and be washed on the regular cycle. During the basketball Final Four, I've been known to eat, and feed my children, pizza for a few nights in a row. Let's see, what else? I don't shave on weekends. I can't stand lima beans. If you serve them, I'm going to pull an Adam and refuse to eat them. I'm sure there's more, but that's as much soul baring as I can handle this early in the morning." He called out, "Guys, let's move it."

When the boys filed out with their backpacks and the throng departed, except for three disappointed puppies, who pressed their faces to the front door, she sent a text to her sister.

I have an idea. Call me.

CHAPTER TWENTY-THREE

"WHEN I TURNED out the horses a few days ago, my young stallion was really interested in one of your mares, following her around. You might be in business sooner than you think."

Tate wasn't displeased. Tripp had an eye for prime horseflesh, and his stallion was a beautiful animal. "I'll send you a stud fee when we find out."

Tripp shook his head. "I should've taken him to the north pasture to graze alone. This first one's on me. I was in a hurry because Hadleigh was having an ultrasound. I can't promise, but I have a suspicion there's going to be a foal."

They carefully loaded the horses in the long new transport trailer. That was an expense Tate had known he'd have to make, so he was resigned to it; besides, he could write it off as a legit business deduction.

When the last animal was in and secured, Tate said—not as casually as he would have liked—"Bex wants her sister to come home to Mustang Creek. Greg is threatening to take Josh away as leverage to get back with Tara. I'm stuck because I really want to interfere, but I'm not sure how this should play out. Bex wants her here for Josh's sake, and like I said, Greg seems to want her back."

Tripp rested his hand on the side on the trailer, his

expression troubled. "That's a tough one. Greg and Tara have a one-sided relationship, and that's his side. He's gotten to do whatever he wants for a long time."

"I see Bex's point." Tate puffed out a breath. "I'm invested in this, too. Josh has changed a lot just in the time I've known him. He deserves to stay here with his friends. It would all be different if his father and mother got along fine and he was moving, say to Denver, for another reason. I did it to my kids. New life. New place. They love it here. They aren't part of an ongoing argument, though."

But if he and Sandra had divorced as planned, they sure might have been. It would be hypocritical to criticize too much.

Tripp shrugged. "Bex was born to fix the world. Accept it. Melody will stylishly decorate it. Hadleigh will be the queen-slash-dictator, and everything will be under control. I say let them handle it. Greg won't stand a chance."

"Hands off?"

"That's my advice. Hands off. This is up to Bex. I understand you *want* to fix it, but she's more than capable of handling it."

Probably good advice. "If he hurts her or Josh, I'm going to—"

"Step back and trust her," Tripp said quietly. "Help pick up the pieces and be there 100 percent. If I know Bex, *she* knows exactly what she's doing."

Tate found his sense of protectiveness hard to conquer, but Tripp was probably right. "Why haven't Bex and her friends done something before now?"

"Tara never did something as drastic as taking off for Denver and actually getting a lawyer. So no one thought she'd go through with a divorce. Intervention only works when the person is prepared to change. Tara and Greg have been together a long time. It's a shame, because I think she does love him, and I think in his dysfunctional way he loves her, but he can't keep his hands off other women. I've seen plenty of men who do the same thing. And women, for that matter, who can't resist other men. People who stray repeatedly. Hadleigh almost married one."

Tate *had* married one.

Tripp was reasonable and levelheaded, so Tate took him at his word. "I'd better get back," he said with reluctance. "My father's going to be in town yet again for something he says is business related. I'm sure he's just micromanaging because I swear he has nothing going on in Mustang Creek. Since Mrs. A. knows this due to a flurry of emails, and they want to take a look at the stable and the horses, I might have a murder investigation interfering with our progress."

"Mrs. A… Yeah, I can see that. How are the puppies?" Tripp grinned.

He grimaced. "Let's see. Messy, undisciplined, they sleep with the boys unless I catch them, eat like horses and grow overnight. All three of them are smart enough to jump down if they hear me coming, but that's no small thud when they hit the floor and there's nothing wrong with my hearing, so I'm not exactly fooled." He sighed. "And they're puppies, so when it's lights out, they sleep through just about anything." He rolled his eyes. "One of my favorite boots has gone missing, but I'm choosing to pretend it'll turn up in one piece."

"Yeah, maybe next spring. If at all." That was followed by a chuckle. "Kind of what I imagined."

"The kids love those damn dogs, so I forgive most infractions."

"I can tell you're already fond of them, too. I have a couple of rules for Ridley and Muggles. Stay off the couch and my favorite chair, and we're all good. Hadleigh is a little more demanding. If she ever catches me feeding them table scraps, my life would be in danger."

"Try having three boys. I've attempted that rule, and they hear but don't listen." Tate shook his head as he got into the truck. "Thanks again for keeping the horses. If there *is* a foal, it's yours. I owe you big-time for all the help."

"We can work it out later."

"Fair enough." He checked the clock on the dash and groaned. "My dad might already be there. Wish me luck."

He needed it.

"Hey, I like your dad. For that matter, I like Mrs. A."

He didn't put the vehicle in gear, the window still rolled down. "I do, too, most of the time, but they don't like each other." Tate added, "The good news is my father likes Bex. The bad news is he's going to wonder why we aren't getting married if he figures out she's living with me, and he'll figure it out pretty quickly."

Tripp said carefully, "It your business, not mine, but I like Bex, too. I think of her as my little sister. Why *aren't* you getting married? Just wondering that myself."

"She told me flat-out not to propose."

Tripp tugged off his work gloves, frowning. "I know her, and that sounds backward to me. She'd be much more likely to accept a proposal than agree to move in without one."

"Something to do with Will. He proposed and then died." Tate stared out the windshield blindly, not seeing the mountains and trees, just being introspective. "I'm good at fixing problems for two little boys who depend on me night and day, but I don't know how to reassure Bex about this one." He threw back his head. "At first I didn't want to ever remarry, but now I feel that she's the one I've been waiting for all my life. We both agree we want more children—and yet she doesn't want to marry me."

"She's *afraid* to marry you. That's different. Yeah, okay, I can see her thinking that way. When she cares, she really cares. Look what she's doing for her sister and Josh. Will was my best friend, and I was there when he died. I took it hard, but not like Bex. There's loving someone, and then there's being in love. Not the same thing."

It wasn't as though he could argue. He'd made the same point himself.

"Wish me luck," he said again.

Tripp let out a raspy chuckle. "Oh, I do. All the way around."

SHE'D SPENT ALMOST an hour on the phone with Tara, wiping her sister's tears from hundreds of miles away, then another hour with her mother and dad, now retired and living in Sacramento. In *that* conversation she omitted the information that although Tara was moving back, into Bex's place, she herself was living elsewhere. She ate lunch at her desk—chicken salad from Bad Billie's. Delicious. That man might look rough around the edges, but he sure could dish out good food. Then she went for a run to clear her head.

Tara had jumped at the chance to return to Mustang Creek and swore she was determined to go through with the divorce. Since the gym manager had called in sick yet again, Bex decided it was a good idea to hire her sister, because it solved two problems at one time. But Tate's practical observation lingered.

It might not turn out the way you want...

At least Josh would be living in a place that was familiar, stay in the same school, and see Ben and Adam on a regular basis, not to mention Tate, who represented stability and positive male authority. She'd have a reliable manager to do the office work and to make sure the center was open without her constant supervision. Her house would be rented, and as long as Tara stood firm, the situation would be good for everyone. Except maybe Greg, but Bex refused to worry about him for now. In any case, if he ever showed an interest, his son wouldn't be in Denver, so she was doing him a favor, too, although that wasn't high on her list of priorities.

Now, if she could only resolve her personal life that neatly...

She was being untrue to the pact, for one thing.

She needed to fess up to Hadleigh and Mel. Just plain admit that she'd chickened out, that even though she'd already admitted Tate was the man she wanted, she was afraid.

She had a feeling they were already aware of it all. They were giving her time to work it out, but that wouldn't last forever. She knew them as well as they knew her. Sooner or later, she was going to have an intervention of epic stature from two pregnant women with very definite opinions.

The run was a great cardio workout, but head cleared? Not really.

It didn't get any better when she bumped down

the lane to the ranch, either. Construction workers all around, two extremely expensive cars she recognized in the driveway, a brand-new horse trailer hitched to Tate's truck and more horses in the fenced pasture. Now all she needed was…

Three boys and their giant puppies came rushing out the door at the sound of her car pulling up. She fended off the dogs semisuccessfully, hugged the boys and wished she wasn't dressed in sweats if Mrs. A. and Tate's father were inside.

They were. One seated stiffly on the chair Bex had picked out and particularly liked, striped in beige, brown and dark blue, the other on Tate's huge leather couch.

The silence was tense. It was clear they weren't speaking to each other.

Tate offered up a smile that silently apologized. He said drily, "We're having an impromptu business meeting." He came over and kissed her then whispered in her ear. "It isn't going well as if you couldn't tell. Feel free to escape while you can. I encourage you to save yourself. That's how much I love you."

"Got it," she whispered back. Then more loudly, "I've been running." She appreciated the opportunity to edge toward the hallway. "I need a shower and I don't want to interrupt. Good luck with the meeting."

She dashed down the hall and selected a clean outfit, a long-sleeved dress and flats in case she was dragged off to dinner somewhere. Thankfully, she'd brought over most of her clothes by now, so she felt prepared for most—if not all—circumstances. She shut the door to the master bath. The jetted tub beckoned, but she chose the shower on the off chance she could help defuse the situation just by returning quickly, decently dressed and with a smile on her face.

She combed her hair after her shower, fluffed it with her fingers and added a touch of lip gloss. When she walked back into the living room, she was glad she'd hurried.

Tate was obviously grateful to see her because all three boys with their canine companions had come bounding in as she entered the room, and he was busy riding herd on the crowd. Mrs. A., in Bex's opinion, could hardly complain if one of the exuberant puppies *she'd* brought over leaped on her.

"Hey, guys." Bex nabbed one of the dogs—she thought it was Joker—by the collar just before he launched himself onto the chair, and tried to deflect his affectionate response. "How about Ben's room and some popcorn?" she suggested to the boys. "You can watch a movie."

That was kind of a bold move, since it wasn't even dinnertime yet and none of them were her children, but it did the trick. The boys went running down the hall, the puppies followed and she prayed the microwave popcorn she'd brought a few days ago was still in the cupboard.

"Well done." Tate's father, when he chose to use it, had the same smile as his son. Up until that moment, the resemblance had just been height, build and bone structure.

But that smile…

Unmistakable.

"Thanks. Well, I'd better go deliver or they'll be back."

"I'll help you." Tate followed her into the kitchen.

She had to say it. "Help me make microwave popcorn? I think I can handle it."

He was unrepentant. "I had to get out of that room for a minute. Besides, the big plastic bowl is on a top shelf, and I'm taller than you are. See? There you have it. I need to help."

"It's that bad in there, huh?"

"Why they agreed they'd both invest is beyond me. It was even their idea." He reached into the cupboard for the large bowl, and he was right, she would've had to stand on one of the stools. Tate handed it over, his face grim. "I'm too far in to change it now, but the second I can buy them both out will be a champagne moment. Individually, they're difficult enough. Together, I need a lasso and some skilled cowboys to keep 'em calm. Other than coming to the conclusion that they should both get into the business, they can't agree on a single thing—except that they like you."

It seemed unfair to laugh at his gloomy expression, but she couldn't help it. "And you, or they wouldn't be here. And they both think breeding horses will be a successful enterprise, although I doubt either of them needs the money. Mrs. A. gives most of hers away as far as I can tell, and I've seen your father's house and car."

"I don't disagree with any of that. I'm just hoping this is worth all the stress of trying to be a diplomat with two pigheaded people used to getting their own way. I'm beginning to think that's not one of my skills."

Bex put the packet of popcorn in the microwave and pushed the start button. "You have other skills."

"Oh, yeah? Cheer me up. What are they?" His voice dropped in timbre.

She tossed out, "You're not a bad kisser."

"*Not bad?* High praise. Jeez, I'm all warm and fuzzy now. What else?" He moved closer, his gaze holding hers.

The popcorn started to pop.

"We can discuss it later."

He ran a fingertip across the curve of her eyebrow. "You bet we will. I hate to break it to you but we're going out to dinner again. Three puppies will have to be incarcerated in Ben's room. And I have no idea how this happened, but Mrs. A. is coming with us. They decided that when I stepped outside to check on the boys and the dogs. My prediction is that she and my father will argue over the restaurant, the table, where we all sit and who knows what else." He added, "You look fantastic, by the way."

It was shaping up to be an interesting evening.

The microwave pinged. Bex said, "I'd better deliver this to the boys. I always try to keep my promises."

"I'm counting on that."

Now, what did he mean? she wondered as she emptied the popcorn into the bowl.

CHAPTER TWENTY-FOUR

THE EVENING WASN'T the disaster he'd feared.

All three boys were reasonably well behaved, as were his father and Mrs. A., if pointedly ignoring each other could be considered polite. At any rate, it was preferable to their constant bickering. Tate and Bex kept the conversation going, but were both relieved when dessert was over and they were back in the truck.

"Could've been worse," Bex remarked as she fastened her seat belt. She wore an elegant long dark coat that was a contrast to her usual no-nonsense jacket and cute snowflake hat.

He was fond of that hat.

"No blood was spilled," Tate said as he pulled out of the lodge parking lot. "We haven't had a chance to talk about today yet." He was conscious of Josh in the backseat, probably not listening, but he wasn't willing to take that chance. "Go well?"

"I believe I've hired a new manager." Bex was just as unwilling to say anything directly. "She's enthusiastic about it all and managed to book a cheap flight for next week," she said. "Which is a good thing considering how your afternoon turned out."

"That's the truth," he muttered. "Left alone, those two would've done who knows what. The next meeting will involve the National Guard if I have my way. Some tear gas would've been handy today. I'd rather there *wasn't* another meeting. But back to Tara and company. What happens now?"

"No idea. It seems like every single time I make a plan, something blasts it off the face of the earth. I'm just waiting for everything to settle down."

"Hey, I have a surprise that might make up for your tough week."

He really did. It had taken some ingenuity to pull it off, too.

Bex looked at him, her eyes green in the reflected streetlight. "Like what?"

"I'm sure I just said *surprise*."

"I don't like surprises. Ask Hadleigh and Mel."

He'd already asked them if she'd like this one. They'd both emphatically said yes, and if anyone would know, they would. "I'm doing my best to change your mind about surprises, and it isn't just for you, anyway."

"That's intriguing." She sounded as if she meant it but still wasn't thrilled.

It was gratifying to drive into his lane with the house so inviting, all lit up in the distance. Once again he felt that true sense of *home*, of having arrived where he was meant to be.

The kids scrambled out of the car. Time for bed. Dogs let out, teeth brushed, pajamas put on, the usual quarrel over some small thing between brothers but they'd been good at dinner so Tate ignored it and allowed them to work it out themselves. Then dogs back in, good-nights said, lights out. He left some of the routine to Bex as he went out to check on the horses. That chore was only going to become more demanding. This venture wasn't going to be nine to five, and he was fine with that.

This was his life, the life he'd chosen, and he wouldn't change it, even if he could at this point. Kids, puppies, horses, his interfering father, Mrs. A. and all. Then there were friends...and Bex.

When he went back inside, she was sitting in her customary chair with a book on her lap, her legs curled under her. The house was quiet. She'd changed into pajama pants and a T-shirt, looking deliciously sleepy and drinking a cup of tea.

"Let me wash up and then it's surprise time. By the way, Flora is an exceptionally affectionate horse."

"She's a sweetheart." Bex glanced at him dubiously and he read a flicker of apprehension on her face.

"No proposal," Tate promised. "I gave my word, remember? But this *is* for us."

Bex relaxed. "Okay."

When he returned after looking in on the boys and the puppies, all asleep, he went over and grasped her hand, easing her from the chair. "Let's go."

She set aside her teacup. "Go? Where?"

"Outside."

"Seriously? I don't even have my coat."

"Yep. Seriously. You don't need a coat." He led her through the kitchen to the French doors onto the back porch.

Tripp was one hell of a good friend. Hadleigh and Mel, too.

He'd had part of the porch screened because Wyoming had its share of insects; he'd intended to put a couple of chairs there and a table. But then another idea had surfaced. The chairs and table would move to the open section of porch. He'd let Bex pick them out later.

There'd previously been drop cloths draped over everything, so she'd just assumed it wasn't finished yet. Thanks to the expanded stable plans, the contractor had done the labor on this project free of charge.

The hot tub was sunk into the deck, and Tripp had come over to open the lid and put the lights on while they were at dinner. Someone else, Hadleigh probably, had set out champagne in an ice bucket and crystal flutes, two plush towels and a plate of those lemon-filled pastries Bex claimed she never got to eat. Everything was arranged on a small ornate table that had, no doubt, been designed by Mel. He'd have to look more closely, but it seemed to echo the background she'd created for the clock.

Star-studded sky and snow-capped mountains as a setting. He couldn't have ordered it and have it turn out better.

"I thought we might need a chance to sit and relax and talk now and then," he explained in a voice that was thick with emotion. "Just you and me, without all the crazy stuff. This isn't an easy gig for either of us. Kids and animals and your work and mine... Like I said, I thought we needed a place for *us*. If you get pregnant, we can't use it for a while, but—"

"I *love* it." Bex interrupted him by pressing a finger to his lips. "I run marathons, remember? I exercise every single day. This is perfect. I've always wanted one but couldn't imagine using it alone."

Her response was what he wanted, right down to the hitch in her voice.

"You're hardly alone. Not around here, anyway. Ready to get in?"

"I don't have a swimsuit. They're all at my house."

He gave a classic male response. "No need for one. I was hoping you'd say that."

"I should go in naked?"

"I like the sound of that." He was opening the champagne, turning the bottle after twisting off the metal cage. "The beauty of this is if any kids come out looking for us, we can just turn on the jets. Besides, they're fast asleep. So, Becca Stuart, no need to be shy."

He'd prefer to call her Becca *Calder.* The cork popped in his hand and he reminded himself that it was all he'd be allowed to pop. Not *the question.*

But he was tempted.

Instead he poured the bubbly into the glasses and felt grateful for good friends. He felt grateful for even more than that as Bex turned her back and started to take off her clothes. She said over her bare shoulder, "I will if you will."

That alone made the rest of the day worth it.

BEX DIPPED A TOE in the warm water, and then slid in. She was going to change her mind about surprises if they were all like this. It felt divine.

"Oh, this is lovely." She murmured the words as she smiled at Tate. "Now I can take boys and dogs and even you in stride."

"*Even* me? I'm feeling pretty special at the moment. Champagne?"

He'd poured it, so why not? She wasn't going anywhere, and he looked so enticing, naked as she was, with his bare chest directly in her line of sight.

This was not the Bex Stuart she knew. That Bex did not get into hot tubs with a naked man.

She didn't move in with a father who had two children, either.

She didn't agree to have his baby.

She didn't go on fishing trips to remote cabins. She didn't do a lot of the things she'd been doing lately, but life changed and you adjusted, and she asked herself, *What am I going to do next that I haven't done before*?

She wasn't going to budge on letting Tate ask her to marry him.

On the other hand, she thought as she accepted the glass he handed her, maybe it would be different if *she* proposed to *him*.

"Okay?" he asked, probably because she was staring at him as though she'd never seen him before.

Bex realized he meant the champagne. She took a sip. "Really nice."

It was. Clean and crisp.

The question was, would he say yes if she did ask? Oh, he wanted to live together and have a baby, but he'd never actually talked about marriage. She was the one who'd requested there be no proposal, no discussion. She had good reasons for that, but he had his own motives for not wanting to travel that path again.

She pondered their bad luck, karma, whatever you wanted to call it, as she sat there admiring the male scenery. Yeah, they both had some issues.

She cleared her throat. "Being out here like this is fabulous."

"Look at the stars." He tilted back his head.

She looked at him instead. "Will you marry me?"

He dumped half a glass of champagne in the tub before he caught himself and sat up. *"What?"*

"If you don't want to, fine, but living together and babies—they do seem to go with…marriage. With commitment."

"I'm not saying no, but if I recall correctly, and I'm sure I do, I wasn't allowed to ask *you* that question."

"You still aren't. It's different if I ask you."

"Why is that?" he asked in a hesitant voice.

"Well, it's a reversal of what happened before, when Will asked me. Do you know what I mean? I realize I'm being superstitious but it just *feels* right, as though I'm in control this time. As though I'm sending a message to the universe."

"I guess I understand. For me, being married to you would be completely different from my first marriage because *you're* different."

From his first wife, he meant. She nodded and went on. "I bet Mel could make you a ring in a few days."

"I'm supposed to wear an engagement ring?"

"I'll have her make something simple, don't worry."

His chest gleamed in the reflected light. "Bex, I do understand what you're saying, but traditionally *I'm* supposed to be the one asking."

"Don't do it," she warned. "And since when is tradition everything it's cracked up to be?"

He laughed. "I won't, I won't. I promise. Can she do a ring for you, too, or is that against the rules?"

Good question. The warm water felt fabulous. Bex sighed. "I know I'm being unreasonable, but I love you. Really love you. That's what scares me and has always scared me, ever since Will. The risk."

"To share my life with you, I'd take just about any risk."

Now she might cry, and she never cried. Those words were better than a proposal. Her eyes stung.

She choked out, "Is that a yes?"

"I don't know how else you'd take it. Yes!"

"Then yes to the engagement ring, too. For me, I mean. Mel can pick it out."

Tate chortled. "Oh, great, so my taste is in question now."

"Well, yeah. Here's an example—that big couch. Half a football team could fit on it."

He poured her more champagne. "That's the beauty of it. Being able to sprawl out, watch sports, spill your beer on it if you doze off…"

"I think it might become a casualty of our prenup agreement."

"I haven't said word one about that!"

"Do you have to? I've met your very businesslike father. In fact, I had dinner with him just tonight."

"I'm never going to ask you to sign anything." He sounded sincere and emphatic.

"Tate, it's okay."

He looked dangerously serious, the steam from the water rising around him, his arms on the side of the tub. "I'm not going to. No. I refuse. You told me I couldn't propose and I went along with that, so it's my turn. I am not going to ask you to sign a piece of paper that essentially says, *I don't trust you.* That I don't trust *us.* I did it once and the marriage didn't work out." He held up one hand to forestall her protest. "Yes, I know what you're going to say—it wouldn't have worked out, anyway, and you're right. But you aren't the only one with a superstition or two."

She set her glass aside and moved across the tub to wind her arms around his neck. Their lips were a whisper apart. "I'd sign it."

"Not an issue." He kissed her. "There isn't going to be one."

"What if I asked you to give up the couch? Would you sign an agreement?"

"Do you have a pen? Wait, I can see you don't." His hands slid along her bare skin. "My answer is, of course I would if you really wanted me to. But my point is that a marriage should be two people loving each other and not a business arrangement."

"No argument there." She grinned as she told him, "You can keep the couch. Puppies and young boys love it. Magnanimous of me, huh?"

Tate grinned in return, a grin that said he was happy with her concession. "They can't hurt it, anyway. You get to pick out the next one. Redecorate the whole house once the monsters, both kids and dogs, stop defiling everything we own with sticky fingerprints and muddy paws and a few other things I won't mention. I'm only going to admit this to you—it's a hot-tub secret—but I walked around for the better part of one day last week before I discovered I had a jellybean stuck to the back of my jeans, courtesy of the giant couch. I know for a fact that you or I didn't leave it there. It was a somewhat emasculating experience. I don't mind having a nickname, but I don't want it to be Jellybean Pants."

"Or even worse, Jelly Butt." Bex was laughing so hard she had to wipe her eyes. "I wish I'd seen that."

"I'm fairly sure some of the construction crew did,

but my sensitivity to humiliating situations has decreased quite a bit since becoming a parent."

"By the way, you'll rue the day you made that offer about redecorating, Mr. Calder. I usually shop with Hadleigh and Melody. They tend to go top-shelf. Maybe you should talk to Spence and Tripp before giving me carte blanche."

"I should start saving my pennies now?"

"I'd say that's an excellent idea."

"Speaking of excellent ideas…" He moved against her. "Have you ever made love in a hot tub?"

"No. You?"

His mouth caressed her neck. "I haven't, but I'm willing to give it a try."

She was, too.

Bex ran her fingers through his hair. "Did you really accept my proposal?"

"I think the real question should be, did you ask a man with two kids, three enormous puppies and no real job at the moment to marry you?"

"I might have."

"No going back now."

Making love in a hot tub under a brilliant vista of stars was, she discovered, another great surprise.

CHAPTER TWENTY-FIVE

"You're engaged?"

"I just said that, Dad," Tate repeated patiently.

"Officially?"

"Would I say so otherwise?"

He was glad to see that his father looked pleased. "Bex is smart and successful. Congratulations."

With a warm sense of humor. And kind. And beautiful and sexy, Tate thought. But all he said was, "Thanks."

"When is the wedding?"

That was something they hadn't decided on yet.

He and Randolph were walking over to the construction site, hands in pockets, collars flipped up against a stiff breeze that had decided to sweep down from the north. Snowlakes floated through the air. Tate shook his head. "I have no idea. Her call. Whenever she wants."

"Your mother was hell-bent on June," his father remarked. "The marriage season, she called it. She got her way, of course. I would've given her anything."

It wasn't a subtle hint, but then, his father wasn't a subtle man.

Tate didn't remember his mother very well. She died when he was about Adam's age, of kidney failure caused by a rare infection, so he and his sons had that in common. His father didn't talk about it, and maybe that was why he so rarely mentioned Sandra in front of Ben and Adam.

"I didn't know that."

Walking next to him, his father glanced over. "Didn't know what? Our anniversary?"

"No. That you loved her so much."

That was taking a chance. His father did *not* use the word *love*.

"Your mother? Of course I did." It was said gruffly.

There was no *of course* about it. "Things between Sandra and me didn't work out. Just because you decide to get married doesn't mean it's a match made in heaven—if you'll forgive the cliché. Ask all the people who file for divorce. Tripp is about the nicest guy I know and he got divorced from his first wife. He and Hadleigh genuinely are a good match, though."

"You and Bex. It's different from before?"

At least he could answer honestly. "Yes. Definitely."

"The first time you swing a bat doesn't mean you'll hit it out of the park."

He could come up with a lot of responses to *that* tired cliché, but Tate didn't bother. "I'm very happy about this."

"Seems to me you should be."

He might as well tell his father straight out. "I'm not asking for a prenup agreement. Just leave the money to the boys. That's fine with me."

Silence except for a raptor screaming in the distance, circling in the sky, the keening sound punctuating the moment. Their boots scraped the gravel as they continued down the drive. Grudgingly, his father said. "You've done okay on your own."

"We've never gone hungry."

"Don't be a smart-ass, son." Ex-military, his dad never skirted around expressing exactly what he thought.

So Tate modified his remarks. "All I'm saying is that Bex is more important to me than the trust fund. You worked hard for it and I admire you for that, but I'll never ask her to sign a piece of paper that says I'm worried this marriage might fail. Maybe I'm being impractical. I don't think so. I freely admit you were right about Sandra. So do whatever you want. There you have it."

"Becca Stuart is nothing like your first wife."

"No, she isn't."

"Glad we can agree on something."

Tate nodded. It was an infrequent occurrence— infrequent enough to deserve comment. Obviously, Aunt Gina was a terrific mediator or the butting of heads through the years would've been that much worse.

"We altered the stable plans a bit," his father said next.

Tate was pleased to see the sides framed in but even without the blueprints in his hands, it did seem to be bigger than he'd expected.

He stopped walking. "You what?"

His father shrugged. "If we gave the structure a second story, it would've blocked your view from some parts of the house, so we decided to extend it at the north end to include bigger living quarters for the hands, and a separate office with a reception area for your buyers."

No wonder his contractor had moved the finish date. Being without all the hammering and the noise of saws and nail guns was going to be a gift on its own. The construction crews were great guys, but he'd be happy when the constant racket was over, and there weren't vehicles coming and going at all hours.

It took him a moment to respond, because he was

still in shock at his father's audacity, but he finally said, "Is there some reason that I, the owner of this property, wasn't consulted on this?"

"Yep. Early wedding present."

Why was it that every conversation he had with Randolph felt surreal? "I only told you a few minutes ago that I'm getting married. And who is *we*?"

"Lettie told me it was a done deal, so we decided this made sense." His father gestured at the stables.

That statement took *surreal* to bizarre. "Lettie, meaning Mrs. A.? You *agreed* on something?"

"We're both reasonable people. She's just overbearing at times. Always wants her way."

It was all Tate could do not to drop to the ground laughing. "*She's* overbearing? Dad, I love you, but reality check."

His father gestured at the expanded structure again. "That isn't a good present?" he asked defensively.

Tate wasn't ungrateful, just bemused at their presumption. "Of course it is," he replied. "And we appreciate it," he added in a soothing voice. Not to mention that Nate Cameron would be hopping up and down with joy. "It's generous and then some. How did Mrs. A. know it was a, uh, done deal?"

"She knows Bex and I know you. We talked it over and came to the conclusion that you'd get married, so we went forward."

They'd *talked*? Never in his presence.

He asked wryly, "Have you named our first child yet?"

"I'm thinking Randolph for a boy, and she suggested Leticia for a girl."

At least he and his dad were joking with each other. That didn't happen often.

His father turned then and gazed up at the mountains. "I like it here. How would you feel if I moved closer?"

GIRLS' NIGHT OUT.

Bex needed one. And after all, she had two designated drivers. The three of them agreed on appetizers and salads they could split, and she ordered a fruity rum drink with pineapple and cherries on a long toothpick before she broke the news.

"I believe the pact worked for all of us. Tate and I are engaged," she announced.

Hadleigh and Melody looked at each other, and Hadleigh extended her hand across the table, palm up. "Pay up, Melody Hogan."

"You got the date wrong," Mel argued. "You said they'd make the big decision before Columbus Day."

"I was off by a week. Sue me."

"Still…"

"Let's face it. I won."

"Not until we have the wedding date and the color of our dresses."

Bex said, "Hello! Sitting right here. Have you two been betting on my personal life?"

"Duh." Hadleigh didn't look repentant, and neither did Mel. "You're our only current link to the not-pregnant world. Just please, please, don't pick purple for the dresses."

Mel interjected, "That's cheating. You can't influence her."

"I was unaware that there were rules, and I *hate* purple."

"I'll admit it doesn't flatter you, but that's her choice, now, isn't it?"

"Well, then I hope she picks brown. Just sayin'. *That* doesn't flatter you."

A low blow, since Melody was wearing a rich brown sweater. In Bex's opinion, it looked very nice on her, and Hadleigh no doubt thought the same. They were both laughing. Bex put a stop to it. "Hey, congratulations might be in order."

Hadleigh did a graceful swirl of dismissal with her hand. "You already know that's how we feel, Bex. Come on."

She did know.

There were some things in this world you could count on and in *her* world, that was one of them. She turned to Mel, "Can you make me an engagement ring?"

"Of course. Diamonds? Ruby? What?"

"It's for him. Something simple. Just a band."

Hadleigh rubbed her temple. "You're going to make the *man* wear an engagement ring?"

"I asked *him*. So it follows, right?"

If anyone understood, it was Hadleigh. They both had loved Will so much, and Hadleigh would know that doing things the wrong way around—at least, according to most people—was a gesture of defiance. And, equally, one of confidence. "I suppose I can follow that convoluted logic," she murmured.

Mel interjected softly, "I'll design one. Of course. Don't make me cry. Anything sets me off these days— a sappy commercial, a cute cat video, *this*..."

Naturally, the rest of dinner involved wedding plans. They both voted that both the ceremony and the reception be held at the new house. They decided she should go with a strapless gown, maybe mermaid-style—they were divided on that—and Bex was fairly sure they'd chosen her lingerie but was afraid to ask.

"I want one of those invitations you make, too. With the ribbons and sculpted edges. I'll look online to find an Old Maid card."

For about the fourth time, Mel and Hadleigh looked at each other in question.

"Inside joke."

Driving home, Bex had to smile.

Tate was on the big couch when she arrived. He switched off the television. "How was dinner?"

"We had healthy salads, along with mozzarella sticks and artichoke dip. So it was a balanced meal—in some ways. And how was yours?"

"The boys wanted pizza. I made pork chops and corn on the cob instead. Maybe I didn't win the Dad of the Year award, but they cannot exist on pizza alone. How are Hadleigh and Melody? Oh, by the way, I think my dad has a thing for Mrs. A."

Bex accidentally dropped her purse on the floor at that casual addition to his question. "What?"

Tate had a noncommittal expression on his face. "I'm not pretending to be a great romantic, but I'd make book on it."

"I've had enough of betting on the love lives of other people."

He seemed mystified.

"Never mind. Back to this interesting theory about your dad. You do remember how they can't even exchange a civil word, right?"

"Let's call it an educated guess. They already gave us a wedding present, by the way."

She shed her coat. "If it is three giraffes, I won't be able to feed them, since I don't know what they eat."

"Even if it was, we'd have space for them now. Dad and Mrs. A. made an executive decision. They went over my head and redesigned the stables. I'm torn between irritation that people are making high-handed decisions for me, and gratitude. It is going to be exactly what Nate Cameron and I wanted. My dad's presumptuous, but he knows what he's doing."

Bex went over and dropped down next to him—which was possible on the giant couch. "Yeah, well, I feel your pain. I get the impression that I'm not going to be picking out my own wedding dress. Hadleigh and Mel have definite ideas. I'm hoping for the shoes." She sighed dramatically. "Should we just elope?"

"No can do. I'm informed June is what my mother would've wanted." His arms went around her.

Bex laid her head on his chest. "I'm fine with June. It's a long way off, but…" Those extra months together would simply prove they'd made the right decision, she thought.

"Maybe we can plan the honeymoon, but I'm an optimist. Mrs. A. may have other ideas."

"I know what I want."

"You do? What? How about St. Kitts? I've flown in there many times."

"No."

"What about Italy?"

"Not this trip."

"You're hard to please. No to the Caribbean and Italy? What do you have in mind?"

"What about the cabin where I fell in love with you

when we were crammed into that tiny bunk? You know, the one with an outhouse and an outdoor shower?"

"The outhouse cabin? *That's* where you want to go?" It was.

"Please, Tate, think about it. That lake is one of the most beautiful places I've ever been, and it's completely private. We can take the boys fishing. Oh, and we can buy a mouse-free mattress for our room."

"I believe you just took *private* out of the equation. You want the *kids* to go with us?"

"I do. They had a lot of fun."

"*I* want a lot of fun." Tate laughed and kissed her temple. "I think that's great. Where else could we leave them? My father's good in some ways, but he always looks at the kids like he never knows what to do with them. Reminds me of growing up. We could leave them with Hadleigh and Mel, but they'll have their hands full. I vote for your idea. Let's take them—and Josh, depending on circumstances. June is perfect. No ice out on the lake, so we can put in the boat and you can lure in the fish. They'll love it."

"Sounds like we've settled on a place."

"And a time. The marriage season. My dad and I never talk about stuff like this, but I think that's going to make him happy."

"Does it make *you* happy?"

"It does."

"This way, Mel and Hadleigh will have time to arrange everything the way they want for our wedding."

He pulled her on top of him. "The details can wait. Kiss me now."

She did—and then kissed him again.

THE SEASON

THE SHEER NUMBER of guests was staggering.

There were probably paw prints on the train of her dress, but it was impossible to rein in Ace, Joker and King, so Bex let it go. Wearing it was a one-time deal, anyway. The dogs were excited with all the extra people around and they went a little wild.

And when it came to the wedding preparation, so had Mrs. A. and Tate's father. Flowers everywhere. Bouquets overflowing the tents they'd rented and set up next to the house. The horses, more than curious, watched the festivities over the pasture fence.

Babies, children, dogs. Hadleigh, Mel and Tara beaming. Tripp and Spence holding their son and daughter respectively, Tara and the rest of her fitness-center staff. Her parents. And of course, Tate waiting for her by the preacher, with Ben, Adam and Josh at his side.

The afternoon was a blur, but she suspected every wedding was like that for the bride. Her dress, selected with the able assistance of Hadleigh and Mel, wasn't strapless, after all. It was sleeveless, and full skirted— and it managed to be both elegant and summery.

Champagne toasts, which Tate only participated in once since he'd be driving to the cabin. Mel and Hadleigh were still breastfeeding, so they didn't take more than a sip, either. In solidarity with her friends and fellow members of the marriage pact, Bex did the same. Then she tossed the bouquet—caught by Junie McFarlane, of all people—and they were out of there.

In her opinion, the reception was more for Tate's father and Mrs. A. anyhow. Three months ago, they'd taken off for someplace tropical and gotten married and then invited practically the entire state of Wyoming to the reception. *This* reception.

Now, she, Tate and the boys were on their way north, to the cabin on the lake. *And* the dogs. Tara had offered to watch them for the week, but the boys had voted that down.

Bex wished she'd changed clothes before they took off, but on the other hand, she wanted to get to the cabin as quickly as possible. Tate did, too. But *he'd* somehow found an opportunity to change into casual clothes.

"For once, my shoes are the only comfortable thing I'm wearing." She slipped one off, anyway. "There's a pair of jeans and sweatshirt in my very near future."

"If it is any consolation at all, you look beautiful." Tate had that half smile hovering on his face.

"I notice you managed to sneak into the house and change." Her tone was accusing. He was wearing jeans, boots and a denim shirt, and she resented how comfortable he looked.

"I wasn't the glowing bride. No one missed me."

She took off the other shoe and considered removing her hose. "Well, this is my one and only rodeo. I'm not doing *that* again."

"I sure hope so, Mrs. Calder."

She was Mrs. Tate Calder. She really was. Becca Stuart Calder. Her throat tightened at that realization. She swallowed and then said, "So now both Mrs. A. and I are Mrs. Calder. That's awkward. What am I supposed to call her?"

"Lettie?"

"Oh, no way." The boys weren't paying any attention from the backseat, so she figured that with her long skirt, the hose could go. Why she'd ever worn panty hose in the first place was a mystery to her. "Are you going to call her that? She's technically your stepmother."

"And your mother-in-law."

He had a point there.

It was difficult to grasp. Mrs. A. was her mother-in-law. Hadleigh and Mel thought it was hilarious.

Wriggling discreetly out of her panty hose, she said hopefully, "Why don't we play a game of Old Maid and the loser gets to decide how to handle it?"

Her husband made a comical face. "In other words, you'd be leaving it up to me? Bex, you're so cute when you're trying to be funny. If you want my suggestion, we ask her what she wants to be called, and that'll settle it. Problem solved."

The sign for the cabin must have been a casualty of the winter, and at first she assumed Tate had missed the drive, but when he pulled in, she recognized the same quaint little place nestled by the lake. The boys started cheering from the backseat, which launched an excited chorus from the dogs. How they'd crammed themselves in the back, everyone belted in, dogs beneath and between them, was beyond her. But the very idea of Tara keeping those critters had been met with a firm refusal—from Tate, as well.

Boys wanted dogs, dogs wanted boys, argument over.

Josh was thrilled at the prospect of a week with his

dog—Joker—who lived at Tate's ranch. Tara had made it clear that although she couldn't cope with a dog herself, she appreciated everything Bex and Tate did for her son. Greg was out of the picture finally, having left the state, so their household was calm. Josh had Tate as an honorary father, a responsibility Tate took very seriously.

All three boys were chattering about the fish they expected to catch. How they were going to fish with five people and three large dogs in a boat was another interesting question. It would be a miracle if they didn't all end up in the lake, but she didn't trust the dogs alone in someone else's house yet, so they certainly couldn't be left outside on their own and the boys didn't want to stray two steps away from them.

Once Tate had parked, doors opened, dogs and boys tumbled out and scattered, and Bex, in her wedding dress, practically fell out of the truck, no shoes…

But Tate caught her, easily lifting her up. "I've got a small surprise."

"I'm still nervous about surprises," she warned him, looping an arm around his neck.

"You love the hot tub."

She did. "So you scored once. Don't get too confident."

He carried her to the front door. "You'll love this one, too, if I can manage this romantic moment first. Here are the keys, mind unlocking?"

She did it, although they were both laughing by the end. The boys had bounded in, pushing her unwieldy long skirt aside, and were arguing about their bunks already, the dogs hopping around.

But when he set her down, she saw her surprise in

the tiny kitchen. "Oh, I can't believe it! Mel made a clock for this place?"

It was designed with the usual artistic genius—a silhouette of the cabin surrounded by trees, the lake represented by tinted glass, the rustic framing... Bex went over to look at it more closely and found herself choking up. "The owners must love it."

"I'm hoping your expression means the owners do love it."

She swung around. "What?"

"My friend Russ was interested in selling for the right price. He doesn't use it often. I thought I'd buy you an outhouse for a wedding present," he joked, "but he wouldn't sell just the outhouse, so I had to buy the whole thing. Thanks to the insane competition between Mrs. A. and my father over the stable, I had the money leftover to do it."

"You *bought* this cabin?"

"The fish in this lake staged an uprising at the idea of you owning this place, but I went ahead with it, anyway. Anything with fins moved to a different county. And to be precise, I did buy you the outhouse. The cabin happens to come with it."

"Tate." She was back in his arms. He really couldn't have given her a more perfect gift...

A moment later she heard Ben in the background, "Yuck. They're kissing *again*."

"They do that a lot." Josh also sounded disgusted.

Adam said, "I never want to kiss a *girl*."

Tate broke it off, but his hands lingered at Bex's waist. "You three settle your argument about where you're going to sleep or do I have to make the decision for you?"

Ben was, as ever, the spokesman. "We got it figured out. Now we want to go down to the lake with the dogs. Can we?"

"With vests, okay? It's getting dark, though, so make it fast. We'll go fishing in the morning."

The congestion at the front door didn't bode well for the outcome of this excursion as they all tried to exit at once, shoving and elbowing each other. Bex predicted, "I'm going to say two dogs and one boy, minimum, will end up in the lake."

"I'll call and raise you another boy."

"This isn't a poker game. At least it's warm out."

"There's no question someone's going to fall." He was watching her intently. "I sure did."

She didn't think they were talking about the boys anymore...

"I love this place." She was definitely the bare-foot bride of Bliss County—although she loved those shoes—and couldn't wait to shed her bra.

"So do I."

"I love *you*."

"And I love you right back."

"Help me out of this dress?"

Tate didn't move a muscle. "We don't have much time before they come streaming back in, asking for popcorn—I blame you for that—and who knows what else. Plus, I'll have to feed the mutts so they can grow even bigger, although they rival small calves already. So I don't have the self-control to help you off with your dress right now."

"I'm going to be stuck in this forever?"

He consulted the cabin clock. "Stop worrying about

that. I might be willing as soon as the boys are settled and the puppies are asleep. You have another hour or so."

"*Might* be willing?"

"Let me amend that. You can count on it." He traced the curve of her breast with a fingertip, his eyes holding a sexy promise for the night ahead. "You were the one who wanted to bring the kids on our honeymoon. Live with the consequences."

"Like you wouldn't worry about them if they weren't right here!"

Tate didn't deny it. "I have a hard time leaving them."

"I know."

"Plus, they love it here. This isn't just a present to you, but to our family."

Bex knew that, too. Josh included. "My wedding present to you," she teased, "is that I accept your gift of the outhouse. I've actually always wanted one."

"Any woman who does *that* is a keeper." He displayed that sexy smile.

"I have another gift for you, as well. A surprise. Maybe even better than yours."

"You hate surprises."

"I love this one." She gestured at the cabin, deliberately revealing her wrist. "And I'm sure you will, too."

The extra charm Melody had made for her bracelet sparkled in the light. He hadn't noticed it earlier—but it had been an eventful day. Tate grabbed her hand and touched the motherhood charm—a baby's shoe. "Does this mean what I think it means?"

She nodded. "I know that once we got engaged, we agreed to wait until after the wedding…but I might've decided to stop using birth control once I was sure I could still fit into my dress if it happened. And…it happened."

The joy on his face was worth the trouble she'd had keeping the secret for the past month. Just as he started to speak, there was some sort of commotion down by the water. Tate gave her a swift kiss and hurried to the window that looked out on the lake.

"Whoops, kid overboard. We called that one."

She'd already guessed. "How many wet dogs will come charging through the door?" she asked, laughing.

"I see at least two in the water. This isn't going to be the most restful honeymoon on record. Let me go address the situation. The dogs can swim and the kid's head is above water, but I should probably fish them out."

"Have fun. I'd help, but remember, I'm wearing a wedding dress."

There was a sensual promise in her husband's eyes when he whispered, "Not for long."

* * * * *

This year, come to Mustang Creek for Christmas!

*Dr. Jax Locke is joining Nate Cameron's veterinary
practice in town and hoping to reconnect with
Charlotte Morgan, originally from—Mustang Creek!
And now on her way back there...*

*Turn the page for an excerpt from Linda Lael Miller's
CHRISTMAS IN MUSTANG CREEK,
available from HQN Books in October.*

Charlotte Morgan shouldn't have checked her bag for the flight from New York to Wyoming. Her layover in Denver had already been far longer than planned because of a storm that was coming in from the West Coast, and now she was—*finally*—waiting by a luggage carousel at the Cheyenne airport. And waiting... As her friend Karin always said, there were two kinds of luggage—carry-on and lost. And hers appeared to be of the lost variety.

December 10 meant it was almost the festive season, but her spirits were definitely on the low side.

This airport mess was typical of the dismal way her luck had been running lately.

Let's see. She'd had to arrange for her aunt Geneva to move into assisted living. Dealing with that, mostly by email and over the phone, hadn't been easy. Then there was the fact that a stranger was staying at Geneva's house, the house Charlotte had grown up in. And—just when she'd thought things couldn't get any worse—she'd been laid off.

Merry, merry Christmas.

Oh, the company, an advertising firm, had given her a generous enough severance package. Her boss had explained that budget cuts were taking a toll on everyone.

Not on him, apparently. *His* job seemed to be safe, unlike her own. It had taken some effort to not say something to that effect, but in truth, she just wanted to go home.

As she watched everyone retrieving luggage while hers was, predictably, nowhere in sight, she realized how ironic it was—as a teenager, she'd been convinced that all she wanted was to leave the small town of Mustang Creek, become successful, meet the right man and never look back. She'd done it. She'd left. She'd gotten a great job. She'd met the right man.

But she sure had looked back.

There was one other hopeful passenger waiting, and they exchanged a shrug of commiseration. The carousel was still moving, so maybe…

Yep, she'd left the small town. Got the dream job—and lost it. Met one Dr. Jaxon Locke, fell in love, and that didn't work, either.

The other passenger won the lottery and his case slid down.

"Happy holidays," he said in sympathy as he hurried away.

Then…a Christmas miracle! Her suitcase actually bumped out—no more than two seconds before she was going to head over to the airline counter to fill in the claim form—and began the journey toward her. Yay! Clean underwear for Christmas.

Aunt Geneva would tell her to count her blessings, and as she heaved her bag off the carousel and wheeled it toward the rental car area, Charlotte actually smiled. Things were already looking up. Oh, she still had to make the drive home with a giant storm roaring in, coasting a clipper from the Arctic, but at least she had her clothing. She'd need to make arrangements to have everything else sold or shipped home but would deal with that headache later. Her ridiculously expensive apartment had been sublet and all the rest of it was in storage.

The snow was coming in sideways when she finally reached her rental car. Nothing like driving an unfamiliar rig in bad weather, she thought, as she climbed into the midsize sedan and turned the key in the ignition.

She was on her way home.

After seven years in New York City.

Back in the day, she'd craved the city life, but now she simply wanted to get back to that big old drafty house, that *comfortable* house, where she'd grown up. Mustang Creek was the kind of small town where, if you sneezed, people were concerned you might be coming down with something and offered you their grandmother's favorite remedy. She wanted the fragrance of grass in the summer, the view of the Tetons, the old grape arbor in the backyard.

She wanted *home*.

Geneva needed her, Charlotte mused as she tried to figure out how to turn on the windshield wipers. But *she* might need this change even more. Losing her job wasn't a financial catastrophe since her aunt had taught her a lot about saving her money. She hated that the vibrant woman she remembered was slowly fading. Still, Charlotte viewed her own changed circumstances as a positive in some ways. They'd be able to spend time together. Quality time. Not just the fly-in, fly-out visits of the past few years. She could take care of the house, maybe use some of her savings to fix it up. The place had needed a new roof for at least ten years. She'd offered to pay for it more than once, but Aunt Geneva, her only living relative, had declined.

Stubborn pride was a family trait, no question about that. She came by hers honestly.

She should've looked more closely at the forecast, she decided when whirls of snow, like errant ghosts, circled her car. Almost no one else was traveling, which was just as well, since she could barely see enough to stay in her own lane. Other than the dim lights of one car some distance behind her, she had the road to herself.

She was happy that she'd grabbed coffee and a sandwich in the Denver airport, although—exhausted as she was—she could've used another coffee right now. She slowed her speed even more as she squinted at the increasing whiteout conditions. There was one other immediate problem she hadn't considered. She didn't have keys to the house. Aunt Geneva had been a seamstress, working at home; she was a wizard with her machine and had probably made most of the wedding dresses in Bliss County for the past half century. So Charlotte had never really needed one.

To be honest, she wasn't even sure there *were* keys. The doors with their beautiful faceted glass panels were original, and to her knowledge the locks had never been replaced. Maybe Aunt Geneva had given keys to the friend who was watching her house and taking care of her beloved cat and dog, but it was already after ten and she wasn't going to get to Mustang Creek anytime soon at this speed.

It seemed wrong to go pounding on the door at midnight when she didn't even know this Millicent Klozz. She certainly didn't want to wake the poor woman from a sound sleep.

"Have Yourself a Merry Little Christmas" came on the radio, and Charlotte turned up the volume. She loved the song, which brought back memories of getting tucked into bed on Christmas Eve, Geneva reading her a story and forbidding her to go downstairs until daybreak.

She'd always heeded this admonition—except for the year she was seven. She'd gone downstairs in the middle of the night—not all the way down that creaky staircase because she'd known she'd get caught—and seen the packages under the tree. When she'd heard Aunt Geneva get up—for a drink of water, judging by the running tap—Charlotte had taken a small liberty and peeked at the gifts. Most of them had *her* name on them.

Then she'd climbed into her aunt's bed and nestled there, eyes wide. When Geneva rolled over, she gave a small scream, obviously not expecting a small face right next to hers, dimly visible in the glow of the hallway night-light.

"Santa was here," Charlotte had informed her excitedly.

"I hope he brought me a new heart," Geneva had replied, after gasping and pressing her hand to her chest. "Lord, child, you startled me."

"He came to our house!"

Charlotte still remembered Geneva hugging her, remembered the warmth of her arms, the loving smile on her face. "Of course he did."

Negotiating a slick turn, Charlotte wondered what her aunt had sacrificed to make sure Santa came to their house every year. As a child she hadn't comprehended the effort that went into raising a toddler. Especially if you'd inherited that responsibility in your late fifties, because your younger sister and her husband had died tragically in a train accident. Geneva had been single and inexperienced with tantrums and packing lunches, and later on, cheerleading practice and track meets, sleepovers with giggling girls…

Her great-aunt had done it all unflinchingly, and when it came time for college, had given her guidance, but let her choose. Now it was Charlotte's turn to give back.

JAXON LOCKE HAD been chased all the way from Idaho by the storm and it was starting to catch up with him, mentally and physically.

He had no idea if he was being an idiot or not, going to Mustang Creek. After their breakup just over a year ago, he'd continued, though casually, to follow Charlotte Morgan on social media (they "liked" each other). A few days before, he'd checked in on her page and discovered that she'd left the firm. Even if she hadn't mentioned her plans to return to Wyoming, he would have known where she was headed.

No part of him believed it was a coincidence that both he and Charlotte had ties to Mustang Creek. She'd been raised there, and he'd been hired by his friend Nate Cameron as a veterinarian in Nate's practice.

He'd met Charlotte—Charlie he called her—through an online dating service. Sort of.

Except he'd cheated. Sort of. He'd sat next to the girlfriend of one of his college roommates at a cocktail party. The event had taken place in midtown Manhattan. He had been working in a nearby Connecticut town at the time, and he'd come into the city for his friend Remy's wedding. This woman had studied him over the rim of her cosmopolitan glass, then asked, "Single?"

No doubt she'd made that assumption because while he'd taken the time to pick out what he considered a nice shirt, he'd still worn jeans and boots. His best boots, expensive, but he probably looked like a cowboy. "Not married, not dating," he'd answered wryly. "The invitation said casual dress. I took it to heart."

Her lips twitched. "You could use a haircut, too, but the look you've got going suits your style. Put you in an Armani suit, give you a five o'clock shadow and you could be on the cover of a magazine. You're from where?"

"Originally, Idaho."

She got right to the point. "I know just the girl for you."

He'd doubted that, not only because she was dressed in three-inch heels, wore too much perfume and spent most of the time talking on her cell phone, but because they were strangers. "You don't know anything about me."

"Sure I do. Remy's mentioned you before. You're an animal doctor, right? You and Remy and a bunch of other guys all met at Ohio State."

He nodded. "We shared a house. And, yes, I'm a veterinarian."

She leaned in a little closer. "I work with this girl who's beautiful, smart and hates the city as much as you obviously do but won't admit it. Loves animals and is from a small town. Here's the catch. She refuses blind dates from friends. I do know that she's recently joined an online dating service. Let me write down her name for you, plus the site info. It won't hurt to check out her profile." Her smile was audacious. "Don't tell her I had anything to do with it."

"Since I don't know your name, that would be impossible."

"We'll do official introductions if the two of you actually get together, okay?"

"Okay with me," he said, figuring nothing would come of this odd conversation, anyway.

"She's a Wyoming girl, Mr. Cowboy. I have a feeling you'll ride off for bluer skies and fresher air soon—and I think she will, too."

The deliberately mysterious woman's cell rang again and while she answered it, she scribbled down *Charlotte Morgan* on a napkin, along with the name of a popular dating site.

Even though he'd basically just been playing along, passing the time, Jax realized he was curious enough to take a look at Ms. Morgan's profile.

He'd never even considered online dating. Later, when he got home, he'd typed in the information and, eventually, been completely...well, the English would have called it *gobsmacked.*

Charlotte Morgan was beautiful, all right. More than beautiful.

They'd exchanged a few tentative, getting-to-know-you emails over the coming days, and one fine day, they agreed to meet for coffee. He'd been doing a stint at a small animal practice just across the state line, so the trip involved trains and various other methods of transportation.

When he met finally Charlie face-to-face, Jax discovered that her pictures hadn't done her justice, and on top of her good looks, she was sexy, intelligent, charming...

A whirlwind romance later, Charlie still lived in New York and he'd had to go back to Idaho to help his dad, also a vet, after he'd had a heart attack.

Jax had missed Charlie, but he'd also learned something about himself. The West was still his home, the place where he belonged. He realized he wanted to stay—not necessarily in Idaho, since his father, once fully recovered, didn't really need his help, but somewhere out there, under that sweeping sky.

He'd asked—okay, practically *begged*—Charlie to join him, but for reasons he still didn't fully understand, she'd dug in her heels. Yes, she longed for the wide-open spaces sometimes, she'd said, but she liked her job, her neighborhood, her friends.

All of a sudden, she claimed to love the city, despite her colleague's assertion to the contrary, back at Remy's wedding reception.

They were at an impasse. He wanted to settle in a small town on the other side of the country. She wanted to stay in the city.

Jax recalled all too well the last time they'd tried to discuss the situation rationally, to arrive at some compromise. They'd just made love, she was still in his arms, but her averted face had made her feelings clear. It was true that she couldn't have a job making the same sort of salary anywhere except a place that was a major financial and cultural center. It was also true that in a small town she couldn't walk down the street and pick from a dozen different types of restaurants. No shopping, no theater, no symphony... The list went on.

A classic standoff. He might be Dr. Locke, but he didn't have a glamorous profession like most of the men she met. He helped cows give birth and he treated horses, driving to some remote places at some strange hours to do so. He vaccinated dogs and cats, spayed and neutered house pets. No, the work wasn't glamorous, but it was satisfying. Jax loved animals, loved his job and honestly couldn't see himself living in a big city for very long. He'd grown up bottle-feeding abandoned kittens and baby goats, ridden horses every day, dug fence posts with the best of them, and rarely went to art galleries or museums, her favorite forms of recreation.

He liked the outdoors, she liked skyscrapers.

Let's call the whole thing off.

They had. Sadly, regretfully, unable to agree, they'd gone their separate ways.

The trouble was, Jax had never been able to get her off his mind.

So he was on his way to Mustang Creek, of all places.

What were the chances he'd know someone from her hometown, wind up practicing there?

Maybe this was more than a coincidence, a meant-to-be kind of thing. Like sitting beside the woman at Remy's shindig—her name turned out to be Kendra Nash—and just happening to hear about Charlie for the first time.

Was fate intervening again? Jax hadn't expected a job offer when he contacted Cameron; he'd just wanted to know if there might be openings in the area.

Charlotte's last Facebook post had said: *Catching a flight back to Wyoming soon. Goodbye, NY. It's been nice but I'm heading home. Merry Christmas.*

Jax punched the hands-free device when his phone rang, startling him a little. Beyond his windshield, the weather was getting worse by the second. "Hello."

"Jax, you're still driving, right? Making progress?"

Nate Cameron, the man he'd be sharing a practice with.

Jax answered a little grimly, "Sort of, if you call thirty miles an hour progress. I was hoping to outrun the storm, but obviously that didn't happen."

"I booked you a room at the motel on Main about two hours ago. Last room, in fact. I'd be happy to have you stay with me, but you'll never find my place in this mess. People miss the drive in broad daylight, never mind the middle of a blizzard. Besides, the way the snow's drifting, I don't care what kind of truck you have, you might get stuck. That's one wicked wind. In town at least they've got the snowplows out."

That sounded like a plan. He was starting to doubt he could even find the town; the road ahead was disappearing before his eyes. "Thanks. I'll call you tomorrow morning."

"Let's just meet up. This is supposed to blow through pretty fast. Betsey's Café is where I usually have breakfast, and it's next to the motel. Eight o'clock?"

"See you then."

When Jax finally saw the lights of Mustang Creek glowing in the distance, he felt a measure of relief. His shoulders ached from the tension, and what he really needed was a soft bed and a good night's sleep.

It wasn't hard to spot what he suspected was the town's only motel. The parking lot was full, and the one car that had been in front of him for miles pulled in, too. After searching for ten minutes or so, he found a parking spot, then grabbed his suitcase and ran for it, flipping his collar up.

The dated lobby was empty except for the clerk and a very dismayed-looking young woman at the counter.

She said, "No rooms?"

"None. I'm sorry. The storm and all." The young man did seem apologetic.

Glossy dark hair swung as she turned around, obviously disappointed, and then she froze. "Jax?"

Charlie. She stared at him, incredulous recognition in those gorgeous green eyes.

"Yep. Hi." He was almost too stunned to speak.

Coincidence? No way. Fate or *something* was definitely messing with his head.

Yes, he'd expected to run into Charlie—Mustang Creek was a small community, after all—but he'd never dreamed she'd be one of the first people he encountered, especially in the middle of a snowstorm.

"What are you doing here?" Charlie's eyes were wide and a little wary. Did she think he was stalking her?

"Job offer," he said lamely.

"Oh…well…" She seemed to be struggling for words, too. Small comfort. "What are the odds of that?"

Good, when a person actively pursues a goal, he thought wryly.

He cleared his throat. "*I* have a room if you need a place to stay."

The clerk hit a few keys on his computer. "You're Dr. Jaxon Locke? Last person to check in tonight. Room 215. Two queen beds. Maybe there's some holiday magic in the air, since you two seem to know each other. Let me get your key cards."

Just then, the sound system began to play "Have Yourself a Merry Little Christmas."

Maybe he would, Jax thought. Maybe he would.

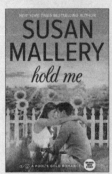 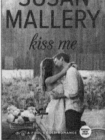 

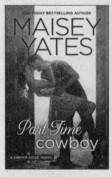 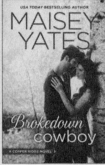 

BESTSELLING AUTHOR COLLECTION

CLASSIC ROMANCES IN COLLECTIBLE VOLUMES

#1 *New York Times* Bestselling Author

LINDA LAEL MILLER

A PROMISE OF PASSION

Tony Morelli had always pursued the things he wanted with single-minded tenacity and authority. It had been a very successful strategy in business, and it had been just as successful with Sharon Harrison. From the moment they met, he and Sharon had had an explosive chemistry. Tony had been sure they would follow their heart-stopping passion into happily-ever-after.

Then everything fell apart— Sharon wanted more, and Tony was no longer sure of their future. But he did know he wasn't ready to let Sharon go. And if a determined seduction had won her once, this time he would wage a passionate war to keep her, no holds barred...

USED-TO-BE LOVERS

"Miller's masterful ability to create living, breathing characters never flags.... [The] romance won't disappoint." —*Publishers Weekly*

Available June 30, 2015, wherever books are sold!

**Plus, ENJOY the bonus story *Into His Private Domain*
by Janice Maynard, included in this 2-in-1 volume!**

www.Harlequin.com

NYTLLM0715

From the creator of *The Originals*, the hit spin-off television show of *The Vampire Diaries*, come three never-before-released prequel stories featuring the Original vampire family, set in 18th century New Orleans.

Family is power. The Original vampire family swore it to each other a thousand years ago. They pledged to remain together always and forever. But even when you're immortal, promises are hard to keep.

Pick up your copies today and visit www.TheOriginalsBooks.com to discover more!